THE
HOPELING

MAGGIE MASTER

Helping talented writers publish exceptional books

The Hopeling

Printed in the United States of America. For information, address Acorn Publishing, LLC
3943 Irvine Blvd. Ste. 218, Irvine, CA 92602

www.acornpublishingllc.com

Interior design by Kat Ross
Cover design by Kristie Radwilowicz

ISBN-13: 979-8-88528-112-6 (hardcover)
ISBN-13: 979-8-88528-111-9 (paperback)
Library of Congress Control Number: 2024914825

For my daughters

"Hope" is the thing with feathers
That perches in the soul
And sings the tune without the words
And never stops at all.

And sweetest in the gale is heard
And sore must be the storm
That could abash the little bird
That kept so many warm

I've heard it in the chillest land
And on the strangest sea
Yet never in extremity,
It asked a crumb of me.

—Emily Dickinson

Author's Note

"Our thoughts and prayers are not enough." President Barack Obama said these words in 2015, after a mass shooting at a community college in Oregon. It was the ninth time in six years he'd been asked to summon words for an event that defies language.

I didn't yet know how his words would come to intersect with *The Hopeling*, only that his sentiment—*We can't pray our way toward the world our kids deserve*—felt at the core of the story I was trying to tell.

I kept writing this story (over two decades) in part because of a common refrain usually echoed after some manmade tragedy: Thoughts and prayers, thoughts and prayers, thoughts and prayers. To me, the concept seemed like a terrifyingly convenient way to disengage from our fellow citizens. I hope this book serves as a foil to that type of response, and that it sparks conversation around what responsibility each of us has toward another.

There are moments in this book that are hard to read. I name that here. But harder to read are the nonfictional headlines from which many of these fictional scenes are taken.

There are plenty of adults who'd prefer to keep kids from reading books on difficult topics. But my hunch is young readers have already heard some variation of any scenario I could possibly share, just listening to the news on the ride home. As a novelist, my aim is to help younger adults make meaning beyond headlines; to form an opinion and act in an often heartbreaking world. Because young people are smart enough to know we can't pray our way out of our problems. In fact, they're probably smarter than most adults. And thank goodness, because our world needs them.

Chapter One

My mom is being so annoying! I called about MindForce II again and she said to stop bothering her at work. Doesn't she understand it was released last night and Logan and Hunter will already be, like, fifteen levels ahead of me? Please, please, please can you make her change her mind? I promise I'll totally be nicer to my little brother and clean up my room and study for my classes and stuff.
—Cole

IPSA WATCHED AS THE LINES APPEARED, JERKING AND sputtering onto the page. The words gushed forth like an earthly tsunami of penmanship crashing onto the page. Although, she realized, "penmanship" was being generous. It was clear the author spent way more time holding a game console than a pen. But his handwriting was the least of Ipsa's concerns.

She closed her eyes and the scene unfolded as if through this teenage boy's own eyes: piles of dirty laundry littered the bedroom floor. Two discarded bags of chips, hastily torn open and mostly empty, left crumbs deep in a shag carpet that smelled of old gym socks. The boy's smelly, bare feet rested on his desk, and he cradled an electronic device in his lap. He attacked the buttons with his thumbs, pausing only to shove his hand, elbow deep, into a bag of bright orange cheese puffs and utter a prayer—for that was the proper title for his jumble of complaints and bargains; and Ipsa was the angel who'd been assigned to read it.

Ipsa opened her eyes and watched the boy's name appear on the paper, the final flourish of some invisible pen. *Cole.* His prayer complete, the parchment sprang to life. It alighted from the desk, flapping slowly, like some delicate paper bird, and hovered a few inches away from Ipsa's nose, patiently awaiting her direction.

She stared at it, glumly. These creatures—hopelings, as they were called—uttered too many prayers. They flooded into the Reading Room from every corner of the hopeling world. Even the youngest seemed to learn how to do it: *I want a lollipop. I. WANT. A. LOLLIPOP!*

Ipsa brushed her own forearm, even though the imitation cheese powder covered Cole's arm, a world away. Unfortunately for Ipsa, seeing into the prayers she read—seeing their world as that particular *hopeling* saw it—was an unwelcome part of her job as a Reader. For a moment, she fantasized about a freak power outage that would disable all his gadgets. Her lips curled as she imagined him, confused and pouty, sitting in his dark and smelly room.

Behind her, someone sniffled.

Ipsa's smile dissolved: Her manager, Eon. He oversaw the entire Prayer Reading Department, yet he somehow managed to spend most of his time hovering over her wings.

"The clock is ticking," Eon said, tapping his naked wrist with a pointer finger.

One of Eon's more annoying habits involved using words or phrases he'd taken straight from the hopeling world (which angels called, simply, There). Like the concept of a "clock," which held little meaning Here, where they measured time in reading sessions and their daily community celebration, and not by ticking clocks or calendars.

Ipsa bit her lip. The prayer fidgeted in the air, like a dog circling the front door for a walk. She knew it was anxious to hear its destination. She looked up across the Reading Room. The sheer volume of prayers required more Readers than Ipsa could count, rows upon rows of reading desks forming concentric circles, like the rings of some earthly redwood. At the room's center stood a glass tower. The Hive droned with a sound like a million angry bees thrashing and swirling. The structure held prayers not yet formed on paper and trembled like a pressure cooker about to burst. Burst with need, thought Ipsa, glancing up at the swirling, invisible chaos within The Hive. A million nagging Coles.

Eon leaned in closer. Beside him stood an angel named Muir, who'd received her wings just a few community Repasts ago. Before her wings had chosen her, Muir had been nothing more than stardust. Now she stood beside Ipsa, an angel with wings that bore the deep crimson of a Prayer Reader. Ipsa glanced from Eon's bald head to Muir's thick crop of rich, black curls, wondering if the stars had given her Eon's rationing of hair.

Muir was the reason that this session was somewhat tolerable. Ipsa had convinced Eon to let her mentor a new Reader. But the unintended consequence seemed to be Eon mentoring *Ipsa*.

"This isn't rocket science." Eon quietly chuckled, adjusting the hem of his cloak, which draped a bit too long over his feet. "Where should this prayer be directed?"

"Into Cole's trash can." The words came out before Ipsa even realized what she was saying—or that she'd said it out loud. Her fingers shot up to her mouth as if to keep anything else from flying out. Sometimes her tongue seemed to have wings of its own.

Muir turned back toward Ipsa, tilting her head in confusion. Her wings jittered. Ipsa's own wings, that same crimson of a Reader, blushed a bright magenta, shrinking down against the fabric of her robe as if trying to disappear. That had come out *wrong*.

Eon puckered his lips like he'd just eaten a bad earthly lemon. "I'm sorry?" His eyes narrowed, flinching back and forth between Ipsa and Muir.

"I…was just making a hopeling joke, of course," Ipsa said, forcing a laugh. She turned her gaze toward Muir. Eon and Muir were the same height, but Eon's skin looked as yellowed and dry as the parchment on a Reader's desk, while Muir's skin was smooth and the color of a young sapling.

"Muir," Ipsa stalled, "why don't you tell us what *you* think. Start with that third line, right there."

Muir leaned toward the wagging paper, trying to conceal her excitement at being this close to a hopeling prayer. She gently pulled it toward her. "*It was released three days ago and Logan and Hunter will already be, like, fifteen levels ahead of me,*" Muir read, carefully repeating the words scrawled sloppily on the paper. "Being concerned that he's behind his friends would be upsetting," Muir began to think aloud through the logic of filing a prayer. "And the sooner he gets his new game, the sooner he'll be able to study for school, which is his livelihood…so I would say this is *highly* urgent!" Muir's face unfolded into a beam of delight. Eon's scowl lifted. He gave a slow nod.

"That was a wonderfully close reading of the text, Muir. Well done," Eon said. "Of course, I might suggest filing it merely as 'Urgent' rather than '*Highly* Urgent,' given there was no mention of any specific deadline, but you'll read more about how to distinguish between those two categories in class."

"You've got to be kidding me!" Ipsa's voice rang out so loudly that several other angels in the row in front of her turned their heads toward her desk. "There is no way this stupid hopeling's request is *remotely* urgent!" The words gushed out of her mouth like a broken hopeling fire hydrant. "As if Mr. Bottomless Cheetos is going to do anything good for anyone besides himself, ever! The best we can hope for is that videogames turn him into a mindless zombie—at least then he'd stop praying."

"Ipsa!" Eon clenched his lips into a tight smile, his words hissed through gritted teeth. "Perhaps you need a refresher around the characteristics of an urgent request: The subject related to that hopeling's livelihood but did not specify a precise timeline."

"If video games are his livelihood, I feel bad for him," Ipsa said, unable to help herself. She shuddered, imagining how much time this hopeling kid had spent with his giant paws glued to those buttons.

"Your job is to read and file prayers based on certain criteria, not offer commentary. *That* is all." Eon's eyes narrowed as he offered an even wider, forced smile. "Given that criteria, how would you file Cole's prayer?"

Ipsa bit her lip, defeated. "Urgent," she whispered, almost as an exhale.

"I'm sorry, I couldn't hear you." Eon leaned in, his lips forming a smug smile.

"UR-GENT," Ipsa said. The prayer perked up, spiraling a few feet in the air before flapping off toward a far corner of the room where the Urgent chute would expedite it directly to the Answering Department.

"Quite right! Quite right!" Eon sang as he moved to put an arm around Muir's shoulder. "Muir, it looks like Felix at the end of the row is about to tackle a challenging prayer. Why don't you go ask him if you can read over his wing for a moment?"

Muir looked at Eon and then at Ipsa, as if trying to process what she'd just observed. "Of course," she said, turning in Felix's direction. "See you in a few prayers, Ipsa."

Eon's smile began to unfold and Ipsa's wings sagged. She knew there would be a lecture. There was always a lecture.

"Was that some kind of stunt?" Eon said. Ipsa looked straight ahead toward her desk where already the next prayer was appearing on a new sheet of paper—but she could feel his glare boring into her.

"If you had really seen him and his disgusting room, you would understand what I meant," Ipsa said. She traced her finger in a loop on the desk, as she often did when a prayer frustrated her. "I think there's a real problem with our Urgent algorithm."

Eon let out an exasperated sigh and his wings slackened in perfect sync. "There's nothing wrong with our algorithm. Somehow, an angel who hasn't even read five hundred prayers managed to land on the right answer. I think the problem, frankly, is *you*."

Ipsa's wings felt like bricks, as they did when she felt

exasperated. Which she felt a lot. "Eon, how could any angel read that prayer and think—"

"It's quite simple," Eon interrupted, folding his arms against his chest. "Your job is very straightforward and requires little commentary. Read a prayer, review its topic and deadline, and file it for the Answering Department. And yet…." Eon paused, deeply inhaling in preparation for another sigh. His wings expanded dramatically with his exhale. "I think assigning you a shadow reader was a mistake."

"No, Eon, please!" Ipsa said, jumping to her feet. As mad as Cole's prayer had made her, she couldn't risk losing Muir. The promise of a mentee had made Prayer Reading slightly bearable. "I'll do anything. I'm very sorry," Ipsa said, reaching back to smooth her agitated wings. "Really, I —I just got a little carried away. It won't happen again."

Eon's wings stood a bit taller. He straightened his coal-gray cloak before putting his hands in his pockets. His eyes narrowed on Ipsa before lifting his chin haughtily. "Topic and deadline."

"Topic and deadline," Ipsa repeated.

Eon turned to walk away.

"Eon!" Ipsa called after him, her voice barely piercing The Hive's blanketing drone. "What about Muir? Can I please keep her?"

"I'll have to think about it," he said. Then, with a swift turn of his heels and flick of his wings, Eon walked away.

Ipsa knew she was right about that awful hopeling's prayer, no matter what Eon said about "topic and deadline." But her problem wasn't just with Cole. She hated her job—a job no other Readers seemed to mind. She looked up and down the nearby rows of desks, each Reader wearing a contented smile as they filed prayer after prayer.

No one else complained that the prayers never stopped coming, or that hopelings couldn't seem to do anything on their own, or that they made so many stupid requests most of the time.

Ipsa began to think maybe Eon was right: *She* was different. *She* was the problem.

She pushed the thought aside, turning instead to the next prayer on the parchment before her. She placed her hand on the prayer.

"OUCH!!!" Ipsa jerked backward, falling out of her chair. She lay on the floor gasping, her fingertips tingling from a searing current that had surged from her fingertips all the way to the tips of her wings.

The angel one table over looked up before returning to his reading. A few others glanced around, and then the disturbance was absorbed into the ambient hum of The Hive. Ipsa righted her chair and lifted herself back onto it, left to wonder how a piece of paper had just knocked her over.

Prayers typically carried some sensation from that hopeling's physical environment: the smell of Cole's disgusting old socks, or parchment soaked with tears from a breakup. But a prayer had never affected Ipsa the way she'd just experienced—as if she'd been struck by earthly lightning. While she had no frame of reference as far as physical pain went, she felt stunned and drained.

"Hi again!" Muir appeared in front of Ipsa's desk, startling the Reader out of her daze. The tips of Muir's wings bloomed rosy pink. "Eon suggested you walk me to class. But he wants to see you first." Muir laid her small hands on the table and innocently leaned over Ipsa's workspace, a smile brightening her face. "What are you reading now?"

"Nothing," Ipsa said, suddenly realizing she must have

taken the prayer down with her when she'd capsized. "Just totally standard prayers. Pretty dull stuff." Ipsa jumped to her feet, stealing furtive glances under her chair and behind her.

"Are you okay?" Muir said, tipping her head to the side.

"Great! Great! I'll just…um, can I just meet you by the entrance in two prayers or so?" Ipsa hoped she sounded casual as she tried to locate the rogue prayer that had electrocuted her and then disappeared.

"Sure!" Muir said, hoisting her satchel over her shoulder. "Don't forget about Eon, though. It sounded kind of important."

"Yes, Eon! Absolutely. Definitely." Ipsa pressed her fingers to her lips to stop herself from talking. She crouched to the ground, scanning the floor for the prayer. She found it perched innocently atop her satchel, uncommonly still. Though she'd barely touched the parchment, it was now a tightly crumpled ball. Ipsa reached down and gave the prayer a timid poke. A thousand images flashed through her mind, too quickly to take shape. Lifting her head above her desk, Ipsa scanned the room.

She looked back down at the prayer, unsure of what to do. The paper now lay still as a piece of hopeling trash.

Ipsa knew she should probably tell Eon.

She also knew Eon would find a way to make this her fault. Whatever *this* even was.

Straightening her back, the angel summoned her most authoritative voice. "Stay put until I get back."

Ipsa threaded her way back through legions of Readers and swirling prayers in search of Eon and another lecture, her wings still pulsing from that strange experience, like small aftershocks from an earthquake.

Chapter Two

Please let this be Jean Paul calling.
—Zoe

"IPSA," MUIR LEANED OVER AND WHISPERED, "WHAT DO YOU think it's like…being a *hopeling*?"

The pair sat in the back row of *Introduction to Prayer Reading*. Ipsa slumped down on the bench beside Muir, hoping no one would recognize Ipsa as an experienced Reader. After she'd hidden the mysterious prayer under her desk, Ipsa learned her penalty for her Cole outburst: attending a remedial class on Prayer Reading. A few hundred crimson-winged angels sat on a series of terraced benches, sloping down toward the stage in the center of the room. Like Muir, they were newly assigned Readers, having only received their wings a few thousand prayers ago.

At the front of the classroom stood Corintine, an angel with wrinkled dark skin and a hunched back. His wings, which sagged, were the color of a ripe eggplant, the deep

10

indigo that signaled his role as an Implementer. Ipsa had attended Corintine's lectures millions of prayers ago. His lectures were, in Ipsa's opinion, as much fun as reading a prayer asking for water to boil.

The new Readers in the room did not seem to agree: Their wings fluttered and fidgeted in anticipation of this first class. Ipsa, on the other hand, couldn't stop thinking about that strange prayer. Typically, hopeling prayers, once out of sight, were out of her mind. With each passing prayer, she couldn't say for sure what had even happened. Had she imagined the sparks? Lost her balance on a wobbly chair? Yet the almost memory of images just out of reach seemed to stay with her.

Muir nudged Ipsa's arm with her elbow, bringing her back to her question about the hopeling world. "Honestly," Ipsa said, grimacing. "I think it would be awful."

"*Really?* You really think so?" Muir said. A look of disappointment clouded her face. "I mean it just seems like some of these hopelings have really interesting lives," Muir said. "Like that woman who traveled all over the world taking pictures of different places? Or that old man who trained his dog to open the refrigerator?" Muir giggled slightly, her eyebrows rising till they nearly touched the border of black coils that framed her forehead.

From the front of the room, Corintine cleared his throat. "Good prayer to you all, and welcome to Introduction to Prayer Reading. By now you've had a chance to familiarize yourself with the Reading Room. I'll help you understand more about how those prayers you've started reading get from There to Here and...." Corintine paused, staring out toward the back of the room, as if he'd forgotten why he was standing there. His wings went limp. The class waited politely.

Ipsa sighed. She hated to dampen Muir's enthusiasm, but in her opinion, the mystique of reading prayers wore off quickly, the way a first snowfall There meant weeks of slush, sopping-wet feet, and yellow snow.

At the front of the room, Corintine leaned slightly. One of the angels in the front row raised her hand.

"Corintine," she said in an encouraging voice. "Where *do* the prayers come from?"

"Wonderful question. Splendid!" Corintine said, awakening from his stupor. "As a Reader, you must think of your desk as a portal between two worlds. You'll learn more about the angel Fortula in your history class, but she was the first angel to summit the Mount of Echoes and discover the source of hopeling prayers…"

Muir leaned in toward Ipsa. "I spent most of recreation time reading about her," she whispered. "How she's the one who found a way to give prayers a physical shape. I can't believe she *built* the Reading Room—right over that mountain peak! Can you imagine what it was like before that?" Muir held her fingers close to her face before pulling them wide apart, as if the space between her fingertips had exploded.

Ipsa winced, imagining Here before the creation of the Reading Room—audible prayers flailing around the ethers of Here, with no Hive to contain them. A geyser of hopeling voices, constantly erupting.

Corintine rambled on. "Yes, indeed, Fortula discovered one of the Three Great Truths of Here, which eventually became known as the Second Arcana—understanding that to be answered, each hopeling prayer must first be *heard*. Separated from the larger orchestra, as it were. As prayers find their way up the Mountain of Echoes, they are contained in The Hive before being routed to your desks.

From there, you file them to the Prayer Answering Department for implementation. Once a prayer receives its answer, it is sent to the Archives and filed away."

The same angel's hand shot up again. "About the Arcanum: We *read* prayers—but how are they *heard*?"

Corintine smiled. "You sound like a hopeling!"

Several angels giggled. Ipsa saw the questioner's wings blush from crimson to a rose hue. How embarrassing to be compared with the likes of a hopeling!

Corintine raised his hand in the air to still the wings tittering in the crowd. "I jest, new angel. It's just that hopelings have difficulty even *listening*, let alone truly *hearing*. An angel, on the other hand, hears with their whole self, with every fiber of their wings. To truly hear isn't to simply ingest a sound, it is to internalize someone's deepest needs. To see the peace and tranquility of a prayer that has been *heard*, that knows it will be *answered*, that is a wonderful thing. Does that make sense, new angel?"

The angel in the front row nodded. Other angels feverishly jotted notes.

Corintine cleared his throat. "Now, where was I? Oh yes, they appear on paper—now this I think you will find *quite* interesting—in the author's own handwriting! Let me show you a few examples." He leaned over and began rummaging through a stack of papers on his desk, mumbling to himself as he searched.

Muir looked over both shoulders, then leaned in close to Ipsa. "Sometimes," Muir began in a hushed but excitable voice, "I think it might be *fun* to be a hopeling."

"Fun?" Ipsa said. "You can't be serious!"

"Well, haven't you ever even *thought* about it?" Muir said, chewing the end of a strand of hair.

"No!" Ipsa said, crinkling her nose. "Not for an earthly

millisecond! I am *so* glad I'm an angel and not a hopeling. For one thing, you know they age There, right? I know it sounds crazy, but it's true!" Ipsa reached into Muir's school satchel and pulled out a thick textbook titled *Growing Up Hopeling*. Flipping to chapter three, she placed the open book on Muir's lap, which featured more than a dozen photos of one hopeling, across the span of their life. "The minute you get really good at one age, one phase of life, bam! Time for the next chapter!"

Almost reflexively, Muir touched her hand to her cheek, cupping her smooth, round face as if it, too, might suddenly age.

"Don't worry," Ipsa said, sensing her concern. "That is what you will always look like!"

Muir shook her head. "Is it also true that they eat all the time? Not just at their Repast?"

Ipsa nodded. "They need to eat to survive. And then they spend the rest of the time *praying* to get rid of the weight they've put on because of what they've eaten, or how it makes them look. It's so absurd!"

Muir's wings began to make a small fanning motion, as if to cool her down. Her brown eyes widened, looking toward the far wall of the room, where several large windows revealed Here's reliably blue sky.

Ipsa seemed to anticipate Muir's question. "Don't get me started about weather-related prayers," Ipsa moaned. "You'll read a prayer about ending a heat wave one day, and then the next thing you know, that same person will be asking for the snow to stop. It's like they can't make up their minds about what they want, ever."

Muir sat staring at Ipsa and began nodding slowly.

"And, you know, new hopelings don't just awaken at some Repast the way we do, fully formed and ready to receive their wings and know their purpose; they have to grow up and figure out something they're good at."

Ipsa paused, coming up for air. Her wings seemed to buzz behind her. Muir's eyes were two hungry orbs taking in Ipsa's every word. "Do you think that maybe—I mean, is it *possible*," Muir said, choosing her words carefully, "hopelings *like* all those different phases of life, all of that choice and uncertainty? That they're okay with not knowing what's next? That all that change is what makes their lives…exciting?"

Corintine coughed again, causing Muir to bolt up in her seat and direct her attention back toward the front of the room. "Your task as prayer readers is rather straightforward," Corintine said, pointing to a chart behind him. "Sorting prayers based primarily on subject matter and earthly time. Topic and deadline, as we like to say. There is simply no point, you see, in sending along a prayer to the Answering Department for a red light to change in traffic." Corintine chuckled almost to himself. "We're not magicians, after all!"

An eager, petite, white-haired angel in the third row of benches shot up her hand.

"Yes, Kora?" Corintine said.

"But I thought time moved slower There."

"It's not that time moves slower so much as hopelings move slower." Corintine chuckled, which unfortunately for his audience, turned into a garbled cough. The room waited. "But even so, we simply cannot be expected to have a prayer go through the entire cycle—reading, filing, and implementation—in a few earthly seconds. As a general rule, any prayer that has a time constraint within about an earthly hour should be routed straight to the "Expired" bin, where they are then sent directly to the Prayer Archives."

Corintine's purple wings began to flap slowly behind him as he walked to the front of his desk and leaned in toward the students with a smile. "But now suppose that same hopeling requested a string of green lights for the *following* day. Can anyone take a guess at how you would file that one?"

Kora's hand shot up again. "Trivial?"

"Exactly right, Kora!" Corintine said, beaming. "All requests pertaining to traffic lights, along with phone calls, hopeling hair, anything relating to a sale on hopeling consumer goods—those are just a few examples—would automatically be filed as Trivial. There is a comprehensive list of Trivial categories starting on page four hundred twenty-nine of your textbooks. I do ask that you memorize them by our next meeting."

Corintine rummaged through a thick stack of papers on his desk, pulling out a yellowed sheet. "Ah, here's another good example of a Trivial prayer from a little girl named Zoe in a hopeling land called Canada. It reads, 'Please let this be Jean Paul calling.'" Corintine let out another chuckle, his round stomach visibly bouncing underneath his mantel.

A large angel spoke up. His waxy head was covered in the same speckling of stardust that blanketed Ipsa's nose and cheeks. "Excuse me, but when do we get to the part about how prayers are *answered*?"

"Prayers are answered by the Answering Department, which sits wholly outside of the role of Readers," Corintine said. "We'll touch on it briefly in an upcoming class."

"Why don't Readers just answer them, since we're already reading and directing them anyway?" the bald angel asked.

"As you will soon find out, prayer *answering* requires a lot of wisdom, and so a very special group of angels are tasked with determining those answers. Your job is simply to sort the prayers to better assist them in Answering." Corintine trailed off and seemed lost in thought. "Now, where was I? If a prayer has not already expired, there are several different pipeline options for an angel to choose from. We've already touched on Trivial. Can anyone name the others for me?"

Rows of angelic hands shot up in the air. Ipsa whispered a goodbye to Muir and slipped out of the room, careful not to let the great oak doors slam shut behind her.

Chapter Three

Hi God, please keep my mom and dad safe and let me have a super good week at school. Help me to remember all the definitions for my spelling test and can you make Bobby stop pinching my arm when Mom's not looking? It really hurts. Oh, and I think my cat, Miss Moffatt, has a cold. She was sneezing a lot this morning. Can you look into that? And also, those children Mrs. Prescott told us about in World Cultures class the other day—the ones that only have chicken broth for lunch? I want to pray for them too. You can give them some of my chicken if you want.

Thanks, God!

—Molly

Having escaped the remainder of Introduction to Reading, Ipsa looked up into the great blue expanse of sky above her. She smiled, closed her eyes and tilted her chin upward, letting the warmth of the sun touch each of the tiny specks of stardust that tattooed her nose and cheeks. Her wings felt restless, itchy. New angels attended classes during what was recreation time for the rest of the community. She could go find Elna, her best friend and a Wreather. But Ipsa felt her wings tugging her in a different direction.

Most of the spaces in Ipsa's world had been fashioned to help angels better understand the "hopeling perspective," as Corintine would say. So much of the scene seemed to burst out of the parchment prayers Ipsa read each day: the cobblestone path, the cherry trees, even the small red bird whistling overhead. With one significant difference: The angels' version, like the cloudless blue sky above her, was unchanging, a state of constant springtime. The cherry blossoms were forever blooming. She glanced down at the footpath, which seemed to gleam—unlike the hopeling sidewalks where flattened gum blotted the path.

If streets always looked like this There—no litter, no weeds—if it was always *springtime*, Ipsa mused, maybe hopelings would spend a little more time *thanking* and a little less time *asking*. But probably not.

Ipsa turned off the walkway and headed toward a bench beside a sycamore tree. She grazed her hand across the trunk, her fingers brushing its flaky bark.

"Hi, Ipsa," said the angel seated on the bench. He spoke without even turning his head to see who was approaching from behind.

"Hi, Dhavi."

That angel's thick hand stroked the wing of a mourning dove that rested in his palm. The bird's feathers were smooth and sleek, and contrasted with the rough, deep wrinkles in Dhavi's hands. Ipsa could barely put her wings around how many years she'd known Dhavi, now her trusted friend. But she couldn't fathom ending a single Repast without confiding in him; Dhavi had a way of making hopelings seem tolerable.

"How were your prayers?" Dhavi asked.

"Just okay," Ipsa said. She paused, wondering if she should tell Dhavi what had happened with her last prayer. She decided she'd read and file it during the next session, and that would be that. "I had a, um, bit of a run-in with Eon."

Dhavi looked straight into her eyes, his own flashing of green and amber. "By 'run-in,' do you mean calling a hopeling—what was it?—a 'bottomless Cheeto' in front of a new Reader?" Dhavi smirked, sending the soft skin around his cheeks rippling. His skin was leathery and the color of wet sand. A scruff of white whiskers covered his cheeks, save for a patch that grew bright red near his chin, as if he'd forgotten to wipe his face after eating a bowl of vismarati at the Repast celebration. His long white hair stayed tucked in a ponytail behind his neck. "If so, then I *did* hear something about that."

Ipsa rolled her eyes. In a world that seemed to house an infinite number of angels, Dhavi seemed to still know everything that happened before she could even tell him. Maybe it wasn't surprising, given his role. Dhavi worked as a Historian in the Chronicles Department. It was his job to remember everything that ever happened There. And apparently, everything that ever happened to *Ipsa*.

"It wasn't my fault!"

"Of course not! It never *is*, is it?" Dhavi said, his cheeks rumbling with a chuckle. How unfortunate that hopelings could never get used to their changing skin, when Dhavi had spent an eternity perfecting his. Every crease, every leathery line seemed to hide some wisdom in its folds. Ipsa's own hands were smooth and firm. She felt her face frown, wondering where her own wisdom might be hidden.

"I'm beginning to think Eon gave me a mentee just to

trap me into some prayer violation or hover all session." Ipsa crossed her arms defiantly, leaving out her suggestion that the hopeling become a zombie. Retelling these spats to Dhavi always made them seem silly, when, in the moment, her wings felt like clenched fists.

"Why do you always assume the worst with Eon? He was giving you some responsibility with Muir," Dhavi said, examining a flake of tree bark as if it housed the answer to Ipsa's frustrations. "He oversees the most important work in our community."

Like Corintine, Eon's purple wings declared his status as an Implementer. Ipsa could still not believe that an angel as annoying as Eon could be so important.

"That hopeling was being awful," Ipsa said, changing the subject.

"That hopeling was being *human*," Dhavi corrected.

"Same thing."

"You *are* a cold-hearted angel, aren't you, Ipsa?" Dhavi's tone offered a playful ring. "Consider why they're even called hopelings in the first place. Do you remember your classes, angel?"

Ipsa rolled her eyes. She hated when Dhavi tried to sneak in a lesson. "Yuka named them, because even in their misery, they clung to the hope that someone would help them, blah blah blah. We give them hope to survive There."

"What about a hopeling you mentioned a few Repasts ago?" Dhavi asked. "He was asking only for his mother to go to Heaven. He didn't sound awful."

Imagine! A hopeling living in some sort of afterlife! The thought was as absurd to Ipsa as suggesting a hopeling's dog could read! Every angel knew that when a hopeling's life expired, that was it. Hopelings *Here*!? Ipsa could scarcely imagine the thought.

"I don't think they're *all* awful," Ipsa said, swirling her toe in the dirt. "Just *most* of them."

Dhavi closed his eyes and shook his head. He let out a small laugh, but Ipsa could tell she was disappointing him.

"I know I'm a terrible Reader—not putting 'Hopelings First' and all that," she said, reciting the well-worn mantra of Here, the very first of their guiding Arcana. "I've tried, really I have, to see it from their point of view, but…" Ipsa trailed off.

"But what?"

"They're so ungrateful!" she said. "Nothing is ever good enough. The prayers never stop coming."

Dhavi spoke softly. "They can't help it, Ipsa. They rely on us in a way *they* can't even fully comprehend. Imagine being a hopeling and relying on something wholly unseen. On *faith*."

"Knowledge, with prudence," Ipsa said in a deeply theatrical voice, reciting a phrase as familiar as her own wings. "It's the Responders who *really* have a wing to pick with hopelings. No wonder they don't even have time to attend Repast. How do they put up with answering all of that need?" Ipsa said.

Dhavi stared deeply into the folds of his hand and Ipsa watched his brow wrinkle into an unfamiliar expression. But the instant passed like a hopeling cloud across the sun. Lifting his head, Dhavi returned her stare with a smile.

"Enough questions for one day, Ipsa."

Chapter Four

Hi Grandpa,

Mark Stevens is such a jerk. All week he's been making fun of my curve ball. Mom said if I really want to win, I should pray. Could you make Mark have a really bad game?

—Jamal

I PSA STARED TOWARD T HE H IVE AND THE CACOPHONY OF unread prayers swirling inside, clambering to be freed, to be *heard,* as Corintine had said. The noise was so much a part of the fabric of the Reading Room that, most of the time, it seemed more like the absence of any sound at all.

Ipsa glanced down the aisle of Readers and observed the angel beside her. She watched as he sent a prayer gliding toward the Highly Urgent chute. She had to admit, the change in the prayer was remarkable: The act of reading had calmed it, left it almost drowsy.

"Darius." Ipsa leaned toward his desk. He looked up,

somewhat startled, a flop of salt-and-pepper hair falling across his forehead.

"Oh, hello, Ipsa," he said, blowing a silver lock from his eyes with a puff of air.

"How are your prayers?" she asked.

"Wonderful!" His eyes dazzled the deep blue of the Endless Lake, the body of water which hemmed their community. Ipsa searched his face for a trace of frustration or dissatisfaction, but he returned an untroubled smile. Darius adjusted his cloak and Ipsa noticed his arm was covered with star marks—the only vestiges from when he'd been stardust. Ipsa's star marks looked like six pink circles on her chest. Darius's formed a series of black swirls that reached to the edge of his wrist.

"What was that last prayer about—the Highly Urgent one? If you don't mind my asking."

Darius paused for a few moments and crinkled his brow. "You know, I'd forgotten already!" The smile returned to his face. "Oh, that's right! It was a hopeling with a broken leg—fell while skiing."

He glanced down at a new prayer, already transcribing itself onto the page, and his crimson wings flexed. "Anyway, back to work."

Ipsa turned back to her desk where a prayer from a hopeling named Jamal floated patiently like some graceful, cream-colored butterfly. Topic and deadline. "Urgent," she commanded, swatting the flapping prayer as if it were an earthly fly.

A new prayer materialized on Ipsa's desk, but the only prayer she could focus on was hiding in a quiet ball beneath her desk. Her wings pulled her toward the floor. Ipsa looked around the room. She'd been waiting for several hundred prayers for a chance to check on it. Now here was her chance: Eon was leading Muir and other new Readers on a tour. The Readers nearby had their heads down, noses to parchment. Looking over her shoulders once more, Ipsa sheepishly ducked her head under the desk. Her wings gravitated toward that small fist of paper as if by some magnetic charge. She leaned in further and, gathering up some cloth from her sleeve, tapped at a fold in the balled paper. Nothing. Still skittish, she tried again, this time with the tip of her finger. No fireworks erupted. She wondered if she'd imagined the whole thing.

Sitting back up in her chair, Ipsa delicately unfolded the balled-up paper, which looked suited for a hopeling waste basket. The idea intrigued her: She knew there were hopelings out there who didn't pray at all and those who prayed all the time. But if a hopeling wanted something, why would they ask and then say, "Never mind?" She began reading:

Wow, I guess I've really hit rock bottom if I'm resorting to praying…

Ipsa stared deeply into the scene unfolding within the battered piece of paper. She stared down at two hands clutching what she recognized as the bars of a hopeling bicycle. They wrung the leather handles as if wrenching a wet towel.

The hopeling's hand then moved to fidget with a small rearview mirror, bending it up slightly, then down. That brief moment allowed Ipsa to catch sight of him. He looked about the age of a teenage boy with rumpled, auburn hair that seemed to point in every which way. A pair of thick glasses slid down his nose. His neck hunched forward, as if he was carrying something heavy on his back.

I haven't even uttered your name in almost a year…And we

both know that I'm not exactly religious. Well, I don't know what you know anymore, or what you are. It's just that I got another note…

The hopeling squeezed a piece of lined paper in his hand that looked torn from a notebook. Ipsa could see writing scrawled across the underside of the paper in thick, black script, though she couldn't make out the words. He let go of the handlebars, the bike swaying as he rocked with his feet, all the while alternately folding and double folding the paper.

I found this one taped to my bike outside the library, which means someone was following me. It said we'd better call it off or I'd see the Second Amendment "up close and personal."

I can't tell Mom and Dad; they've been through enough. But if anything happened to me, I don't think Mom would survive. Annie, if you can hear me—

"What have you got there?"

The sound of Eon's voice startled Ipsa; the boy and his bike dissipated, leaving her staring, once again, at a wrinkled piece of parchment on her desk.

Ipsa's wings froze. Where had Eon come from? She feared he could sniff out prayers neglected from the previous session.

"Just churning through my prayers!" Ipsa said. She spoke in an overly cheerful tone, hoping he would go away. Call *it* off? She wondered what this boy meant when he said "if anything happened to me." For the first time, a prayer was getting *interesting*.

She hunched over, hoping her wings might block his

view. When Ipsa was seated, Eon stood no taller than the top of her head. He leaned over Ipsa's shoulder, scanning her desk. His eyes widened for an instant.

"Oh!" Eon exclaimed in a friendly tone as natural as a tree sprouting feathers. "I've been *looking* for that prayer! It must have been *misdirected*."

Before Ipsa could register what was happening, Eon reached over her shoulder and snatched the paper. *Misdirected?* In all her Repasts, she'd never heard of a prayer being *misdirected*. Prayers were prayers were prayers. It was a random shuffle, each one pulled from the droning masses swirling within The Hive to the next available Reader.

Ipsa felt her wings stiffen. "But I was in the *middle* of that prayer," Ipsa said, reaching for the note now clutched in Eon's bony hand. "Can I please finish reading it so I can file it?"

"Oh, don't worry about this silly prayer. You've really done some great work this session! I'll take care of it. Sorry about the confusion. Repast will be starting any moment, and I know Muir will be looking for you, anxious for you to pass on some more of your reading wisdom. There's so much she can learn from you!" Eon said the last line with an actual wink. His voice had a singsong quality she'd never heard before—certainly not directed toward her. Beyond that, had he just *complimented* her?

"Eon, I think that hopeling needs help, and something about it…" Ipsa began, but Eon was already halfway across the vast room. Ipsa was left to stare down at her desk, trying to figure out what had just happened. But the more she struggled to recall the specific details—the boy's frantic folding and unfolding of that mysterious note, the tremble in his voice—the faster those images seemed to fade into the distance, the way hopeling dreams were said to do.

Chapter Five

Allah,

If we could just have a little bit of electricity—so I can turn on the light for my homework—it would be a blessing. I have my exams the day after tomorrow. As always, please watch over my brothers and keep the school safe.

—Sabeen

IPSA COULDN'T SHAKE HER ENCOUNTER WITH EON OVER THE unfinished prayer. Equally odd was the sensation of actually *caring* about it. Unless prayers offered some funny story to share with Elna at Repast, Ipsa barely remembered them. But this prayer was different. She couldn't shake a memory of this rumpled boy and the desperate tone of his prayer: Had it been fear?

Trying to refocus on the prayer springing to life on her desk, Ipsa quickly skimmed it: The petition related to school, which was considered a livelihood, with a deadline of the next two earthly days—and so she directed the parchment toward the Highly Urgent chute. The prayer began flapping upward, but it suddenly froze just above Ipsa's forehead. Ipsa glanced down at the topmost piece of parchment on her desk, where a new prayer was unfolding in the large and shaky scrawl of a toddler just learning his letters. That writing, too, stopped in mid-sentence, as if some invisible hand had suddenly lifted its orange crayon from the page.

"Time for Repast!" Darius smiled at Ipsa as he pushed away from the neighboring desk. "Looks like this prayer will have to wait!"

Normally, Ipsa was grateful for the ability to put hopelings out of her mind and chat with Elna, but her thoughts kept turning over the mysterious hopeling prayer and Eon's odd reaction. She wanted to speak with Dhavi about it, but just as Eon had said, Muir stood waiting for her just outside the Reading Room, clutching her school satchel beneath her arm.

"I can barely wait to start reading my own prayers," Muir gushed. "I'm so glad I was assigned to be a Reader. I mean, what about the ones that are *group* prayers? I mean, does someone write their prayer ahead of time and then pass it out to everyone?" Muir giggled at the idea, slipping a ring of curls behind her ear.

Ipsa tried to feign excitement, but her thoughts were a world away on a balled-up piece of paper.

"Do you think I could sit with you and your friend Elna at Repast?" Muir asked. "She seems so lovely. I don't think she made my wings or anything, of course, but I bet anything she crafted yours, didn't she? You can tell just by looking. They're so beautiful…" Muir went on and on without coming up for air as Ipsa glanced over her shoulder toward the pathway that led to Dhavi's bench. She sighed. Their conversation would have to wait.

"IPSA! Over here!" Scouring the wingtips poking up through the thick crowds, Ipsa spotted the golden pair belonging to Elna. She could feel Muir's hand clinging to the fabric of her mantel, eager to stay close to Ipsa amidst a technicolor of wings.

The coloration of an angel's wings helped distinguish an angel's role Here, and so, as they threaded through the crowd, Ipsa knew which angels worked in the Contemplations Department because their wings were sky blue, while the wings of Harvesters—those who gathered Kluna from the fields—flashed an olive green. Ipsa's own wings shone a deep crimson, rich and speckled as an earthly apple.

The Wreathing House, where Elna worked, crafted wings for newly arrived angels, woven from the fields of Kluna that surrounded their community.

Elna embraced her best friend. To stare at Elna's wings was to watch the sun reflecting on a moving sea. They seemed to sparkle with gold even as they changed, flashing blue undertones that complemented Elna's pale skin. "I couldn't find you at Meditation," she said. "Where were you? And how's your new mentee?!"

Muir stumbled past Ipsa and extended her small almond hand toward Elna.

"That's me," Muir said, her wings blushing. "My name is Muir. The wings you make are so beautiful."

"Thank you!" Elna replied, breaking into a wide smile. Elna's skin was pale as an egg, and her eyes winked a deep blue. "Ipsa, you should bring Muir around all the time!"

The trio found a seat on the grassy embankment just beside a low stone table brimming with bowls of vismarati, which resembled hopeling grapes. Angels felt no hunger, nor did they feel the need to eat in excess. Ipsa reached her fingers into the mound and plucked out a single piece of the fruit.

Elna gracefully fanned her mantel beneath her as she knelt down onto the soft ground. Ipsa hunched over slightly, her elbows resting on her knees, but Elna's back seemed to pull effortlessly upward. Elna's head, like Eon's, had no hair. But unlike Eon's, the top of her head looked much as her cheeks did: soft and smooth.

"Elna," Muir blurted out. "Is it true that the first angel seeded the ground and, the next day, there were fields of Kluna as far as the horizon?"

"Yuka's gift," Elna said, nodding. "Every patch of Kluna that grows here came from that first seed. They're harvested and then soaked for thirteen Repasts in vismarati juice." Elna reached forward and popped one in her mouth. "Just as Yuka did, millions of Repasts ago."

"And then you weave them," Muir said, her eyes wide.

"We let them dry first!" Elna smiled. "But yes, then we weave them."

Muir's finger rested on another factoid in her book. "If the colors are always changing, how do you know who will become a Reader or a Harvester?"

To stare upon a field of Kluna, seemed, for Ipsa, a bit like trying to take in a hopeling rainbow after a sun shower. Kluna grew in vivid pinks, bold yellows, muted greens, soft blues, and every shade in between. But the petals were constantly changing hues, as if unable to decide which color they wanted to be. Elna might begin her work on a pair that were Contemplations blue, but by the end of her threading, they would be the color of sunrise. As such, Elna never knew which departments might receive new angels that Repast, since the colors were unpredictable until the very last moment before a pairing.

"Your guess is as good as mine, Muir!" Elna smiled. "But it makes Repast exciting, even for me!" She ran her palm over the top of her smooth scalp. "So, tell me what's new in the hopeling world!"

Elna's department was one of a few Here that had no direct interaction with There, limiting her knowledge of hopelings to second-hand stories from Ipsa, along with whatever she could remember from the classes she'd taken as a new angel, now so many Repasts ago. Ipsa could still remember meeting Elna at the Learning Commons and giggling as they'd found a seat next to each other in their history class.

Ipsa once again pushed the odd prayer out of her head and launched into the retelling of another prayer from that session, about a young hopeling who had gotten his head stuck in between two poles in the stairs.

"Oh Ipsa, that is too funny!" Elna said, pressing a hand against her lips. Ipsa smiled, noticing Elna's star marks, three small markings on the inside of her wrist, leftover from her journey Here. Unlike Ipsa's star marks, Elna's actually looked like three delicate stars.

"How many new angels this Repast?" Ipsa asked.

"Oh, my," Elna said, pressing her hand to her cheek, "a few thousand, at least." Her lithe back bowed forward toward Ipsa, like a flower following the setting sun. Even at play, Ipsa marveled at how graceful her friend appeared.

"Should I get out my bell?" Ipsa said, and they both giggled.

"I don't understand," Muir's face scrunched up. "Why a bell?"

Ipsa sighed a long, drawn-out breath. "Muir, I forget

that you're new. Hopelings really think that the universe turns around them. An angel receiving their wings is one of the most magical and important moments Here." Ipsa straightened her back, her wings seeming to puff up behind her, flapping once or twice. "Our wings choose *us*. We don't just sprout a pair the moment some hopeling rings a doorbell, just because they saw it in some movie!"

"Oh." Muir blushed, looking slightly embarrassed.

"Muir, don't let Ipsa ruin all hopelings for you," Elna said, good-naturedly. "She likes to poke fun, but I think they sound sort of charming."

Ipsa rolled her eyes. "Charming? No way!"

"Enough about hopelings," Elna said, motioning toward the front. "The ceremony is about to begin!"

The trio turned their wings toward the stage before them, where a few hundred angels shuffled across the floor in a practiced line. Ipsa shook her head, still thinking about the absurdity of a bell magically granting wings. Repast—which occurred each day as a celebratory break—marked the most important moment of an angel's life: the matching of wings. The gathering assembled every angel in the community in an amphitheater that from every spot offered clear views of the stage at its center, which abutted the Wreathing House. Ipsa read prayers from hopeling sporting events—stadiums, they were called—but those venues were clamshells compared to the size of the Repast Field, which might have covered the ground of an entire hopeling city.

As a few hundred angels shuffled up the stairs and onto the stage, the audience began to hum and sing the chorus that welcomed each batch of new angels to the ceremony.

Stardust to angels, your wings flock to thee,
Your soul shall it capture, then named shall you be!
From a place in the sky, like countless untold,
Angels to stardust, our circle unfolds.

"Angels. Friends," a voice boomed from the front of the stage, rich and melodic as a single trumpet. Thodius headed the Wreathing House and led each pairing ceremony, his voice at once intimate and electrifying.

"I am honored to welcome you to one of the most joyful moments we experience Here: the welcoming of our newest angels and the fitting of wings."

A slow rumble sounded through the ampitheater as the crowd fluttered their wings in approval. Thodius paused, a wide smile spreading across his face. His wings—which like Eon's, were the deep indigo of an Implementer—seemed to expand another foot as the gentle applause rippled through the arena.

One Repast, when it had been Elna's turn to bring out the new wings, Ipsa had found a seat close to the stage, just below the stage. Having read many prayers in which hopeling women pined for some Prince Charming they'd seen in an earthly movie theater, Ipsa imagined Thodius fit that bill exactly: His eyes glittered a dazzling green, framed by a set of eyebrows that arched perfectly below a smooth brow. A wave of night black hair seemed to curve across his forehead, without a single lock out of place. Like Dhavi, he had been created with a burnish of whiskers, but unlike Dhavi's mange of grey and red scruff, Thodius's subtle beard only softened his sharp jawline. If angels cared at all for physical beauty, Ipsa thought, the crowd would be far too distracted to ever hear a word Thodius said.

"Friends," Thodius repeated, spreading his arms toward

the crowd on the lawn. "I'll now read the most ancient words of our history, our creation story." As he spoke, a petite angel with alabaster skin and grey hair joined Thodius on stage, grasping a thick leather-bound book nearly half her size. Tugging on a thick ribbon, she opened the book to a specific page and held it out for Thodius to read.

Ipsa let out a low groan. "Here we go again," she whispered under her breath. Despite the fact that Repast occurred each day, Thodius started every instance reading the same passage from the same book, using the exact same tone of voice. She found the ritual terribly boring, although looking around, every other angel seemed rapt with attention, waiting on Thodius's every word. Ipsa rolled her eyes and began mouthing the words as he spoke them onstage.

"With the first stardust of the universe, angels were born more than three million Repasts ago. The first angel, Yuka, was formed with wings. But the second angel, Ren, had no wings. And so Yuka became the first Wreather. Taking a bit of her own wing, she buried it in a field of green grass. When the sun rose a second time, the field was thick with Kluna, a gift for Ren and every angel born of Here since."

Thodius looked up at the sky, closing his eyes dreamily, before he slowly lowered his gaze back to the book before him.

"Those first angels had a choice: They could spend an eternity living in repose and comfort, or they could help these creatures, the counter image of angels—so physically similar yet lacking the many gifts bestowed on us by the universe. And so, we began answering their prayers. We gave them our language, gave them fire. Most of all, we gave them hope to survive their dangerous world. And so, we call them…"

"Hopelings," Ipsa mouthed silently, mimicking Thodius's speech. She reached for another piece of vismarati, knowing that Thodius would pause at this moment for dramatic effect. She chewed, swallowed, and then commenced imitating his recitation once more.

Thodius took in a deep breath that caused both his chest and purple wings to expand. He bowed his head toward the smaller angel standing in front of him. She closed the book and scurried off. Thodius turned toward the crowd of new angels seated onstage.

"And so it shall be that these angels, the newest members of our family Here, born of the dust of stars in the time of their own making and choosing, will find their new form as others have before them—Yuka's gift of knowledge and magic bestowed upon them, just as it was to Ren, so many Repasts ago. You shall be complete only upon sacred union with your wings." Thodius paused and turned his head upward. "It is your destiny."

Ipsa tugged at Muir's mantel and leaned in close. "Crazy that only a few Repasts ago you were angel dust," she said. "Can you remember anything from that time?" Muir shook her head slowly and then lifted her head toward the sky, as if the distant glimmer of some faraway star might jar her memory.

"Enough whispering!" Elna hushed. "It's time for the first pairings!"

As Elna spoke, two heavy doors at the back of the stage began to creak open. Out stepped a slender angel with light brown skin and a close crop of jet-black hair whom Elna had introduced to Ipsa a few Repasts ago, named Argo. He stood gazing out at the crowd for a moment, taking in the sea of angels before him. He took a step forward, but his arm seemed tethered to something inside, which pulled him back toward the interior of the Wreathing House. Taking his other fist, he gave a strong tug, leaning the weight of his body toward the crowd. Suddenly, three objects, then four, then six swooped down below the doorway and out into the open air of the stage, before soaring up toward the sky. Each was stopped only by the length of string tethered to Argo, who was moving somewhat frantically below. Soon there were too many to count.

"Wings!" Muir whispered with excitement, her eyes never leaving the chaotic tangle fluttering above the stage.

Hundreds of wings of nearly every color soared through the sky. Argo struggled to remain firmly on the ground as the pairs danced frantically above. Ipsa thought he looked like a frazzled hopeling dog walker being pulled down a sidewalk.

Elna saw a pair of golden wings flitting back and forth nervously behind Argo. "I always get excited to meet the new Wreathers!"

Ipsa nodded to her friend and saw that it looked like there were at least two dozen pairs of crimson wings, the color of her own department.

Muir leaned in with a whisper, pointing toward the far side of the stage. "Why don't I see any purple wings—for the Implementers, like Thodius and Corintine?"

Ipsa smiled. So much of the time, she felt out of place Here, as if she was doing everything wrong. With Muir, Ipsa felt like she actually knew the answers. "Implementers aren't chosen when they get their wings. They're selected by the other Implementers to join the group once they've been Here for maybe a billion Repasts—I'm not sure what the criteria are exactly, but they could be chosen from any department Here. It's a really big honor."

Muir squinted at the group of Implementers seated in two rows on the stage to the left of Thodius. "Like Eon."

Ipsa cast an annoyed glance toward a seat in the second row near the edge of the stage. Eon sat tapping his foot and looking like he had somewhere else to be.

"Unfortunately," Ipsa said. "I guess it's probably because he oversees the biggest department Here, so they figured they needed to include him."

An Implementer with grayish pink hair in the front row shifted her wings slightly, once again obscuring Eon's small frame from view.

Muir nodded, her eyes wide as she tried to remember everything Ipsa relayed.

"Argo, everyone, shall we begin?" Thodius's voice boomed. The soft flutter of angel wings in the crowd gave their answer. "As we know, even as stardust, these angels had a very specific destiny, a destiny they will find out at this Repast, when they pair their wings. While hopelings may speak of having a 'soul,' they cannot truly understand what that concept means, for they will never experience the state of divine knowledge and contentment that comes with the pairing of one's wings." He paused, nodding his head along with the masses in the crowd bobbing theirs in agreement. "But of course, with this greatest of gifts comes the responsibility of knowing that we must always watch over, protect, and give hope to those poor wingless creatures who have been made in our image—but can never truly be angels." Thodius said his last line slowly, pausing a beat after each word for dramatic effect.

"Release the first pair!" Thodius shouted, and Argo eagerly let one cord unravel from his hand. It was a pair of dazzling wings that seemed to sparkle like jewels flashing in the sun, giving off glints of pink, amber, and turquoise. But its underbelly gleamed distinctly black.

"The Statistics Department!" Elna sang, clapping her hands together softly.

"What does that department do again?" Muir asked.

"They keep records of most activities There," Elna whispered, leaning toward Muir while never taking her eyes off the stage below. "They can tell you exactly how many hopelings live There at any given time, track climate, and all sorts of things that might help the Answering Department better answer prayers."

Freed from its constraint, the pair of ebony wings pumped upward, high above the stage, until they soared far above the top of the Wreathing House. They somersaulted, then glided, then twirled, all before spiraling back down toward the stage at a high speed. The crowd in the amphitheater fluttered their wings with approval and enthusiasm. The pair skidded to a halt above the group of wingless angels who stood in a line at the front of the stage. The wings paused just overhead, suspending themselves with an occasional flap. That pair began to inch across the row now, like a dog tracking a scent—a few feet forward, then a pause, then a few more. After dancing back and forth several times, the flash of black shot up high into the air one final time and then, pausing for a moment, suspended in mid-air, they opened themselves wide and swooped down softly to land gracefully on the back of a large olive-skinned angel with gangly arms. That angel, who up until that moment had been staring out into the crowd somewhat vacantly, looked at once like a key had just turned in a lock at his back. He smiled and took a step forward toward the crowd.

"Angel, tell us: What is your name?" Thodius said.

"Meko," the angel replied, sharing the new title as if he'd always known it.

"Meko, the Statistics Department welcomes you!" Thodius said, and waft of flutters filled the space as members of that department stood up, amidst the crowd, and bowed slightly, their wings tapping together as a greeting.

Ipsa took a closer look at Meko's wings: They offered an outward rendering of an angel's soul, taking up exactly as much space as they needed to in any given moment, expanding in moments of joy or flight, relaxing in moments of tranquility.

Onstage, Meko bowed slightly and retook his seat. Another hundred or more angels remained standing.

"Another pair! And another!" Thodius said, and Argo released a pair of emerald green wings that easily found their way to the back of an angel with ravishing red hair the length of her back.

"The Harvesters welcome you!" Thodius said.

"The Harvesters…" Muir trailed off, hoping Ipsa would fill in the blank of her new angel knowledge. She tugged at Ipsa's sleeve to be sure she'd heard her.

"They're the ones who collect the Kluna to make wings," Ipsa whispered, her eyes still following the flapping wings onstage.

Muir scanned the skirmish of wings tangling above the stage. "I don't see any orange wings," she said. "Aren't the Answering Department's wings orange?"

"Those are very rare," Elna said.

Muir looked across the Repast Field, her nose crinkling: "But I don't see any of them, anywhere—in the crowd, I mean."

"They don't come to Repast," Ipsa said, her wings clapping together as a pair of blue wings made a graceful somersault onto a new Contemplator's back. "They're too busy."

"Their work is far too important," Elna added. "Hopelings First."

Argo let slip another cord from his grasp, and then another, until there remained only two angels standing before them and seven pairs of wings floating somewhat lazily above, as if they had no plans to choose an angel. Thodius signaled to Argo, who went to retrieve those chords and cull the remaining wings back together, disappearing through the doors at the back of the stage.

The pair of wingless angels shifted down the stage slightly. Another hundred or so new angels climbed the stage to await their wings. Argo re-emerged back through the great opening, a new group of pecking wings tangling and tumbling after him. Again, he released them one after another. This time, every angel onstage found a pair, even the two angels from the first grouping. The process continued several more times until all of the wingless angels had crossed the stage to find a pair of wings.

Thodius cleared his throat. "There is, of course, just one more bit of ceremony before we return to the important work of our departments. Just as we have welcomed new angels from stardust, so too, do we allow others to return to that from whence we all came, realizing that, in much the same way, the moment of choosing is decided by those very wings that gave us each life. Now, to whom will we bid a safe return to stardust this Repast?"

Across the space, angels turned their heads this way and that, wondering which angels would answer the call to return to the stars. Slowly, in the distance, Ipsa saw a thin woman with a long braid down her back, a Harvester. Elsewhere, hundreds of others rose from their tables, their wings carrying them softly down to the stage. As each landed, Argo stood by the doors to the Wreathing House, ready to direct the line of angels inside.

Ipsa turned her head this way and that, wondering if any more angels would heed the call. This portion of the Repast seemed unscripted. No angel, not even Thodius, could predict which angels would appear onstage. Their wings alone held the answer of when they would be called upon to return to the stars from which they'd come.

"Where are they going?" Muir asked, tugging urgently at Ipsa's sleeve.

"To swim the Endless Lake," Ipsa said, not looking at Muir. Near their table, a short and round man with leathery brown skin and wings of the same color also rose. She wondered if Dhavi knew him from the Chronicling Department.

"Swim?" Muir said, confused. "Why would they swim if they could fly?"

"Millions of Repasts ago, a group of angels rose and made their way from the Repast Field down to the shores of the Endless Lake," Elna said. "Their wings just seemed to lift off of them, flying off toward the horizon line, while those first angels smiled, like *they knew that was going to happen.* Then they walked into the water and started swimming after them."

"Where did they go?" Muir said, breathless.

"Legend has it, Yuka once sent a Harvester to follow them, to understand where they were swimming to—even rescue them," Elna said, her hands absentmindedly rolling a couple vismarati in her palm as she spoke.

"And?" said Muir, leaning forward.

"The Harvester eventually gave up," Elna said, her eyes sparkling. "His wings ached and the shoreline had disappeared. All he could report back was that these angels were swimming with a purpose and in a steady stream, toward a horizon line that no other angel has reached."

"Where do you think they go?"

Elna squinted, as if the question caught her by surprise. "Why, back to stardust, of course!" she said. "There! I think that's everyone for now!"

In fact, the last angel was heading through the doorway, Argo slowly closing the doors behind them. Thodius turned back toward the crowd. "Friends, thank you as always for your hard work today, and for joining us in this celebration to welcome the newest members into our community. Although they can't join us for Repast, I speak on behalf of all of the Responders in the Answering Department when I say that your enthusiasm and dedication allow our community to truly put Hopelings First."

At a mention of the Responders, Muir perked up. "There!" she said, pointing down to three pairs of pumpkin-colored wings in the front row. "There's a group of new Responders!"

Almost on cue, the group of Responders stood and followed Argo through a side entrance. Group by group, Thodius celebrated each department's special and critical role Here. He saved the Readers for last, which made Ipsa feel both special and guilty for not caring more about her work. "My dear Readers, as you know, as the Second Arcanum tells us: Prayers must be heard to be answered. Your work is vital. Thank you."

Ipsa looked around the crowd. This was the moment each Repast when angels seemed to relish in their service to a world of hopelings who, as Thodius noted, would never have souls or wings the way they did, who had only an inkling of the complex world that offered their species protection and survival. Ipsa watched those seated around her smile and laugh, each angel so content. Elna chatted easily with Muir, as if they were old friends. These were the moments when Ipsa wondered if perhaps there was a hollow inside her own wings, something that, somehow, her own angel soul was missing. But she kept that emptiness to herself.

Chapter Six

Please, please, please, please, PLEASE let there be a snow day tomorrow.

    —Aidan

IPSA RETURNED TO THE READING ROOM FOLLOWING REPAST to read and file prayers. Almost mindlessly, she went through the motions of topic and deadline, topic and deadline. Finally, she sent a prayer about a snow day winging toward the Weather prayer slot in the far upper corner of the Reading Room when, suddenly, that prayer paused in motion above her, just as the loops of a new prayer slowed to an indiscernible pace. They'd reached the end of their daily work sessions.

Ipsa turned her head to see Darius reflexively smile and push himself up from his chair. His eyes met Ipsa's. "Recreation time! See you next session, Ipsa!" He turned and walked away without pushing in his chair, a half-read prayer floundering around his desk, waiting for direction.

Ipsa looked down at her own table: A nearly finished prayer on her desk twitched slightly, as if it itched to get its last words out. But it would need to wait.

Ipsa headed straight to Dhavi's bench, but it was empty. She couldn't shake the image of that hopeling teen from the mysterious prayer, twisting and tensing his piece of folded paper. So she did something she'd never done before: visit Dhavi at his dwelling—a small thatched cottage that sat in the opposite direction from the communal Rest Houses. Almost without exception, angels Here did not have private quarters, even within the Rest Houses, which were simply large open gathering spaces where, at sunset, angels could meditate and gaze up toward the stars from which they'd been created, until the sun rose again on another blue sky. Another Repast. Only the Responders lived away from the community.

That Dhavi lived and worked in solitude, within this small cottage down a serpentine footpath, was uncommon. But Ipsa figured that, much like the Answering Department, Dhavi's work must be very important. Lifting her hand, she gently rapped her knuckles on the door.

"Come in," Dhavi's deep, familiar voice called from behind the oak door. He spoke as if he'd been expecting her.

Ipsa pushed open the heavy wooden door and found Dhavi seated, reading a book in the corner of the room. She inhaled deeply. The air felt thick and smelled of spice. The inner cottage was small—three angels with their wings at full mast would fit tightly in the main living space—yet it felt inviting. Books filled the room—more than she had ever seen, even within the Learning Space—stacked high on shelves and in haphazard columns on the floor. In another corner, a long sheet of paper stretched across a large table, the paper sketched with a mountain range of zigging and zagging lines overlayed with smaller etchings and scribbles. Several journals sat on top of the paper, spilling open to pages covered in Dhavi's loopy script.

From what Ipsa understood, Dhavi kept the recorded history of There—drawn from the information pooled at various departments, including Prayer Reading and Statistics—capturing a timeline of the hopeling world and the events that shaped it.

A crackling sound behind her caused Ipsa to turn around, startled by the wild dance of yellows, reds, and ambers flickering inside a hole in Dhavi's wall. This was fire! She had heard about it—it was, after all, an answer to one of the first prayers Yuka ever answered, the prayer for warmth— and she'd seen it secondhand a few times in prayers, but Ipsa had never seen a real fire—they had no need of its heat, as it was never cold Here, and no use for it in cooking, as their Repast dishes required no oven. It had never occurred to her that angels would use fire.

"So, what do you think of the place?" Dhavi asked, interrupting her inspection. Ipsa's wings blushed pink. Taking any interest in material things was so "earthly," and she'd been caught right in the act.

"Dhavi, is that a…*fire*?" Ipsa asked, her eyes drawn once again to the flecks of color, swirling in constant motion.

"Not if you tell on me!" Dhavi chuckled, and, leaning his left arm over the side of his chair, opened his palm to reveal a few scraps of paper. He cast them softly toward the hearth, sending gold flecks swirling into the air. They vanished as quickly as they appeared.

Ipsa didn't know which was more ridiculous: the idea of her telling on Dhavi or the thought of him as a rebel angel. Not that she could recall any explicit rule against having a fire. In any event, rules Here were not so much rules as the accepted guidelines for how all angels behaved. *Hopelings First. Share knowledge, with prudence.* Angels felt content to adhere to a way of life, to their Arcana, not necessarily a set of rules or laws. But Ipsa forced herself to push the thought aside; she had not come all this way to talk about rules or even fire.

Ipsa thought about their last conversation as she watched the dwindling fire spitting out its last sparks.

"I read a prayer, Dhavi," Ipsa began, taking a seat across from him.

"Well, I should hope so! Otherwise Eon really *would* have an excuse to send you to the Transcription team!" Dhavi chuckled.

Ipsa smirked and glided her right hand down the arm of her chair, absentmindedly sifting the wooly covering between her thumb and forefinger. She leaned forward, filling in some of the space between herself and Dhavi.

"It's just that I've never read a prayer like this one before," Ipsa continued, surprised at her own timidity.

"Well, tell me about it." The angel's eyes flickered, as if from the fire's reflection.

"There was a hopeling boy. Well, not really a boy, but not quite a man either—I think he was what they call a teenager," Ipsa finally decided. "And something was wrong. Someone had left him a note, but he was afraid to tell his parents about it, and it seemed like that someone might hurt him if he didn't do…or not do…*something*. I think he might be in danger, Dhavi."

"I see…I think. And what exactly was he praying for? What was the note about?" Dhavi asked. He stopped poking at the burning logs and turned toward Ipsa.

"That's the problem! I was just about to find out when

Eon showed up and snatched the prayer right off my desk. He said it had been 'misdirected.' Since when are prayers misdirected?!"

Ipsa trained her eyes on the bits of wool twisting in her fingers.

"Misdirecting aside, you've read prayers before where a hopeling was in some kind of difficulty? You usually just brush them aside. Why was this one different?"

Ipsa hesitated, recalling the mysterious sensation she'd felt when she first handled the prayer. She'd never kept anything from Dhavi, but she also still didn't know quite what to make of what she'd seen. After so many prayers and the Repast, it seemed blurry and fuzzy and hard to describe, and so Ipsa couldn't say with total certainty that anything out of the ordinary *really* had happened.

"I don't know Dhavi, I just, I mean, aren't you always telling me I should be more invested in my prayers?" Ipsa said. "I'm just trying to show a little *concern*, a little *sensitivity*."

"Yes, Ipsa, and the sun that makes every star in the sky is just some self-contained, big yellow ball of fire. What else are you going to sell me today?"

Ipsa met Dhavi's gaze and wished that, just once, he couldn't read her as plainly as the books at his feet.

"This one was different, Dhavi. I can't really explain it. I…I just *felt* something I've never felt before. Somehow, I know this prayer is important. I know it's a prayer I should help get answered. And I feel responsible for making sure that happens." Ipsa's voice trembled.

She watched and waited for Dhavi to speak. He leaned back deep in his chair, his brow wrinkled. He turned toward the crackling embers of flame, as if searching their movements for an answer. His expression seemed guarded. Ipsa realized it was the same look she had seen for that fleeting instant in the park during their last conversation.

Finally, Dhavi spoke softly, his gaze fixed on the dancing flames. "Tell me everything you remember about the prayer."

She recounted every detail from start to finish—from its strange sensation to the way the teenager kept reaching up from the bike's handlebars to rumple his red hair. And how *nice* Eon had seemed when he took away the prayer. Dhavi's face stayed in the same strained wrinkle throughout her story, but when she finished, his face seemed to unfold, and his lips, which had been tightly pursed, relaxed slightly. Ipsa felt a wash of relief in her wings, having unburdened this to Dhavi. She knew he would tell her just what to do.

Dhavi studied the grooves in his palm for several moments and then turned his eyes again toward the last embers of the dying fire. "Ipsa." His voice sounded thick and dry. "Thank you for sharing that, but I'm tired. You must go now."

Chapter Seven

If by some miracle, you could make it stop raining in time for my wedding tomorrow I would REALLY appreciate it. I know everyone says it's good luck to have rain on your wedding day, but I'm pretty sure that's just something people say to make the bride feel better as she's trudging across the lawn wearing galoshes under her dress while seven waddling bridesmaids attempt to shield her from the elements with an electric-blue tarp. Please don't make me wear galoshes and a blue tarp on my wedding day.

   —The soon-to-be Mrs. Jill Golden

"Ipsa! Do you realize what this is?" Muir said as she and Ipsa looked at a flapping piece of parchment smelling of hopeling nail polish. "It's my five millionth prayer! Corintine said that once we get to five million, I can read unsupervised. Isn't that exciting?"

"That's wonderful," Ipsa said flatly. She stared past the prayer, at nothing in particular. It had been five Repasts since she'd spoken to Dhavi about the teenage hopeling's mysterious prayer, and she'd been struggling to focus on her incoming prayers ever since. She couldn't understand why he had asked her to leave his cottage so abruptly. Had she done something wrong?

Muir waved her hand in front of Ipsa's nose, waking her from her trance. "So, what do you think? A hopeling whose wedding is going to be rained out...I was going to say, *trivial,*"—Muir giggled—"mostly because I figured that's what you'd say. But then I wondered if marriage for some people is considered their livelihood, and it's in the next twenty-four hours, but now I'm catching myself because I realize it goes to WEATHER!"

The prayer flapped in half, hovering at eye level, waiting for Muir's command.

"Well, Ipsa?" Muir nudged Ipsa's arm.

"Huh?"

"It's Weather, right? That's where this prayer goes?" Muir said.

"Oh, right. Yes, Weather," Ipsa replied.

Muir beamed and cleared her throat. "Weather," she commanded in a firm voice. The prayer dutifully bounded away toward its destination, as if it were a dog chasing after a tennis ball.

"Ipsa, is everything okay? You've seemed distracted lately," Muir said.

"Oh, nope, just bored, I guess," Ipsa said. As she often did when she was distracted, Ipsa found her fingers tracing circles in the wood, then curving down in a serpentine twist from top to bottom, over and over again.

"I mean, I was *so* nervous when I read my first prayer— do you remember? The one about the little girl's hamster?"

Muir jabbered away a mile a minute, but Ipsa wasn't listening. What she needed was a way to get ahold of that hopeling's prayer and find out who was following him, and what he was supposed to "call off." The question was how? She closed her eyes and tried to remember the prayer. It was dim, but the memory was there—*he* was there—wringing his hands across the braided leather of his handlebars, rocking back and forth, debating, worrying. Ipsa looked deeper into the scene, hoping for some clue. She remembered him fidgeting with the note in his hands…adjusting the mirror…tussling his hair…and there! Just as his hand had swept up toward his forehead, a jingling: Two pendants hung from a chain around his neck. She slowed the memory down and zoomed in. The metal glinted in the late afternoon sun, casting the divots in dark shadow—letters stamped into the metal. She almost had it —the first letter was big…a C. That was it! Con…Conw… Conwa—

"Ipsa? Did you hear me?" Muir laid a hand on Ipsa's shoulder, snapping her out of the prayer. Ipsa felt a moment of frustration—she'd almost had it—followed by a tinge of guilt: Muir was so excited about her prayers, and Ipsa had not paid her the slightest attention.

"I'm sorry, Muir." Ipsa sighed. "Say that last part again?"

Unaware that Ipsa had been—quite literally—in another world, Muir continued on with her gleeful prattle. "I said, do you think my First Prayer is already in the Prayer Archives? I mean, isn't that exciting to think I might already have a prayer answered and archived?"

The Prayer Archives! Ipsa suddenly felt foolish. Jumping up from her seat, she seized Muir's shoulders. "Oh Muir, you're going to make a tremendous Reader!" And with that Ipsa darted out of the room, leaving Muir staring after her, her head cocked to one side.

IPSA WAITED BEHIND A NEARBY EUCALYPTUS TREE FOR THE bells signaling the start of Repast. Moments later, she saw a line of hazel-colored wingtips peaking above the hedge, the Archivists heading to their daily ceremony. Ipsa paused. Was she actually about to sneak into the Archives in search of some hopeling's file, a hopeling whose name she only half knew? Con-something? Since reading the teen hopeling's prayer, Ipsa had experienced a raft of unsettling sensations she'd never felt before. Faced with the daunting task of tracking this prayer down, she added hopelessness to that list.

The Prayer Archives stood a dozen wingspans away from the Reading Room, in an ivy-covered building that was almost forgotten, which seemed fitting given its purpose. The building reached up hundreds of wingspans overhead, with shelves of prayer files stacked as tightly as a container of hopeling sardines, right up to the ceiling. Ipsa padded along a glass floor, which, she vaguely remembered from class, shifted upward once an entire shelf of hopelings was dead and thus their files no longer relevant. And so, legions more shelves descended into the caverns below, dating all the way back to the very first hopelings who'd prayed for fire. The inside of the Archives smelled musty and damp, like the mingling of too many soggy hopeling emotions in one place. Ipsa heard whispers overhead and raised her chin toward the ceiling. A line of prayers flapped through the air in a steady train until they began branching off around corners and down different rows. She spied one prayer about half a row down, just above her head, steadying itself in the air. As if by the push of a button, one of the files on the shelf sprang out and open, allowing the hovering prayer to slip snugly inside, like a child tucked firmly between the sheets. The file slapped shut and squeezed back into place on the shelf.

Ipsa paused for a moment, staring hard through the glass into the cavernous space below her feet. She had never stood in this space before, never seen this many prayers in one space besides the Reading Room. She felt a strange tension in her wings, aware of both the circulation of newly answered prayers overhead and the coldness of glass on her feet, concealing files from hopelings who had long ago stopped praying.

She walked past the rows and rows of files toward a table which housed a pile of massive books. She brushed her hand over the covers, each one labeled with the name of a different country There. Taking a guess, she opened the one marked "United States" and began thumbing her way through an alphabetical list of living hopelings. The names printed across the pages were miniscule—invisible to a hopeling's eye. Ipsa poured over them with the speed of a comet: *Connery, Convery, Conville, Conwakowski, Conwajinski....* Ipsa looked over her shoulder: Above her, a seemingly endless train of prayers chugged along toward their destinations. *Conwall, Conwalt... Conwan, Conwanda, Conwar, Conwatson.... Conway.* Her finger paused. It was the same word that had been imprinted on the metal tag around the hopeling's neck, she was sure of it. Ipsa's wings fluttered, then tensed. She leaned in closer: Indented below the name *Conway* were at least a thousand hopelings who shared that last name. But her fingertip paused, almost on its own, under one name:

Conway, Isaac. 14. Booker T. Washington School of Arts and Technology, Farmington, Connecticut, USA.

Isaac Conway. The moment Ipsa read the name she felt

somehow foolish it had taken her so long, as if she'd always known it. Silently, she felt her lips forming the name over and over again.

Ipsa's wings jittered, sending a tingle across her shoulders. She hadn't learned many specifics about the Archives in her Reading coursework. Ipsa knew how to send a prayer to be sorted but had no idea how to retrieve an entire hopeling's prayer file. She had a name, but no idea where to begin looking amongst the endless rows of shelves. Taking a chance, she called in a hushed voice, "Prayer folder: Isaac Conway."

For a moment, her voice echoed through the vast caverns of the Archives, eclipsing the sound of the answered-prayer train overhead. But then she heard a noise in the distance, a noise that grew louder and louder, until an object came into sight from around the corner of a nearby bookcase. From a distance, it looked like an upside-down paper fan, but as it came closer, Ipsa saw its edges were the hard covers of the file, with a thick pile of prayers swaying from side to side as the file made its way toward Ipsa, until it landed with a soft *plop* on the large table beside her.

Ipsa's wings trembled as she leapt for the file, then wilted: Clearly there was some mistake. Almost all of the files on nearby shelves seemed ready to burst at the seams, nearly overflowing with sheets of paper. Isaac Conway's prayer file, on the other hand, looked anemic, filled with only a few dozen prayers.

Ipsa thumbed through his earliest few prayers, resting on a neatly printed piece of yellowed parchment from eight earthly years before:

God,
Are you also Santa Claus, the Tooth Fairy, and the Easter

Bunny? Because I have reason to believe that those are all actually my mom and dad. (They aren't very careful.) There's no point in asking for your help with Grandma's hip if you're made up, too. Please advise (or don't—if you're really my parents).
—Isaac

Ipsa didn't know what to make of this prayer. Isaac couldn't have been more than six years old at the time. Instinctively, she flipped to the back of the file to find the prayer she was looking for—the prayer that Eon had snatched from her desk.

It wasn't there. That meant it was still being answered. The last entry, dated from nearly one hopeling year ago, was inked with a stark, black pen, the writing almost carved into the paper.

IF YOU REALLY DO EXIST, I WILL NEVER FORGIVE YOU.

Ipsa felt a chill up her wings. Forgive them for *what?* She placed her palm on the paper to transport herself into the memory of that prayer, but at that moment, the heavy mahogany door to the Archives slammed shut. Repast must have ended. Shoving Isaac's file underneath the folds of her mantel, Ipsa waited behind a shelf until she heard a set of footsteps fading from earshot. Ipsa tiptoed to the door, careful not to let it slam on her way out, Isaac Conway's file tucked safely away.

Chapter Eight

I salute Shiva, who burns the sorrow of poverty, who is the lord of the universe. Please don't make my pitaaji be a waste picker for much longer. It's dangerous. Besides, Maji can never seem to get the smell off of him.

—Gomin

"Where have you been?" Elna spoke in a loud whisper as soon as she turned to see Ipsa. "You've already missed four hundred assignments!"

When Ipsa exited the Archives, the main square and paths stood empty; in the Reading Room, prayers still floated over desks, waiting for instruction. Whomever had entered the Archives, they were not returning from the end of Repast.

Ipsa scanned Elna's face, her own wings clenched tightly against her back. This was not nervousness, Ipsa realized, but sadness. She studied her friend's bright, inquiring eyes and suddenly understood that there was a secret between them. There were no secrets Here. Elna and Ipsa always shared everything—every intricate detail of a new pair of wings and every ridiculous hopeling prayer. But something within Ipsa told her that this was one prayer— one hopeling—she could not share with Elna. At least until she had more answers.

Down below on the stage, Thodius held court as a Wreather named Jolie attempted to corral a few dozen wings that had not yet been assigned. "That pair he just released?" Elna said, pointing toward a sage green pair delicately flapping and swooping over the stage. "I made those!"

"They look beautiful," Ipsa said, hoping Elna would not sense her distraction. Ipsa kept one arm around her waist, where, under her mantel, she'd concealed Isaac's file. The prayers twitched like fish out of water, unaccustomed to being outside of a tightly stacked shelf.

"I'm sorry I was late," Ipsa said.

Elna offered an untroubled smile. "That's okay. Muir found me," Elna said, turning her head toward another cluster of angels. "Although I think she went to say hello to an angel in her history class."

Ipsa bit her lip. "How long do you think it takes for the Responders to answer a prayer?" she said.

Elna squinted, causing two creases to appear around her large, blue eyes. "To be answered? Goodness, I've never thought about it. Why?" Elna said.

"No reason. It's not important." Ipsa glanced up at the stage, where Thodius paraded in front of the remaining assignees. The pack of wings tugged and swayed against Jolie's grip. Scanning the benches where the Implementers sat, Ipsa's eyes stopped on Bracchius, the purple-winged angel who ran the Archives.

"Do you remember if Bracchius left the ceremony and returned?"

Elna furrowed her brow. "Which one is Bracchius again? I can never keep the Implementers straight."

Ipsa pointed at him on the stage.

"Oh, *him*! I don't think so." Elna turned her gaze back to the angel who had just stepped forward to claim his wings. "Ha! That makes at least three dozen Harvesters this Repast!" Then, leaning slightly back toward Ipsa, she added, "But you know who didn't show up? Your favorite manager. I'm not sure when Eon has missed a Repast before!"

Ipsa quickly scanned the benches twice; there was no sign of Eon.

"That's strange," Ipsa murmured. Isaac's file twitched and Ipsa slapped her hand against her side.

"Are you okay?" Elna said, giving her a funny look.

"Oh, I'm fine. Look, here comes Muir!" Ipsa said.

Muir waved as she threaded back through the crowd. "Ipsa! There you are!"

At that moment, the gentle applause of wings grew louder. The final angel onstage had found their pair.

"Every pair was assigned this time!" Elna said. "I feel a little bad when one angel has to wait until the next grouping."

Thodius stepped to the edge of the stage, his arms spread wide, offering his daily call for exiting angels.

One by one, a few hundred angels alighted from their various tables, forming a winged procession toward the stage as a gentle rain of applause filled the arena. Underneath Ipsa's mantel, Isaac Conway's file wriggled about, as if longing for a breath of fresh air.

At last, Thodius prepared to close out the Repast. "It is

now time for us to return to our individual callings. Thank you as always for your hard work today and for joining us in this celebration to welcome the newest members into our community. Although they can't join us for Repast, I speak on behalf of all of the Responders when I say that your enthusiasm and dedication allow our community to truly put Hopelings First."

"Ready to head back?" Muir nodded toward Ipsa.

"I forgot: Dhavi asked me to, um, run an errand for him to the Statistics Department, so I was going to stop by on my way back." Ipsa studied Muir's expression for any trace of suspicion but found none.

That wasn't surprising: Her friend would have had no reason to suspect Ipsa's story.

No one lied Here.

Chapter Nine

Please don't let me throw up.
   —Isaac

IPSA HEADED IN THE DIRECTION OF THE STATISTICS Department until she was certain that both Muir and Elna were safely out of sight. It was only then that she veered away from the procession of angels dispersing from Repast, in search of an inconspicuous place to read Isaac's file. Rounding the back of the Statistics Department to a small clearing, Ipsa paused and looked in both directions. Tilting her face upward toward the bright blue sky, she spread her wings to their full span and lifted off to fly.

She headed in the direction of the Rest Houses, which sat nestled alongside the Endless Lake. During work sessions, the space lay vacant. The spaces were not true houses in the sense of four walls and a roof, like Dhavi's cottage. Instead, they were open and vast platforms clustered at varying heights along the mountain range that marked the edge of their community.

Ipsa knew well the ancient story Elna had shared with Muir at a recent Repast: How, at an early Repast, some angels rose and made their way to the Endless Lake. How they'd smiled as their wings seemed to push off from their backs toward the horizon line. How these untethered angels walked toward the water and began swimming, as if to follow their airborne other halves into some great abyss.

Once, many Repasts ago, Ipsa had convinced Elna to spend their entire recreation period flying across the water to see how far they could go—perhaps even catch sight of the stream of the Departing. They flew for ages but found nothing except more water. When they finally returned, they were late for their next session. Ipsa smiled, remembering how free she'd felt as they pumped their wings across the shimmering amber ripples below them. But then Thodius had cautioned Elna about being tardy, and so she'd made Ipsa promise they would never act so recklessly again. Ipsa hadn't felt reckless; she'd felt exhilarated.

Ipsa's wings tingled as she pulled Isaac's file into the open air. She knew she could only spare a few prayers' worth of time before she'd be missed at her desk. She hesitated for a moment, wondering about Eon's absence at Repast. But her wings, an eager co-conspirator, curved to form a cottony hammock for Ipsa to sit in, their flutters keeping Ipsa suspended in the air a few feet above the ground.

Settling in, Ipsa immediately began poring over Isaac's file. She skimmed each prayer hoping to find a few worth really seeing into. There were fewer than one hundred in the entire file, compared to the thousands of a typical hopeling teen. Of those, many seemed to be scripted prayers and involved a young Isaac kneeling bedside, his fists pressed into the valleys of his comforter, parroting rote phrases as his mother hovered nearby.

Ipsa pressed her hand to one from a ten-year-old Isaac, standing at the edge of a stage, overlooking an auditorium filled with hopelings. Looking down, she saw Isaac's feet shifting back and forth. His hands felt slimy and wet. An older, female hopeling stood at a podium in the center of the stage. The woman cleared her throat and adjusted the hem of her magenta blazer, which made her look like a fuzzy pink lollipop.

"It is my distinct honor to introduce our next debater, whom I should note is the youngest ever to qualify for the state championships," she said. The crowd offered a polite round of applause.

Ipsa's vantage point, limited to what she could see through Isaac's own eyes, swiveled away from the podium to the front row, where Ipsa recognized from previous prayers, Isaac's mother and father. When Mrs. Conway made eye contact with Isaac, she started clapping her palms together. "Isaac! We love you, sweetheart!" Mrs. Conway jabbed at the person seated next to her with an elbow to get her attention. But the hopeling, slumped low in their chair, intently reading a magazine or book, did not even glance up from behind the book binding. They wore strappy sandals revealing a pair of slender pale feet and toes painted a bright neon pink. Ipsa wondered if this was Isaac's older sister, whom he'd often referenced during his mother's enforced bedtime prayers. Whoever it was, she tapped her foot impatiently like she had somewhere else to be.

Isaac's focus shifted back to the hopeling in pink at the front of the stage, taking Ipsa's view with him.

"Here to make his case against our reigning middle school debate champion on the topic of leadership and the question of a moral imperative, please welcome to the stage: Isaac Conway!"

Isaac looked down at his clammy hands, which he shoved into the pockets of his khakis.

His parents both jumped to their feet in the front row, cheering wildly.

Isaac closed his eyes, leaving Ipsa in the dark. Then, she heard him whisper: *Please, don't let me throw up.*

Ipsa looked up from the prayer, flipping to the final page in the file, scrawled in angry black ink. *IF YOU REALLY DO EXIST, I WILL NEVER FORGIVE YOU.* Pressing her palm to the page, she closed her eyes to center herself inside the memory. Isaac had uttered that final prayer while lying face down on a bed, a pillow over his head. In that darkness, Ipsa could make out almost nothing else except a red and blue flashing light spilling onto the ceiling. He was alone. It felt like a dead end. She flung the open prayer file toward the ground in frustration. As if to reply, the file slammed itself shut with a loud clap. None of these prayers offered any clues about the prayer she'd found beneath her desk; nothing that explained why present-day Isaac sounded so scared.

All Ipsa could surmise from Isaac's stingy prayer history was that he was a really busy kid. Isaac's childhood, from what Ipsa could gather, was a flurry of debate camps, school plays, and Model United Nations conferences.

His family lived in Farmington, Connecticut, and he had two parents and his older sister—possibly the hopeling with the pink toenails from the debate audience. Ipsa knew from Isaac's bedtime prayers her name was Annie.

It was that last detail that suddenly struck Ipsa. She'd

heard that name before. Ipsa squeezed her eyelids shut; her wings ceased their fluttering, bringing her softly to the floor of the Rest House as she harnessed the memory. She opened her eyes wide. That day on his bicycle, Isaac had called out a name in his prayer: Annie.

Ipsa looked up, tapping her left foot as if to a steady drumbeat. Her gaze settled on the vast sea of water in front of her. She picked up the file and flipped open the back cover to the last page of angry scrawl, not so much a prayer as a threat, followed by earthly silence for nearly a year.

Ipsa closed her eyes and traced a circle and then a squiggle with her finger on the floor of the Rest House. Then she opened her eyes. The Reader in Ipsa knew there was only one circumstance in which a hopeling directed a prayer toward another hopeling.

Annie was dead.

Chapter Ten

Padre,

Please watch over Luciano during surgery. That's all I can ask.
—Antionetta

IPSA STOWED ISAAC CONWAY'S PRAYER FILE IN A ROCKY CRAG in the pocket of space just beneath one of the Rest Houses. She'd flattened it with a heavy rock to keep it from alighting, then returned to the Reading Room and slipped into her chair. Having read her five millionth prayer, Muir had finally been assigned her own reading table two wingspans across the room. Ipsa missed Muir's company, but she also felt glad for the break. She had to admit it had been exhausting keeping this secret, the mystery of Isaac Conway, from her new friend.

The prayer file, which she could picture twitching and fussing in its hiding place, burned hot in Ipsa's mind. Her realization about Isaac's sister was the only lead. And it meant there was only one possible thing to do next: Return to the Archives and find Annie Conway's file. But her wings agitated. She had removed a file from the Archives. If she'd worried about Eon's reaction to some back talk, Ipsa could only imagine the penalty for stealing a hopeling's file from their repository.

Yet every fiber in Ipsa's wings seemed to pull her back toward the Archives in search of clues that might shed light on Isaac's predicament. Six Repasts had passed since she'd found that crumpled prayer. And while angels measured time in Repasts—accomplishing more in an earthly hour than most hopelings could within an entire day—the sun rose and set Here with the same cadence as There. Six sunsets meant six Repasts, meant six earthly days. At least Ipsa knew this: The prayer had not yet been archived, which meant that it was still with the Answering Department. There was still time to see if Annie Conway's file could shed any light on Isaac's prayer. Ipsa would wait for Recreation and double back to the Archives again.

Several times that session, Ipsa caught herself in a daze, a forgotten prayer wagging in the air before her. Twice, when she glanced up from her station, she thought she'd caught Eon watching her. She tried to double down and plow through her prayers, trying not to raise attention to herself.

Ipsa was about to command a prayer from a hopeling named Antoinetta when the prayer froze, as did all the prayers throughout the room. The Hive still rumbled and popped, like a boiling pot of earthly water, but their reading session was over. Rising from her desk, Ipsa joined the procession of angels exiting the Reading Room for Recreation. She spied Muir looking for her, but Ipsa ducked in front of a broad-shouldered angel with widespread wings, then slipped behind a large oak tree to wait for the throngs to clear. Then, quickening her step, she hastened toward a wall of rosebushes that bordered the entrance to the Archives. Ipsa spied the purple wings of Bracchius as he closed the massive double doors, having ushered out the last few workers. Ipsa dropped to her knees behind a hedge and waited for ten deep breaths. Then she slipped inside the Archives in search of Annie Conway's file.

Ipsa retraced her steps to the area of the old library from where Isaac's file had emerged. "Prayer File: Annie Conway," she called out into the caverns, her voice ping-ponging across the glass floor. Her wings felt jittery, as if she'd just flown the length of the Endless Lake. Isaac had specifically called to Annie in his last prayer. She must hold some clue to the danger Isaac now felt.

Ipsa heard a dull clatter down a nearby row of files, followed by a rhythmic series of oomphs. A few moments later, a file the thickness of a hopeling dictionary rounded the corner. As it heaved itself toward Ipsa, the book's binding pulled downward under the weight of thousands of pages. Each airborne flap seemed a feat. Ipsa's wings sparkled bright pink as the volume landed with a thud at her feet.

The angel hammocked her wings beneath her and began to read, choosing a spot in the middle of the book. Where Isaac's prayers seemed forced and short, Annie's could go on for pages at a time, as if gossiping with a friend. Ipsa leafed through prayer after prayer, searching for clues about Isaac's troubles, but she mostly found the insignificant wish lists of a young hopeling—just the sorts of prayers Ipsa hated.

She looked back down and thumbed toward the back third of the file and paused on one prayer—from when Annie was around thirteen.

Dear God,

I know you probably know (since you know everything) but I feel kind of bad now and I just wanted to explain why I did what (you probably already know) I did. Brooke has a gigantic crush on Tommy Gibbons. Melissa thought it would be really funny if we started leaving notes in her locker, signing them from Tommy. And it was really funny—while we were writing them. But then when Brooke didn't know I was watching, I saw her open one of the letters. She looked so excited that, suddenly, I felt kind of bad about the whole thing. I'm just not really sure how to tell Melissa we should stop. So, I guess all I really wanted to say is I'm sorry.
—Annie.

Ipsa rolled her eyes. Flipping through a few more pages, the angel scanned them for Isaac's name. She didn't have to look far. From what Ipsa could gather, the Conway siblings didn't always get along. She read on:

Seriously God, you have GOT to make Isaac stop telling on me. Also, it's not even remotely fair that he gets to go to Washington to visit Aunt Sydney when I've never gotten to go, and I'm practically two years older than him. Just because he's in the stupid Model UN. How come Isaac always gets to go everywhere?

Ipsa flipped to a prayer from later that same year. Annie would have been thirteen and Isaac, nearly twelve.

Please make him go away!

Ipsa placed her hand on the prayer and closed her eyes. Annie stood in the back corner of a large soccer field, a pair of friends beside her casually leaning against the chain-link fence that separated the field from a wooded area. Past the soccer field, Ipsa saw a playground and, beyond it, a one-story sprawling brick building, which she assumed was the Conways' middle school.

Annie's right thumb shot into her mouth to bite at a nail, causing Ipsa to taste a bitter mix of nail polish, moisturizer, and orange peels.

"Should I wear my hair up, like this," the blonde girl next to Annie said, lifting her hair in a twist behind her head, "or down, with a chunky braid that goes all the way to the back?" She let her hair fall back down in thick plaits behind her shoulders. "Annie, how are you going to do your hair?"

"I'm not sure," Annie said. "My mom is so annoying; you know she doesn't like it when I wear my hair down."

"Oh my God!" The other girl beside them tugged on Annie's sleeve to get her attention. "Tommy totally just looked over here!"

Ipsa's gaze drifted over to a group of gangly boys playing touch football down the field. A taller boy with ash-brown hair lifted the ball overhead triumphantly. As he jogged back, he gave a quick glance over his shoulder in the direction where Annie stood.

The two girls beside Annie devolved into giggles as they turned away from the boys, clinging to the fence. "He's totally going to ask you!" the blonde said.

"Oh Melissa, shut up!" Annie said, her eyes rolling.

Out of the corner of Annie's eye, Ipsa saw a small, skinny figure walking diagonally across the field, right toward the trio.

"Oh no," Annie groaned. The other girl cupped her hand over her eyes to shield the afternoon sun. Isaac made his way toward the trio. He looked scrawny, like a strong gust of wind might send him to the far corner of the field, and he wore a faded *Star Wars* T-shirt. His hair color was bright orange—it reminded Ipsa of the Responders' wings. And unlike the rumpled mess of hair she'd seen from his prayer on the bike, his hair was cropped close to his head, making his ears seem bigger.

"Oh, come on, Annie," the friend said. "I think he's adorable. He's gonna be a total heartbreaker once he gets to high school—he'll have all the drama girls swooning."

"Bekah, you're so gross," Annie said. "He's a total pest. I can't wait to get away from him next year."

Please make him go away! Annie whispered under her breath.

Ipsa thought about what Corintine had mentioned in Muir's Introduction to Reading class: Prayers in which the turnaround time was simply too short to be answered. A moment later, Isaac was standing right in front of Annie, his wire-rimmed glasses shifting down his nose. He pushed them up with a thrust of his left hand.

"Hey, Isaac." Bekah dragged out his name in a singsong voice. Ipsa felt Annie's arm jerk toward Bekah, elbowing her in the side.

"What do you *want?*" Annie asked.

"Good day, Bekah," Isaac said in an overly formal tone. Then he turned toward the brunette and gave a mock bow. "Melissa."

He turned toward his sister. "Mom was pissed you left without me this morning."

"Aren't you always saying seventh graders don't need chaperones?" Annie said, rolling her eyes and making Ipsa feel like she'd just done a cartwheel. "I had a field hockey meeting before first period."

A spring breeze blew across the field. Ipsa felt the cool air upwelling beneath Annie's skirt. Her hands pressed down to still the fabric.

"Mom said to remind you that it's your week to do laundry. And to start dinner when you get home."

"Annie, you *promised* we'd do drills this afternoon!" Melissa said, her hands on her hips.

"I know," Annie said, tapping her foot. "Isaac, can't you handle it?"

"Yeah…that's a hard no, sis," Isaac said. "I've got regional debate semi-finals on Thursday, and I need to prep."

Melissa groaned.

Annie folded her arms. "What if I do your dishwasher duty for the next two weeks?"

"No can do," he said. "These are the *regionals*."

"Yeah, and Saturday's game is against Mount Claire's. They haven't lost a game all season," Annie said. "And there's a scout coming from St. Ignatius Prep."

"Annie, I am not going to Booker T. without you next year!" Bekah said, swooping her arm dramatically around Annie's shoulder.

Isaac shook his head.

"Well, I don't really care, because I'm not coming home," Annie said defensively.

"Fine with me, but when Mom and Dad get home and there's no dinner and the house smells like dirty socks, they're going to be pretty mad."

Annie narrowed her eyes—shrinking Ipsa's view of the scene. "I hate you, do you know that?"

Isaac shrugged, turned, and started walking away. "Suit yourself," he called. "Just don't say I didn't warn you." He turned back toward Bekah, flashing a charming smile: "See you around, *Bekah*."

Ipsa felt Annie's sneaker kick the dirt hard in anger. "God forbid Isaac not have five hours to stand in front of his mirror practicing his pros and cons about universal health care," she said. Ipsa felt the fleshy softness of Annie's bottom lip clench between her teeth. "The world comes to a halt if Isaac has debate or play practice. Meanwhile, my parents have missed the last four games and don't even care that I have a shot at a scholarship to play for the best high school in Connecticut."

"Forget him." Melissa pulled out a small notebook and pen from her back pocket. "Let's figure out who should ask Bekah to the dance and then send them an anonymous note!"

"No way," Bekah screamed, reaching for the paper.

Annie's eyes glanced up for a moment as she watched Isaac, hands in his pockets, scuffing his way across the chalky dry soccer field, kicking up dust as he went. Annie took one step forward as if to call after her brother but reached her hand out to take the crumpled list of names from Melissa instead.

Chapter Eleven

Please keep us safe.
  —Annie

BACK IN THE ARCHIVES, IPSA LOOKED UP FROM THE PRAYER. There was an entire chapter devoted to sibling rivalry in *Introduction to Hopeling Psychology*. She flipped over Annie's file so that the back cover lay on top. Opening it, she lifted the top corner of the last prayer, bringing Ipsa's face close to the parchment. She looked at the date: October. About a year after the prayer on the soccer field. Annie would have been fourteen and what hopelings called a freshman.

Please, keep us safe.

Ipsa placed her hand on the page. She couldn't see much except inky darkness. The cramped space smelled like hopeling sweat and tennis shoes. Adjusting to the dark, Ipsa realized it was not a room, but a large closet, a few slits of light slipping through a vent at the bottom of the door. Annie's hand dripped with sweat, her fingers fumbling to find something in the black, groping first at what felt like a net, then a face mask, and then, finally, another hand. Annie slipped her own fingers around it and squeezed. Ipsa felt Annie's chest seizing up and down, her heart banging beneath her rib cage as if it might pound its way out.

Ipsa felt a body wedged behind Annie. They let out a small, fluttering whimper.

"Be quiet," hissed yet another voice.

Annie took a gulp of air and seemed to hold her breath. For a moment, there was absolute stillness. Then, beyond the door, a series of fireworks.

The prayer went black.

That was it: the end of the file. Ipsa thought about the final prayer in Isaac's file—the one where he told whoever he was praying to that he'd never forgive them: The date of the last prayer in his file matched this one. A small shiver went up her wings. Ipsa had never felt cold, but this sensation seemed close.

She knew now with more certainty: Annie was dead.

Ipsa jerked her hand away from the page. Taking her foot, she slid the file a few feet across the floor, as if to distance herself from the prayer she'd just experienced.

A noise pulled her back into the present moment. The padding of footsteps a few rows away. One of the Archivists must have returned. How had she not heard the door open?

Quiet as an earthly church mouse, Ipsa crept toward the nearest stack, hiding Annie's prayer file behind her back. Lifting herself on her tiptoes, Ipsa peered out over the brim of files in the bookcase, trying to determine the Archivist's whereabouts. A nasally sniffle rattled through the large room. Ipsa's wings stiffened like a thousand porcupine needles. She knew that sniffle. Scanning the row beyond hers, she jerked back and crouched down in panic. It wasn't an archivist; it was *Eon*. She'd been so busy trying to evade Muir that she'd forgotten all about him.

"Is someone… *here*?" Eon's high-pitched voice echoed through the massive room, as if bouncing off the files of every hopeling that had ever lived. Ipsa felt her wings lurch. Eon's footsteps drew closer with nowhere to hide. She looked up, considering the rafters, but her wings felt like two blocks of ice. Angels didn't skip Recreation to sneak into other departments. Ipsa tried desperately to squeeze the massive file onto the shelf in front of her, but it squirmed and fought her, realizing this was not its proper spot. "Come on!" Ipsa hissed. "Work with me!"

She could hear the pace of footsteps coming closer, slow and measured, like an earthly clock tolling midnight. Having cornered his prey, Eon was taking his time.

"Hello?" another voice abruptly called from a row in the distance. Ipsa jerked her head up. Was it…*Muir?*

Eon's footsteps paused, then turned away from Ipsa.

"Good prayer, Eon!" Ipsa heard Muir say. "Thank goodness you're here! I was lost!"

Eon seemed as surprised at this development as Ipsa was. "*Muir?* Whatever brought you into the Archives?" Eon asked. "Shouldn't you be in class?" Ipsa could hear the agitation in Eon's voice at not having caught the angel he'd been hoping for.

"I'm so sorry! You see, I was looking for the Statistics Department and realize now that I entered the wrong building." Muir's words gushed forward. "I thought that on my way to class I might follow up with them to find out more about weather patterns There. Ipsa and I read a prayer from a pregnant hopeling bracing for a hurricane. I wanted to find out more…I hope that was okay."

"Well, *normally* you need to come to *me* for those sorts of things, and then *I* will check on the matter with the Statistics Department. We do have a *system* in place…"

Ipsa strained to hear the conversation as the other two angels walked further away toward the door. Their voices trailed off and the main door slammed.

Ipsa felt her wings slacken. She sank down to the cool glass beneath her, clutching Annie's file. Ipsa thought about what Muir had said to Eon: why she had accidentally stumbled into the Archives. As Muir's mentor, Ipsa had read every one of the new angel's early prayers—and knew this much: Muir had not read any prayers from a pregnant hopeling about a hurricane.

Muir had just lied to Eon.

Chapter Twelve

How might all beings realize the Path of Awakening to find happiness and peace?
Namo Amida Buddha.
—Patakin

IPSA SAT FROZEN IN PLACE BEHIND THE ROW OF BOOKCASES for what felt like a million prayers. Finally she snuck out, Annie's file squirming under Ipsa's mantel. The sun had already dipped past the tower behind the Repast Field. With sunset came the end of Recreation and the start of evening meditation at the Rest Houses. But Ipsa knew she needed to see Dhavi first.

She raised her hand to knock, then paused. She hadn't seen him since their conversation when he had abruptly asked her to leave. She took a deep breath and offered a timid knock.

His familiar rasp responded through the thick wood. "Come in."

Ipsa crooked her head shyly inside the warm, firelit room. "It's Ipsa," she said softly. "Is it still all right that I come in?"

"Of course, of *course!*" Dhavi's voice seemed to smile.

"I thought…" Ipsa paused, unsure how to continue, "I thought maybe I'd upset you. You asked me to leave so suddenly during my last visit I thought that—maybe you didn't want me to come back."

"Don't be silly. I'm glad you're here," Dhavi said. "I need your forgiveness. It was wrong of me to send you away without an explanation. You gave me a lot to think about with your teenager's prayer."

Ipsa felt a wave of relief wash over her. She hadn't realized until that moment just how much Dhavi's opinion mattered to her. The relief quickly took a backseat to a rising sense of panic: How could she admit she'd been sneaking into the Archives and stealing files?

"Dhavi, I followed up on that prayer." Ipsa blurted out. "I found the hopeling's name—Isaac Conway—and I figured if I went to the Archives, I could read the rest of the prayer, but it wasn't there yet, and the last prayer was from almost a year ago."

"Isaac Conway…" Dhavi said.

"There's more: He mentioned his sister's name in his last prayer and so, um, I looked up her file too, but something happened to her. To Annie. I mean, her prayers stop just like Isaac's do, down to the day, and I think she… Well, anyway, all I know is that I'm no farther along in trying to help Isaac than I was when I first came to you about it. But Eon came into the Archives and nearly found me and now I don't know what to do."

Ipsa's wings drooped over her shoulders, exhausted.

Her eyes trained to the corner of a gold-trimmed book at her feet, afraid to meet Dhavi's gaze.

Dhavi stared at the fire for what felt like a hopeling century.

"Isaac. Annie." Dhavi repeated the names, slowly. "That's a lot of information. And what about Eon? Did he see you?"

"No, he—no." Ipsa started to share Muir's appearance at the Archives but stopped herself.

Dhavi uncrossed his legs and leaned forward. "Ipsa, this is hard for me to say, since it's so heartening to see you taking an interest in hopelings. But I suspect it will be even harder for you to *hear*." Dhavi paused. "This is not your prayer to read anymore, and it's not yours to answer. You need to let this prayer go. Return the files and go back to your other prayers. There is nothing more you can do for Isaac."

"But Dhavi, I don't understand!" Ipsa put her hands on her hips. "I'm doing the thing everybody says to do: Putting 'Hopelings first!' I can't be the only angel who's ever asked to follow up on a prayer! What's the big deal?"

"Ipsa, the follow-up is not your responsibility. But *your* job is so critical: to read prayers—to *hear* them."

Ipsa rolled her eyes, her wings flexing. "Prayers must be heard to be answered. Yes, I know Dhavi, but—"

"Then please, do what I've asked, and let's talk more after next Repast. In the meantime, just promise me you'll put those files back, will you?"

Ipsa stared into Dhavi's eyes and nodded dutifully. She was getting very good at lying.

Chapter Thirteen

Lord,

    Why can't every child feel as loved as my son?
—Elenora

Closing the door behind her, Ipsa walked a few paces to a large bush where she'd hidden Annie Conway's file wedged between two branches. Unhappy with its confinement, the file squirmed this way and that.

"Oh, just relax," Ipsa said, easing it out of the space. "Wouldn't you rather be outside in the fresh air than cooped up in some old, dusty Archive?" As if in reply, the file smacked against her chest.

Dhavi's response had frustrated her, but he hadn't closed the door to helping. He'd said they would talk after next Repast. Perhaps he'd realize what she was asking for wasn't all that much.

In the meantime, Ipsa didn't quite know where to go or what to do. The Rest Houses would be buzzing with angels settling in for evening meditations. So she opted instead for the Contemplations Garden.

The Contemplations Garden was the one possible stopover that existed for a prayer before heading to the Answering Department. If an angel filed a prayer as a Contemplation, it defied an easy answer. Ipsa thought of a prayer she'd read recently: *How might all beings realize the Path of Awakening to find happiness and peace?* If she were a Responder, she wouldn't have known where to begin answering that prayer. And so, the Contemplators reviewed those prayers and then offered guidance on how Responders might attempt to reply. That guidance almost always presented itself in a creative manner: a swirl of colors exploding on canvas, or a sculpture reaching well into the tree canopy overhead.

Sometimes, during Recreation, Ipsa would convince Elna to spend their free time threading through the haphazard art gallery of hopeling ideas and emotions. It was one of the few places where Ipsa could find feelings of beauty about There, a world to which she felt so unwillingly tethered. Even Ipsa had to admit that the prayers that arrived in Contemplations were usually not selfish. And the way her blue-winged peers reflected those prayers back could, at times, take Ipsa's breath away.

Ipsa entered the green space through an archway of morning glory. She at once saw a new piece of work: A canvas the length and size of a hopeling school bus, covered with swirls and brushstrokes of every color imaginable, along with bits of different prayers. Pressing her finger to the canvas, she traced the rising peak of an amber mountain crafted with the question: *Why can't every child feel as loved as my son?* Ipsa's fingers dipped down into a turquoise lake of color to her right, where a spiral of words seemed to flow toward some unseen whirlpool behind the canvas. ...*I hope to find where my deep gladness and the world's deep hunger meet.* Ipsa's palm grazed the ridges and valleys of paint as she walked the length of the canvas. The fabric was pulled taut between two large oak trees. Ipsa moved behind the canvas, finding a perfect space to sit undetected.

The grass felt soft and cool as she pulled out Annie's file. The cover of the file felt like peach fuzz. Could Dhavi really expect her to give up her only lead? Ipsa pressed her fingers against the edge of the cover and opened to an arbitrary prayer near the back of the book, a few months after the soccer field prayer.

Ipsa looked around and saw Isaac and his parents seated around a circular table, which she realized was a hopeling dinner table. Annie held a fork, which seemed to be endlessly twisting and retwisting a mound of spaghetti. To her left sat Isaac. He was wearing different glasses, but his hair was still cut short as peach fuzz. She recognized his parents from Isaac's debate stage prayer. Up close, Mr. Conway looked older: His hair—bright orange like Isaac's —showed specks of gray, and two thick creases hemmed his forehead. He wore a blue golf shirt. Mrs. Conway wore an apron over a silk blouse; a suit jacket hung on the chair behind her. The sleeves of her blouse were rolled up past her elbows. Two gold bracelets jangled on her wrist as she reached forward to pick up a bowl in the middle of the table.

"Would anyone like salad?" she said.

"Thanks, dear," Mr. Conway said, reaching across to take the bowl from her and setting it down on his side of the table, still untouched.

"Annie, honey, I'd really like you to have some salad," Mrs. Conway pressed.

"I told you: I don't like green peppers," Annie said, still twirling her pasta. Ipsa could feel the rhythmic tapping of Annie's foot beneath the table.

"Ike, tell Mom about the letter you got today!" Mr. Conway said with an excited smile.

"I just"—Isaac paused, his mouth full of food, then swallowed—"found out who I'll be rooming with at the conference, and the guy is the son of a congresswoman from Oregon. How cool is that?"

"That's *so* neat," Mrs. Conway said. "I have a feeling these are individuals that you're going to stay in touch with for a long time—young men and women who'll go on to do *big* things."

"Mom, can I sleep over Bekah's tomorrow night?" Annie said, interrupting.

Mrs. Conway tilted her head slightly, a look of confusion on her face. "But Annie, we drive Isaac to the conference tomorrow, and then we're going to have dinner with your father's old roommate, Mr. Gallagher, and his family. They were nice enough to offer to have us over before the drive back, and I know they're anxious to meet you."

"Isaac doesn't have to meet them!"

Mrs. Conway sighed, her shoulders slumping toward her elbows. "That's because orientation starts at two p.m., dear."

Annie picked up her fork again only to let it clatter back onto her plate, as if for dramatic effect. "This is so amazingly unfair. Isaac gets to go to some fancy camp this summer, and I have to spend my break babysitting some old lady and can't even spend the first weekend of summer hanging out with my friends because I have to drive my brother to his stupid camp."

"Anne Dorsett Conway, please watch your tone," her

father said, resting his hand, which held a butter knife, on the side of the table.

Her mother placed her hands on the edge of the table, as if she was sitting at a piano. "Annie, you know what an honor it was for Isaac to be accepted. They only take two students from each state and—"

"Right, how could I forget, because he's such a genius," Annie responded snidely.

"Considering you thought Calculus was a class about calculators, I feel like your bar for 'genius' is pretty low," Isaac said, then stuck out his tongue at her.

"Isaac!" Mrs. Conway shouted.

"Enough! Both of you!" Mr. Conway said, laying the knife on the edge of his plate, a square pad of butter untouched on its tip. "I, for one, will be glad to have a summer without this constant bickering. Annie, you know very well why you're spending the summer 'babysitting some old lady,' as you put it. You should be glad you found a job to pay the Stinsons back for the window."

"It was an accident!"

"And I've told you one hundred times to bring the net out from the garage before you start hitting in that direction. Maybe this time it will finally get through to you."

Mrs. Conway began to smooth the wrinkles on the tablecloth, as if it might have a similar effect on the conversation. "Besides," she interjected, "think of it as service. Poor Mrs. Elmer sits alone all day long. I know her son just wants her to have a little company and someone to make sure she's eating lunch and taking her medicine."

"Her house smells like cats. I'm going to leave smelling like cats."

"You already do," Isaac murmured under his breath.

"Shut up! I hate you!" Annie yelled.

"Annie, that is it!" Mrs. Conway said, slamming one hand down onto the table, sending rumples across the smooth plane she'd just created. "We do not use that word in this house. Go to your room!"

"Didn't you hear what he said? He started it!" Annie jerked her seat back. "This is so unfair. My life is so totally unfair. All I want to do is spend one night with my friends, and instead you're making me drive five hours to drop my awful brother off at his smarty-pants summer camp. I can't believe how unfair this is."

"I'm sorry you feel that way," her father said.

Isaac leaned in close to her ear. "I'll try and bring back some pointers on crafting an effective argument—they typically don't recommend just saying 'this is so unfair' over and over again," he whispered.

"I hate this place! I hate all of you!"

Ipsa's vision of the table was obscured by the pools of water brimming in Annie's eyes.

"Go to your room," Mrs. Conway said firmly. She looked exhausted.

Annie ran up the stairs, her feet pounding each board as she went. She slammed her door dramatically before throwing herself onto the bed, sobbing.

Please God, get me out of here. Anywhere but here.

The prayer ended and Ipsa blinked away the sensation of tears. Annie was dramatic! She had a nice house, someone making her dinner, a healthy family, and yet she was *still* miserable, picking fights about how bad her life was.

Looking back down, Ipsa studied the prayer again, her hand pressing the paper. She flipped through a few more prayers, but they all seemed like a variation of the same dinner table fight. Ipsa closed the file, frustrated.

❦

"Ipsa!" Muir said, her right hand waving a prayer in the air. "Flat tire and late to a job interview: 'Expired' because of the flat tire, or 'Highly Urgent' because of the job interview?" Muir still frequently ran to Ipsa with uncertainties about her filing decisions, second-guessing her choices.

"Um, I don't know, probably Expired." Ipsa turned her head in each direction to ensure no one was listening. "Muir, I need to talk to you about the Archives."

"Oh, yes," Muir spoke quickly, her eyes glued to a nail in the wooden floor. "I guess the whole department must know about my silly mix-up! I can't even believe how embarrassing that was! I hope you didn't get in trouble…I mean, as my former mentor."

"No, that's not it," Ipsa said. "I only bring it up because…" Ipsa hesitated. "Muir, is it possible that you went to the Archives…to find *me*?" Muir's eyes flashed up to meet Ipsa's gaze.

"I'm sorry." Muir's wings quivered as she spoke, her voice a delicate whisper. "I—I don't know what sort of mess I've gotten myself into. I only wanted to see if you were okay, because you'd seemed so distracted earlier that reading session. But then I heard Eon and I got scared, and I didn't want to get you in trouble or think I was following you, so I made up the story about the hurricane." Muir took a huge swallow of air. "I'm so sick about it, Ipsa! I've never told an untruth! Please don't think less of me and please don't tell Eon! Honestly, I didn't even realize what I was saying as it came out of my mouth."

"Muir," Ipsa soothed, "of course I'm not going to tell on you."

A visible wave of relief flooded Muir's face, bringing the rose back to the brown of her cheeks.

Ipsa paused, unsure how much more to say. "And Muir?"

"Yes?"

"Thanks for looking out for me."

Muir took a step closer. Her soft features reminded Ipsa of a hopeling who hadn't stretched out yet. "Can I ask you a question?"

Ipsa stared back into Muir's concerned eyes. "Anything."

"What were *you* doing in the Archives?"

Muir didn't quite fit the mold of most angels. Maybe it was because she had only received her wings a few Repasts ago. Muir seemed to care so deeply about so much—about the prayers she read, about Ipsa. Not that other angels didn't care; they just didn't seem to *remember* to care in quite the same way—didn't see that it mattered all that much to their daily work and life. Ipsa worried it would be a matter of time before Muir settled into that pleasant nonchalance that seemed to be the hallmark of her world.

Every time Ipsa closed her eyes, she pictured Dhavi's trusting face asking her to return the Conways' files. Suddenly, the thought of telling another lie, and to Muir, who had risked her wings for Ipsa, seemed wrong.

Ipsa leaned in close. "I went to look for a prayer."

Chapter Fourteen

Oh my God, please don't let me vomit all over this boat.
  —Rigoberto

When Repast finally arrived, Ipsa and Muir made a beeline for the door and found a nearby tree to wait out the crowds of other Readers filing out of the Reading Room toward the Repast Field.

Ipsa glanced from side to side. "About six or seven Repasts ago, I read this prayer—or I started to read it—and it just was *unusual*. I got this funny feeling from it."

"You mean like when I read that prayer from the seasick hopeling?" Muir asked innocently.

"No, not that sort of feeling. It wasn't the prayer, exactly, it was *me*."

Muir squinted her eyes, clearly confused.

"I don't know how to describe it," Ipsa said. "But ever since, I just can't stop thinking about it."

"What was it about, exactly?" Muir said.

"Eon took it away from me before I could finish. Said it had been 'misdirected.'"

Muir's eyes widened. "We haven't learned about misdirected prayers in class yet."

"Yeah, well, I've been reading for a long time and that was the first I've ever heard of it," Ipsa said.

"You think that Eon made it up?"

"I think he didn't want me to finish that prayer for some reason," Ipsa said, leaning her wings against the thick tree trunk behind her.

"That's why you went to the Archives," Muir said.

Ipsa nodded. "I figured even though by that point it would have been answered already, at least I'd know what it was about."

Muir's eyes widened. "Well?"

"It hasn't been answered yet. So...I took the file with me." Ipsa said the last part quickly, her toes tracing the roots of the tree through the dirt.

"YOU TOOK—" Muir lowered her voice. "You took a prayer file with you?!" Her wings agitated behind her.

"*Two*," Ipsa said, sheepishly. "I took his sister's file in case I could learn anything about him from her prayers. But I didn't learn much other than basically everyone annoys her. Oh, and she has no patience."

Muir struggled to contain a giggle.

"What could possibly be funny about this?" Ipsa asked, folding her arms.

"I'm sorry!" Muir said, her wings blushing a rosy pink. "It just occurred to me that I know someone else like that."

Remembering the topic at hand, Muir's expression grew serious. "You took a file from the Archives..." Muir's voice trailed off. Her wings slowed to an even, slow pulse, like she was deep in thought.

Ipsa drew her finger to her teeth, biting down on a nail the way she'd seen Annie do in her prayers. Why had she shared this secret? What if Muir told Eon?

Muir took a deep breath, then locked eyes with Ipsa. "Well," Muir said. "What do we do now?"

Chapter Fifteen

Mon Dieu,

In History & Geography class today, we had to report on a natural disaster in the news—earthquakes, tidal waves, mudslides, and other awful stuff. Are the people who live in those places bad? Is that why you keep punishing them?

—Claude

IPSA COULDN'T EXPLAIN HER FASCINATION WITH ANNIE Conway. The hopeling's prayer file was slowly becoming worn and dog-eared from Ipsa's constant skimming. She marveled at how wildly some hopelings could swing from a trivial request to a serious contemplation to a legitimate need. She had read billions of prayers, but never two from the same hopeling. She had never considered one human life, threaded together through a tapestry of prayers.

Ipsa turned to a prayer toward the end of Annie's file.

Isaac frustrates me so much! I know he's good at EVERY-THING, but why does he always have to rub it in? I didn't get the field hockey scholarship to St. Ignatius. Isaac is good at everything: acting, debate, student council…Field hockey is the only thing I've ever been good at—and now it turns out I'm not good enough. To be honest…it wasn't even about field hockey. I really wanted a fresh start, a chance to make some new friends at a new school. Melissa can be so mean sometimes, and that's not really who I want to be.

The majority of Annie's prayers were the usual hopeling drivel, but Ipsa also saw how much Annie struggled with her place in a family that seemed to orbit her brother's sun. Ipsa tried to imagine what it was like to exist within a family unit There; what it must be like to be a teenage girl living very much outside of the bubble of Isaac, looking in.

Still, like most hopelings, Annie only seemed to remember the grievances. There were plenty of prayers in Annie's file that showed she actually had a pretty loving family. Times when Isaac or her parents put Annie's needs above Isaac. Like a prayer from when Annie was five or six, on a family trip to the zoo. She'd gotten lost, then sobbed for ten minutes straight. The security guard had given Annie a popsicle just to distract her while they paged the Conways. Ipsa licked her lips, the taste of iced raspberry suddenly on her tongue. She remembered how Mrs. Conway had appeared, sprinting frantically toward her daughter, arms outspread. Ipsa felt a tightening in her own chest as Mrs. Conway pressed Annie against her ribs, felt the fierce love of that hug, a hug that signaled Annie sat squarely beside her brother at the center of Mrs. Conway's universe.

Ipsa wasn't quite sure why the zoo prayer had crystalized, and it tugged at her wings. Perhaps she'd missed an important clue the first time she read it. Ipsa leafed through Annie's file but didn't see it. She went page by page a second time, careful not to miss a single entry in case she'd misremembered Annie's age in the prayer. Ipsa could find no mention of a trip to the zoo. She paged through the file a third time. It wasn't there.

Ipsa looked up. Her wings went pale. She'd lost a prayer.

Chapter Sixteen

Dios,

    I need your help. Paulo's been on the donor list for three years now, and we've never had a match. Paulo is MY heart. Please help us. I don't see much point in living without him.

    —Flavia

TERROR GRIPPED IPSA'S WINGS. SHE'D LOST A PRAYER FROM Annie's file. A file she'd stolen from the Archives and sworn to Dhavi she'd return. Her wings felt rigid and heavy, their usual beet color faded like sun-bleached cloth.

The start of the session only added to Ipsa's anxiety. She closed her eyes to see into a prayer about a heart transplant, but instead of a hospital room, she found herself at the Conways' dinner table staring at a paper with the number 59 circled at the top in thick red ink. Annie's hand glumly pushed it across the table toward Mr. Conway.

Why can't I be as smart as Isaac?

Ipsa's eyes snapped open. The space where her wings

met her shoulders ached. She didn't have to open Annie's prayer file to know this prayer, too, would be missing; she was positive she'd never read it before. It felt new as Flavia's prayer about Paulo. But Annie was dead. There were no new Annie prayers coming from the Conways' dinner table. Ipsa took her forefinger and discreetly slipped it into her mouth, wondering if Annie's awful nail-biting habit might quell her anxiety.

A sniffle behind Ipsa caused her hand to shoot back down into her lap.

"Good prayer to you, Ipsa." Eon stood behind her, his eyes scanning her up and down.

"Hello, Eon," Ipsa said, trying to evoke the placid tone of other Readers. She had avoided speaking with Eon directly for several Repasts, but she'd also felt certain she was being watched, especially when she couldn't see him.

Eon leaned against her desk. Ipsa had never noticed his hands before. A long star mark, like the one etched into her own knee, ran between his thumb and pointer finger. "You've been very distracted lately," he said, tilting his head. "Yet, *oddly*, also rather amenable to reading—not bringing your usual *commentary* to the work."

Ipsa's wings betrayed her with the slightest twitch. Eon's eyes flicked toward her back.

"My, your wings are looking pale," he said. "Is everything quite alright?"

Ipsa swallowed deeply. "I think having a mentee has just, um, given me a lot to think about. A lot of responsibility and all that." Ipsa feared her wings would betray her at any moment with their trembling. "Thank you for checking in. I'm really fine."

Eon cocked his head to the side and leaned back a bit farther, his fingers tapping the edge of the desk. Ipsa sat in silence for what felt like a dozen prayers. Finally, Eon stood to smooth his robe. "Very well then," he said. "Just wanted to make sure you had everything you needed. I wouldn't want you feeling like you're in over your head."

Eon held her gaze for several beats before striding down the long row of desks.

Only when Eon was out of sight did Ipsa let out a long, slow exhale, her wings sagging over her shoulders.

At Repast, Ipsa jumped out of her seat. But instead of heading toward the Repast Field, Ipsa stole to the back of the Contemplations Garden, retrieved Annie's file, and then headed toward Dhavi's cottage, as if pulled by some invisible string. She needed help fixing this. Dhavi never attended the Repast wing-pairing ceremony. She hoped that meant that he would be there now.

Ipsa had nearly reached the cottage door when the sound of footsteps caused her to duck into the brush. A black-haired angel appeared on the path. The angel, who bore the purple wings of an Implementer, seemed distracted. Ipsa recognized her face from the Repast stage. She paused for a moment, cocking her head slightly toward where Ipsa hid, then lifted upward into the sky, slowly shrinking from sight.

Standing at the threshold of Dhavi's house, Ipsa tried to still her buzzing wings. Every time she closed her eyes, additional prayers from Annie's life spilled into her head. Once or twice, the angel closed her eyes and saw Ipsa's own face, standing in front of a mirror in Annie's room. Annie wasn't even there, wasn't even praying. It was just *Ipsa*.

She raised her arm to knock, but the door opened before her knuckles touched wood. Dhavi stood in the doorway, a look on his face she had never seen before.

"Did anyone see you?" Dhavi asked, glancing around

the path. He placed his hand behind Ipsa's wings and pulled her into the cottage.

"There was an angel on the path just now. An Implementer—but I don't think she saw me."

"Jana." Dhavi mumbled the name, his eyes scanning the floor. "Imagine my surprise *and* my disappointment when I went to the Archives and found Isaac and Annie's files had not been replaced." Dhavi looked down, his neck seemed too heavy to hold upright.

"You went…to the *Archives?*" Ipsa stumbled over her words. Her wings burned. It hadn't occurred to her that Dhavi could simply walk into the Archives to access any file he wanted. Of *course* he could, given his role as an earthly Historian. Ipsa wrapped her arm tightly around her waist, where, under her mantel, she'd stashed Annie's file.

"I did. And then I wondered how long you would avoid me."

Ipsa said nothing, her eyes bolted to the floor like nails into the wood.

"Ipsa, I asked you to do that. For me." Dhavi's voice was stern. "You made a promise."

Ipsa winced. "I'm sorry."

Dhavi's words sliced through the air. "This wasn't just some whim. This was for your own good."

"Why can't we read any hopeling's file we want?"

"These weren't just *any* hopelings," Dhavi said, quickly turning his face away from her.

"I don't understand," Ipsa said. The room felt on fire. Ipsa wiped away a bead of sweat from her forehead with the back of her palm, a small lock of her normally wavy hair tightening into a tendril.

"Now, you're here, breathless, when you should be at Repast," Dhavi said. "What was so urgent?"

A splitting log crackled in the fireplace.

Ipsa swallowed hard. "I can't find a prayer."

"You lost a prayer?" Dhavi said, the creases above his eyebrows forming deep valleys.

"Yes…no. I mean, I don't know," Ipsa fumbled. She pulled out Annie's file and began clawing at page after page. "I mean, I thought so, at first, but I can't remember reading it the first time. I can *see* the scene as if I'd read it, so I know I must have—although I can't find it anywhere in the file."

"Whose file?"

"Annie's. I've checked and rechecked. Read each page three times, but—"

"It's not there," Dhavi said.

"No, and I've gone back to my desk and the Rest House, and everywhere it could possibly be, and I don't see how I could have lost it."

"How did you know it was missing?" he asked.

"I just remembered it. But if it wasn't in the file, how could I remember it? It's just…"

Ipsa's temples pulsed. Every time she closed her eyes there were others—other moments, other memories, like a movie reel from Annie's childhood, flooding her mind without a single word written on a page.

She bit her lip. "It's not just that one prayer." She scanned Dhavi's face, but he offered no reaction. "It's like I have some whole extra file filled with moments from Annie's life in my head. Is that why we can't read entire files?" Ipsa's voice cracked.

Dhavi remained silent. Ipsa jolted to her feet and began pacing the length of the room, winding around stacks of books.

"Maybe they were removed from the file at some point,

but the memories stayed with the file? Is that a thing? Or… or maybe she changed her mind and decided not to send it?"

Ipsa continued to offer theory after theory, each met with silence. She bit down on her bottom lip to keep it from quivering. "Dhavi, what's wrong? Why do I have this hopeling's entire life racing through my head?"

Dhavi leaned back, his head lifted toward the oak beams overhead. Ipsa tried to recall lessons from her classes with Corintine, from the textbooks she'd half studied. Her flustered wings bumped into a glass jar on Dhavi's table, causing a soft reverberation, like the faintest chime of a bell. A bell, she thought, remembering the silly hopeling story she'd shared with Muir many Repasts ago. A ridiculous joke. Hopelings didn't become angels. It wasn't possible.

And yet.

Dhavi slowly lowered his gaze to meet her helpless stare. His lips remained pursed. The ultimate answer came from Ipsa's own mouth, rising up from inside her wings, somewhere deep within her soul.

Speaking slowly, as if sounding out a new reality, Ipsa asked: "Am I…Was *I*…Annie?"

Chapter Seventeen

Hey Mom,

I graduated from college today. Just like I promised you I would! I wanted to make you proud. I wish you were here with me to celebrate, but I know you can hear me. I love you, Ma.

—Terrence

THE TRUTH FINALLY ERUPTED FROM WITHIN IPSA, SPEWING up as if with the force of every prayer in all the world, gushing into the Hive all at once.

"It's NOT true, Dhavi!!" Ipsa's voice roared, hot as lava. She felt anger, felt betrayal. "Tell me this isn't true. Tell me I'm not *her*, that I'm not…that I *wasn't*…" She could barely bring herself to say it. "A *hopeling*."

Yet images raced through her mind—more images from someone else's past—*Annie's* past. Ipsa clutched the arm of a nearby chair for support, waiting for Dhavi to respond, her wings fanning wildly. Dhavi rose silently from his seat and moved toward the fire, allowing his brown wings to stretch out to their full span, nearly the width of the narrow room. Reaching his hands toward the flames, he rubbed them together.

"Answer me, please!" Ipsa pleaded. "This doesn't make any sense. Hopelings don't become angels. Everybody knows *that*. It's what we've been taught for an eternity. It's what all the books say. What about Repast and stardust? Why would they tell us an untruth?" Then Ipsa's eyes widened in misery as a new thought occurred to her: "Or does everyone know but me?"

Dhavi's hands ceased moving and his head turned back in her direction. "No, Ipsa. Very few angels know—nor can they. That is very important."

Feeling her wings buckling under the weight of her body, Ipsa slunk back down into a chair. "So, it's true then —I was a hopeling?" She swallowed, slumping lower in her seat. "We were *all* hopelings? Even you?"

Dhavi didn't answer right away.

"Yes, it's true," he said finally. "We were hopelings, first. And yes, even me." Dhavi's voice hung low and heavy, like an earthly morning fog.

"Hopelings, first," Ipsa said. Those words. Invoked at every Repast, they formed the founding principle of their world. It wasn't some mantra about selflessly caring for lesser beings. It was their origin, hiding in plain sight.

Those moments when she'd caught her own reflection in Annie's mirror—she'd seen herself because Annie's face and her face were one and the same. The long thick hair that Annie usually kept contained in a ponytail and complained about crimping with the summer heat—that was Ipsa's hair. Pulling up her mantel, Ipsa traced the raised star mark that ran three inches from below her shin over the curve of her left knee. Ipsa recalled a prayer from when

Annie was nine in an emergency room—she'd slipped on a mossy rock by the ocean. This was not some unique feature formed from stardust. This was a hopeling scar. Annie's scar.

"It can't be possible." Ipsa shook her head. "Annie only died a year ago. I've been Here forever."

"This place has a way of making you feel like you've been Here a lifetime, doesn't it?" Dhavi grimaced. "But you received your wings three hundred and, I think, *sixty* Repasts ago."

"Dhavi, what about the end of Repast?" Ipsa asked. "When some angels leave to return to stardust? Are they actually going back There? Back to earth?"

Dhavi ran his fingers across his forehead. "We don't know," he said. "The story of the ancient Wreather is true: No one has ever traveled where our departing angels are headed."

A million thoughts careened through Ipsa's mind, a million past prayers she'd read replayed themselves, as if on a hopeling TV screen. She thought of Elna and Muir, who were, at that moment, watching thousands of nameless angels receive their wings at Repast.

"Why keep it from us, Dhavi?"

Dhavi spoke slowly. "Ipsa, do you remember your very first lessons? About our world?"

"Of course," Ipsa said impatiently, tracing the scar on her knee. "Yuka, the first angel, was born with wings, but the second angel, Jan, had no wings, so Yuka took a piece of her own wings and buried it in the dirt. By the second sunrise there were Kluna fields everywhere. Yuka's gift." Ipsa paused, jerking her body forward. "Is that a lie too?"

"Not a lie exactly," Dhavi said quickly. "An embellishment, perhaps, missing pieces of the larger story. The rest is something that, in our entire history, only a few dozen Implementers have known…"

"Dhavi," Ipsa whispered. "Please."

Dhavi scratched at his beard, rubbing the one corner of his chin where the whiskers transitioned from grey to orange. He closed his eyes, taking a deep breath. "Yuka awoke alone in a new land on the shore of an ocean—a scared hopeling without wings. She knew nothing of this place, but it didn't take long for her to realize there was magic growing in the fields that surrounded the mountaintop."

"Kluna," Ipsa spoke the word almost to herself.

"She pulled at those soft flowers, hoping to make a blanket to cover her nakedness. The blanket clung to her back as if it were a second skin; picked her up and carried her like a bird. She realized that these wings offered not just warmth and security, but power. She closed her eyes and dreamed of fire, and suddenly, it was before her. Everywhere, she could hear the voice of her mate, her children, though she could not see them. They asked for so many things, and they prayed desperately for Yuka, calling her name, asking her to return home."

Dhavi raised his chin, sending his fingers up and down the scruff of his neck. "This separation felt like torture. Sometimes, she ate fistfuls of grapes growing on a far slope and, for a time, she felt almost drowsy with contentment, the voices of her loved ones blurred. Yuka called those fruits 'vismarati' because, in her old language, it meant 'to forget.'"

Dhavi continued, "When her mate appeared one day, confused and disoriented, she rushed to him to explain: We were humans, first. But she saw the wild fear in his eyes as he, too, began to hear the cries and whispers from his hopeling children. And so, Yuka did the most selfless thing she could: She fed him vismarati. She pressed those grapes into wine, soaked some Kluna, and fitted him with wings. To forget. She chose to spare him: That was her real gift. Knowledge in its full, raw form felt brutal."

"Knowledge…with prudence," Ipsa said, repeating the well-worn Arcanum in a mocking tone. "The books weren't talking about hopelings and how much *they* could know about Here—they were talking about us."

"Ipsa, you don't understand—" Dhavi's voice sounded hoarse.

"Of course I don't, Dhavi!" Ipsa screamed, slamming her palm down on the cover of Annie's file. "I don't understand the most basic things, like how long I've been Here! Is that why they shove bowls of vismarati in front of us at Repast? In case we start to 'unforget'? Why are you even telling me any of this?" Ipsa demanded.

Dhavi let out another deep exhale. "I guess I'd prefer if we could just be honest."

"Who's we?" Ipsa asked.

"The Implementers."

"But you're not an Implementer!" Ipsa pawed at his wings as if they might suddenly turn violet. "Your wings are brown!" Ipsa said.

Dhavi sighed. "Purple was never really my color."

"But you don't go to Repast! All of the other Implementers are there, on stage, every time."

"I suppose I lean into my role as contrarian in the group." Dhavi half smiled, half grimaced toward the fire. "Sometimes the spectacle is a bit hard to stomach."

"But if you don't agree with it, why don't you try and change it?" Ipsa narrowed her eyes.

"A hopeling might not like cold weather, but they can't

keep the snow from falling." Dhavi sat back down in his chair. "Sometimes, all they can do is move someplace warm."

Ipsa's mind burned, choked by Annie's memories. She tried separate them from her own memories of Here: so many trusted conversations with Dhavi—always, she realized now, with this incredible secret between them.

Her wings burned, but her words came like ice. "So that's what you did?" she hissed. "Moved someplace warmer? Stopped attending Repast? But continued lying to me and everyone else?" Swarming around her head, too, were hundreds of other prayers, past prayers she had read from billions of hopelings whining and complaining. How could she have been one of *them*?

"It's never that simple."

"It seems pretty simple to me." Ipsa's voice thundered through the small room. "I am, it turns out, everything I always said I couldn't stand. And you're just some coward who decided to run away from his problems."

Ipsa shot up from the couch. Swinging the door open, she raced out into the open air and flung herself upward. As Dhavi stepped into the open doorway, Ipsa's winged figure was already shrinking into the sky, shooting away like a blazing red firecracker.

Ipsa pumped her wings in a delirious frenzy as she zigzagged through the air, unsure even of where she was headed. No longer did any part of this world feel like home. She thought about all the angels gathered at Repast, welcoming the community's newest angels. The idea of watching the charade of Thodius explaining their history turned her stomach. So Ipsa flew until her wings ached, flew as long as the day she and Elna had attempted to cross the Endless Lake, so giddy in each other's company, so blissfully ignorant about who they once were.

Ipsa had once read a prayer from a hopeling who'd lost his memory in a car accident. He'd prayed for those memories to come back, for the faces of loved ones to suddenly mean something to him. That was much how she felt in this moment. Ipsa didn't *feel* like Annie. She wasn't even sure she *liked* Annie. And yet there was some kind of connection she couldn't ignore—a connection to Isaac she had felt from the very moment she had touched that crumpled prayer beneath her desk.

She flew over fields of Kluna that stretched as far as she could see. She'd read a prayer recently from a hopeling in an airplane—a contemplation marveling at how humans could engineer a machine to carry them above the clouds. She looked down at the fields below. If that hopeling were with her now, he would marvel that, in this world, they'd found a way to tether the clouds to the earth, for they looked just as those wisps of air and water did from that hopeling's plane window.

Ipsa let her wings slow, touching down. As she slowly threaded her way beneath the blooming crowns, she plucked off a dandelion yellow bud, rubbing its downy fluff between her fingers. This was the stuff of wings— this, she thought, and some mind-erasing grapes. At the end of the day, was this all that separated them from hopelings?

She held the piece of Kluna up close to her nose, observing the yellow change to a swirl of turquoise and magenta. She scanned the Technicolor field. It looked like a hopeling rainbow on the ground. Her own wings itched in this space, as if their very threads tugged toward the earth from which they'd sprouted. Finally, she yielded, collapsing to the dirt. It was dark beneath the canopy of this giant harvest, and the earth felt cool.

Ipsa lay there for what felt like a million prayers, staring up through the blooms, past the blinking, changing canopy of color. Pressed to the ground, her wings began to relax. Closing her eyes, Ipsa imagined the Meditation bell gonging in her ear. She tried to focus on the darkness of her closed eyelids, but as she lay in this secret space her mind kept returning to Annie. What would Annie do in this situation? Bitterly, Ipsa knew the answer: She would have prayed.

Ipsa sat up, leaning her back against a thick stalk of Kluna. She set Annie's file on her lap, unopened, for what felt like an entire Repast. Finally, she turned to the first page —the first fleeting asks of a toddler. She had read all of these prayers countless times, but now, sitting here beneath the Kluna branches, she read them with new eyes.

Thumbing through, she paused on a single prayer, entered the day after Isaac left for debate camp.

Hi God,
I want you to know that I don't really hate Isaac. There are
even times when he's kind of cool, in his own stupid way, like
when he destroyed dad's argument about why we couldn't
watch R-rated movies, or the way he can charm the girl at
Scoops into giving us an extra topping. Anyway, I just wanted
to say that I didn't really mean most of that other stuff I said
before. I was just pretty angry.
—Annie

Ipsa opened her eyes. Clutching that prayer in her hands, she noticed her hands for the first time since she fled Dhavi's cottage. It all made sense now, how different every angel looked Here. Annie had died at fourteen. Her hands were soft—the hands of a fourteen-year-old. She thought about Dhavi's: so wrinkled and leathery. Or Muir, who, with her round cheeks and height could have passed for any hopeling fifth grader. And Elna, who looked a bit like the high school senior who used to babysit Isaac and Annie— just minus the hair. It wasn't that angels never changed, she realized bitterly; they had just stopped changing.

The answers to who Annie was—who *Ipsa* was—were right there on paper, clear as the blue sky above her. Annie was loving, then hateful; she could be selfish, then generous. She had little fears—like what she'd look like with braces— and bigger ones—like her Aunt Patty's cancer. She was a fourteen-year-old hopeling.

Just the kind of hopeling Ipsa had trained herself to loathe.

Ipsa flipped again to Annie's final prayer spoken in the darkness of a closet that smelled like a hopeling gym bag. How had things ended so abruptly for her?

Suddenly Ipsa unfurled her wings and bolted upright. She knew, or at least she thought she knew, how to find out what she needed to know about Annie's death.

Chapter Eighteen

Please God, let her pick up. Pick up the phone, Annie, pick up the phone.
   —Evelyn

IPSA ENTERED THE ARCHIVES WITH A RECKLESS DISREGARD for whether she might be seen. Luckily, the halls were still empty of angels. Sitting in a dark corner on the cold glass floor, Ipsa stared at Mrs. Conway's file, unsure she really wanted to know what had happened.

Flipping to the date of Annie's final prayer, Ipsa laid her hand on the parchment that bore Mrs. Conway's tight cursive script and closed her eyes. She could see a maroon van parked in the driveway of Annie's house. The home seemed enormous by angel standards, ten times as large as Dhavi's cottage. The front door was bright red with a gold knocker. The numbers 4-0-5 hung in gold along the door's frame. Ipsa watched as Mrs. Conway shut the car door and carried in three bags of groceries.

Ipsa's ears pulsed, listening to the home's collective heartbeat—the lumping together of a thousand little sounds and murmurs: the backyard sprinklers ticking, the slow kerplunk from a leaky faucet in the upstairs bathroom. Mrs. Conway bustled around the kitchen, reaching up on her toes to stuff a bag of popcorn on the top shelf of a cabinet. Ipsa could hear, almost *feel* the rhythmic purr of Annie's cat, Frida Collins, as she lay curled up on the pile of dirty clothes in the back of Annie's bedroom closet. Ipsa took it all in with one inhale, breathing in every single inch of that house. Only then did she hear the knock at the door.

An elderly woman braced herself with a cane. Her cheeks mimicked the droopy fuzz of an elephant's skin, covered in a million tiny wrinkles. Ipsa wondered if Dhavi had been older or younger than this woman when he died. She wondered if she could forgive him long enough to ask him about it.

"Good morning, Mrs. Stinson," Mrs. Conway said. "Did Annie hit another hockey ball into your yard again? I've been reminding her to use the net."

"No, no, dear, that's not why I'm here." Mrs. Stinson's lips flattened in on themselves, as if she'd swallowed something bitter. "Have you…uh, have you seen the news?"

Ipsa's view tilted as Mrs. Conway cocked her head toward her left shoulder. "The news? I'm just home between meetings trying to throw some groceries in the fridge. What's on the news?"

Mrs. Stinson swallowed hard. "Have you heard from Annie at all? She's at Booker T. Washington this year, isn't she?"

Ipsa felt the hairs raise on Mrs. Conway's arms, the chill managing to transmit all the way to Ipsa's own wings.

"Mrs. Stinson, what's going on?" Mrs. Conway began to hedge backward now, receding from the doorway, grasping for the edge of the dining room table for her purse, fumbling around the inside, pulling out her keys, a wallet, a fistful of receipts. She dumped the bag onto the table, her phone finally clattering on polished wood.

"There's been a shooting…at the high school."

Mrs. Conway's fingers moved fast, too fast, as if her thumbs were not connecting with her brain. She could not seem to press the series of numbers on the screen she needed to. Ipsa's view was obscured by the blur of Mrs. Conway's tears.

Please God, let her pick up. Pick up the phone, Annie, pick up the phone.

Ipsa felt the cold hard screen of the phone against Mrs. Conway's ear, as if pressing hard enough might transport her to the other side, to wherever that ring was sounding. Seven long rings and then a voice—Ipsa's voice, *Annie's* voice—a prerecording telling friends to text her and that, if this was her parents calling, she was *definitely* at the library.

Mrs. Conway pressed a red button on the phone and tried again.

And again.

Annie never answered.

Ipsa pulled herself out of the scene, recalling Annie's last prayer. The heat and sweat of bodies too close together. Annie holding her breath, as if to render herself invisible. Ipsa flinched, recalling the fireworks on the other side of the door.

There's been a shooting at the high school.

Ipsa learned details through small petitions whispered in assembly halls filled with screaming, wailing parents, men in suits and badges standing before them, people in the audience balling up fact sheets and helpline numbers and throwing them back at the podium, like an angry orchard heaving its poisoned fruit.

Annie had been a freshman. She'd prayed so many times for that field hockey scholarship. For some reason, her prayers hadn't been answered, and instead of being five miles away at St. Ignatius, she'd been in first-period algebra at Booker T. Washington. They'd heard the shots in a courtyard first and fled to the gym, into a storage closet next to the boiler room. But somehow, he'd found them. He'd been looking, not for Annie, but for some hopeling named Chelsea.

She tried to understand how one hopeling could do this to another. The gunman had asked Chelsea to homecoming and she'd laughed in front of the entire homeroom. She had laughed just like Melissa and Annie had laughed at their classmate Brooke. Maybe, like Annie, she'd felt badly after, wished she could go back and undo that laugh, take it back. But she couldn't. And he'd returned the next day with his father's guns.

Ipsa tipped her head back against the stack behind her. Pulling down the fabric of her cloak, she placed her fingertips to the pink flesh that bloomed in a perfect, raised circle at her collar bone. Slowly, she moved her hand across her chest to a second and third spot, a fourth and fifth. Six star marks on her chest that weren't star marks at all.

Ipsa flipped further ahead in the file—a haze of garbled, disjointed, almost illegible prayers—not so much prayers as verbalized hate; unleashed in full, if incoherent, fury on one person: the shooter. "That monster" was the phrase Mrs. Conway used.

More recently, the prayers had begun to come back into focus, as if Mrs. Conway had adjusted the camera lens through which she saw the world. They were more legible and sober. These prayers focused on Isaac, on his welfare and safety. Ipsa leaned forward, her wings tense. She saw him, in these prayers, as his mother saw him: standing up unexpectedly at a town hall, then in front of a herd of reporters shoving microphones in his face. Then, later, before larger crowds or under canned studio lights, a microphone clipped to his shirt, engaging with reporter after reporter. He told Annie's story, demanding that the people in charge keep other kids safe from guns. Watching these prayers, Ipsa forced herself to blink. There was Isaac, on national TV, this fourteen-year-old boy with rumpled hair and glasses, head-to-head against slick men in suits, men trying to make Annie's death about everything but the gun that killed her: The shooter was sick. Their country was experiencing a mental health epidemic. Schools needed better security.

But Isaac was prepared. All the endless debates that had made Annie roll her eyes, with her, with his parents, with some congressman's son, had, in fact, been in preparation for this.

And he was ready.

Ipsa looked up from the file. She remembered every word from Isaac's prayer that day outside the library.

I haven't even uttered your name in almost a year…And we both know that I'm not exactly religious. Well, I don't know what you know anymore, or what you are. It's just that I got another note…I found this one taped to my bike outside the library, which means someone was following me. It said we'd better call it off or I'd see the Second Amendment "up close and personal."

I can't tell Mom and Dad; they've been through enough. But if anything happened to me, I don't think Mom would survive. Annie, if you can hear me—

Cradling Mrs. Conway's file on the cold floor of the dusty building, Ipsa ached for that woman. She imagined a vase shattered into fragments yet still expected to be a vessel to this other still blooming flower, for Isaac. Ipsa wondered: How does someone glue themself back together when the biggest pieces have been taken away, forever?

She re-shelved the file in a daze. She no longer knew what was true in the world. Maybe there really was a place called Hell, some eternal hopeling jail where confused and angry boys with guns were sent for taking the lives of fourteen people. But Ipsa had to wonder whether staying behind on earth, wrapped in a hundred million moments of aching emptiness, wasn't the worst punishment of all.

Chapter Nineteen

Shang di,

Ma had a baby today, but she is a girl. Please, can we keep her?
—Zhang

"Ipsa, you've been acting strange lately," Elna said, gently untwisting her wrist from Ipsa's grip.

Ipsa had reached over the Repast table and lifted Elna's wrist in her hand, turning it over with her thumb. Ipsa had always marveled that Elna's star marks—three small, blue-black stars that marked the inside of Elna's wrist—actually *looked* like stars. She'd read enough prayers from hopelings screaming from the pain to know what these marks really were: tattoos, leftover from whomever Elna had been There.

Ipsa had avoided the previous Recreation and Meditation sessions, unable to look Elna in the eye without wondering who *she* had been There. But Ipsa also knew she couldn't just stop attending Repast. Joining in this celebration—which Thodius called "an opportunity"—suddenly felt like a requirement.

Ipsa had not been able to take her eyes off of Elna—off of whoever this angel had been—since she'd arrived. Graceful, willowy Elna looked the age of a 20-year-old hopeling, except for her bald scalp. Only sick teenagers had heads that smooth: They prayed for the cancer medicine to stop making their hair fall out.

As Elna pulled her hand back, Ipsa rubbed the star marks across her own nose. She thought of Mr. Conway's and Isaac's arms, covered with similar markings, like someone had taken a shaker of pepper across their skin: nothing more than hopeling freckles. She touched the raised pink flesh of the six near-perfect circles along her chest. Bullet holes.

She felt like a fool.

"Ipsa?" Elna asked again. "Did you hear me? Is everything all right?"

Ipsa shook her head as if to shake out the unanswered questions. "Nothing. Yes, I'm sorry. I, just, I have a lot of prayers to read right now."

"Oh." Elna's brow furrowed for a moment, then smoothed as her face broke into an untroubled smile. She reached down and plucked four pieces of vismarati from the common bowl on the table, offering them to Ipsa.

Ipsa shook her head.

"Well, I'm glad that I get to spend a little bit of time with you!"

Ipsa studied Elna's face closely as she spoke. "You have lovely eyes."

"Thank you." Elna's golden wings blushed to a deeper

bronze. She popped the vismarati into her mouth. "What made you say that?"

"I don't know, I was just thinking how different we are," Ipsa said. "I mean, if we all come from the same stardust, did you ever wonder why we all look so different? Why you have no hair and I have too much of it?"

Ipsa knew she was playing with fire, dancing around this subject with an angel who could not fathom this secret. As if: just by asking the question, her friend would suddenly awaken from the fog of her own identity.

"Too much hair?!" Elna laughed, wholly oblivious to the weight of Ipsa's questions. "I think you're perfect, Ipsa! Just look up and you have your answer, silly! No two stars are the same, so why would we be?"

Ipsa looked into the azure blue pools of Elna's eyes. No spark of recognition blinked back. Looking down toward the first grouping of new angels on the stage, Ipsa scrutinized each one for signs of There that might still be clinging to their newly arrived selves. She wondered whether, at this moment, somewhere in another world, one hundred families had just received the kind of news that had broken Mrs. Conway. Or maybe angels didn't appear Here that quickly. Ipsa had no idea. Dhavi gave no details, no putty with which to caulk the leaks springing inside of her, threatening to wash her away with the tide. Maybe there was another place, an intermediary stop between Here and There. And yet she thought about Muir, so new to Here. Muir seemed more curious, more interesting than other angels Ipsa knew. Like Elna had been when they'd first met, in class. Ipsa remembered the sparkle in Elna's eyes: she'd recognized wonder there. Was vibrancy something that faded over time? A gradual shedding of their hopeling skins as they transitioned toward contentment and blissful indifference? Annie had died almost one hopeling year ago: What if, at the one-year mark, Ipsa, too, suddenly ceased to wonder?

"How many Repasts ago were you created, Elna?"

"You're full of funny wonderings!" Elna laughed but gave an odd look. "Who knows? Would you like to throw me one of those hopeling parties you've always told me about—with cake and candles?! That *would* be a bit of fun…"

Ipsa strained to remember the day of her own wing choosing. Maybe that was why Here had so little emphasis on time, she thought bitterly. History was so much easier to manipulate when every Repast melded together as one fuzzy past.

"Annie!" Muir whispered into Ipsa's ear, jolting the Reader back to the present moment.

"What did you call me?!" Ipsa whipped around in a startled voice. Muir knelt close beside Ipsa's shoulder, laying a few books from her survey class on the Repast table.

Muir looked puzzled. "I'd been trying to remember the name of that hopeling you told me about. The one who…*you know.*" Muir widened her eyes, as if wanting Ipsa to silently fill in the blank: *The one whose prayer file you stole from the Archives in your top-secret search to answer Isaac's prayer.*

"I saw you and suddenly I just remembered the name!" Muir looked in either direction and lowered her voice: "Annie."

"Oh." Ipsa let out a deep exhale. Ever since leaving Dhavi's cottage, she'd felt as though this new secret about her past was emblazoned on her face. How could she possibly keep that knowledge to herself?

She looked up at Muir's soft brown face, lost for a

moment wondering about Muir's hopeling story. What sorts of things had she liked to do? How had she died? And who had been left behind There by the death of this young girl?

"I haven't really found out anything new, Muir." Ipsa spoke quickly, turning her face toward the table.

"Are you okay?" Muir asked gently. "You look—how do the hopelings say it?—like you've seen a ghost."

"I've been saying the same thing!" Elna said, leaning over to give Muir a warm hug of welcome. "Muir, I've been meaning to ask: Are you friendly with Sim from the Statistics Department?"

"Oh yes! Sim is SO funny!" Muir giggled, as if remembering a joke.

"He seemed very nice. I met him last Repast—since Ipsa abandoned me." Elna gave Ipsa a genial wink. "Anyway, he said he knows you."

Muir's smile widened. "We received our wings during the same Repast—in different groupings on stage, but still! He was chosen to be a Hair Surveyor within the Statistics Department. He sits next to me in my survey class." Muir giggled for a moment. "Ipsa, you would get a kick out of him: He does the best impersonations of hopelings! After last class, Sim reenacted a scene where some hopeling left his car windows down while driving through a car wash and got completely soaked!"

Ipsa locked eyes with Muir, suddenly awakening from her stupor. "He's a Hair Surveyor." She repeated it slowly, her breath halted. She'd never been to the Statistics Department, but the moment Muir shared Sim's role, some distant memory from a long ago survey class clicked in Ipsa's mind: Hair Surveyors collected and stored hopeling hairs.

"His work is so fascinating!" Elna continued. "I had no idea a single strand of hair could tell you so much about a hopeling—for as 'long' as they had the hair," Elna chuckled, pleased with her pun.

Ipsa's wings fluttered. Piecing a handful of hairs together, then, an angel could get a rather complete picture of a hopeling. Ipsa had been so absorbed by her newfound knowledge about her past that she'd almost forgotten *why* she'd begun her search in the first place: to help answer Isaac's prayer.

Muir tilted her head slightly, confused by Ipsa's reaction. Then it clicked: "Oh, of course! *Isaac!*" She immediately gasped and covered her mouth, looking over at Elna.

"Who is Isaac?" Elna said, glancing back and forth between Ipsa and Muir. "Seriously, what is going *on* with you two?"

"It's nothing. I'm just trying to stay on top of some repeat hopeling prayers," Ipsa said, looking down at the table.

"Ipsa." Elna spoke again, meeting her friend's searching gaze.

"I didn't want to get you involved. It's a prayer I read, a prayer I'm trying to answer. But Eon told me it had been misdirected and—"

"Can a prayer be misdirected?" Elna asked.

Ipsa smiled for the first time in many prayers, her wings suddenly lighter at the prospect of unburdening even a little of this worry to her friend.

"Muir, I feel like such an idiot that someone in the Statistics Department didn't occur to me sooner," Ipsa said.

"*You* feel like an idiot? I see Sim for class every Repast!" Muir said.

Elna shook her head, her lips pursed. "I know that Eon can be tiresome, but all of this sneaking about and reading up on this hopeling—it sounds very *rash*. Can't you just explain to Eon your questions—"

Ipsa interrupted, her mind focused on getting those hairs. "Let me see your book," Ipsa said, pointing toward one of the textbooks that Muir had strewn across the stone table, titled *A Brief History of Here and There*. Ipsa scanned the first pages with her forefinger. "An overview of the Departments of Here, page five hundred forty-three!" she read, her voice tingling with excitement as she flipped to the back half of the book, thumbing her way toward the page in question.

Elna frowned, crossing her arms in front of her chest. "Ipsa, this seems like meddling. Can't we just enjoy the Repast ceremony?"

"Here it is!" Ipsa cleared her throat and began to read aloud. "'The Statistics Department, Surveying Division. The Surveying Division is the fourth largest division within that Department (after Weather, Species Cataloguing, and Geographical Population Patterns), and is overseen by the angel Belarusse. The survey and capture process allows for the retrieval of critical information about hopelings, primarily for the purposes of prayer answering as well as tracking certain statistics (see *Languages Division collaboration*). In addition to offering vital information about an individual (diet, weight, climate, etc.), hopeling hairs serve as a record of events taken place during the course of that hair's viability and offer additional context on specific hopelings, when required, for more complex prayers. Hairs may be collected from within almost any prayer. (Hair Collection: see *Collections Division*.)'"

Ipsa looked up from the textbook on her lap. *"Additional context on specific hopelings, when required, for more complex prayers."* She had just found a way to find out more about Isaac's troubles. She smiled, remembering the disheveled mop of hair she'd seen in the bicycle mirror. He didn't pray much anymore, but he also wasn't making regular trips to a barber.

A burst of energy pulsed through Ipsa's wings.

"Muir, I need to meet Sim."

Chapter Twenty

I work next to an Israeli named Benyamin on the factory line. He's funny and very nice. During the water shortages last year, he would sneak in bottles for my family. His daughter is having surgery tomorrow. I know they're not your people, but would you look after her? Allahu Akbar.

—Fauza Ahmed

THE SURVEYING DIVISION OF THE STATISTICS DEPARTMENT seemed, to Ipsa, the stuff of hopeling science-fiction movies. A series of clear tubes snaked throughout a vast, open complex, with an opening at the workspace of each Surveyor. The room echoed with an undulating series of WOOSH after WOOSH, as if the listener were standing near a hopeling runway where, every few seconds, a plane was taking off.

Ipsa studied Sim, wondering—as she did with nearly every angel she met now—about his life as a hopeling. His skin was a few shades darker than Muir's, and his eyes flashed an olive green with flecks of orange—as if he'd blended the wings of Harvester and Responder in a single wink. He looked to be a twenty-five-year-old hopeling—or at least he had been, before his last prayer.

"So, how does it all work?" Ipsa immediately started in with her questions. "Where do you keep hairs archived? How do you keep track of all of them? How quickly do new hairs come online?"

"Uh-oh, you're really a spy for the Implementers, aren't you?! You going to turn me in for stray hairs?" Sim grinned.

Ipsa laughed. "I'm just curious! This is so much different from the Reading Room. Plus, I think I, um, missed some of the details about Surveying when we went over the Statistics Department in class," Ipsa said sheepishly.

"I'm excited to share what we do," Sim said. "We don't get a lot of visitors, and I feel like I'm finally getting the hang of how this place runs!"

Getting the hang of it, because, like Muir, Sim had only recently received his wings. Ipsa thought of his laugh and easy charm and wondered when that would fade.

They crossed a metal bridge and Ipsa could see below floors and floors of what looked like storage areas surrounding an atrium. Sim walked a wing's length ahead, and Ipsa observed him for a moment with the same sadness she did with Muir. She felt as though she were holding a hopeling hourglass, watching sand spill down through the small opening. When all the sand finally rested at the bottom, what would be left of this funny Hair Surveyor with a twinkle in his eyes? Likely just one more angel content with simply being content.

Sim motioned for Ipsa to come to the left railing of the bridge.

"See that, right there?" he said, signaling toward a large screen. "That is where we monitor rate of influx into the department at any given time. We can isolate for certain geographic areas, geothermal conditions, and other factors you might want to disaggregate: like regional crops, local population density, stuff like that." Sim's ebony wings blushed with a tint of scarlet. "I, um, really love talking about this!"

Ipsa smiled. "You can get all of that from a single hopeling hair?"

"Oh sure! And loads of other stuff too—I mean, besides the actual replay of events in that hopeling's life."

"And how does that part work?" Ipsa leaned her elbows on the railing, trying to sound casual.

"In my opinion, it is even more interesting than prayer reading," Sim said, then quickly added, "No offense." He continued, "Basically, every moment in the life of that hopeling—I mean, at least during the life of *that* strand of hair—is recorded There. A Surveyor can watch this entire stream of events happen in one continuous movie reel, if you want to use a hopeling analogy. It's so much more efficient and streamlined, because you can just see an entire chunk of time instead of one timestamp, the way you do with prayers."

Ipsa bit her lip, trying not to smile. This was exactly what she needed in order to get answers about Isaac. "How often do you get new ones—for each hopeling, I mean?"

"We don't have a lot of control over that part, at least in my department. They just get sent to us from the Collectors, who work with the Archivists, and then we catalogue and input them, but it usually ends up being fairly current."

Ipsa waved one hand in the air in a sweeping gesture. "We do all this so prayers can be answered faster, better?"

"Well, I mean, if you ask *me* there are hundreds of uses and critical arguments for tracking hopeling hairs," Sim said, extending his arms out wide. "But yes, one use is for the prayer context thing. Except—" He paused.

"Except what?"

"Well, I mean, that's a big reason we cite in all the textbooks and everything, and it totally makes sense, but in the few dozen Repasts since I arrived, we've never had a Responder request a hair," Sim said, running his fingernails through his close crop of yellow hair, which Ipsa now realized, looked like it had likely been dyed. Sim thought for a second, and then chuckled. "If we were just sitting around waiting on the Answering Department to request hairs, this would be one dusty workspace!"

Sim leaned in toward her. "Ipsa, can I ask you something?"

"Of course!"

"Why did you really come here?"

Ipsa's eyes met Sim's and, in that moment, somehow, she knew she could trust him. *Knowledge, with prudence.*

"I need hairs belonging to a specific hopeling."

Sim looked puzzled. "Why would you need a hopeling's hairs?"

Ipsa laughed nervously. "It's like you said, Sim. I'm really a spy." She winked knowingly at him. "But I promise I won't turn you in for those grimy containers over there if you help me."

Sim broke out in a wide grin that showed his entire top row of teeth, sparkling white. "I want to help you—whatever the *real* reason is—but what you're asking—"

"I know. It's big."

"Pretty big and pretty out there."

"Can I ask you to trust me and when I can tell you more, I will?" Ipsa's eyes pleaded with Sim, whose brow was deeply furrowed.

Then his face relaxed and he half smiled.

"This is definitely the strangest request I've ever had, but for some reason, I feel like I'm about to say 'yes.'" He flashed a goofy grin and scratched the back of his head.

Ipsa followed Sim through the labyrinth of snaking tubes that turned and twisted overhead. She ducked her head as the tubes rocketed past every few seconds, even though they were well out of reach.

"You get used to the noise," Sim said with a wink.

"So, do you run this place?" Ipsa said, half in jest.

"Just the part that deals with North America," Sim said. For once, he didn't seem to be joking.

They stepped onto a circular pad on the floor, then sped downward. Level after level they dropped, the air getting increasingly colder.

"Where are we going?" Ipsa said.

"The storage vaults. Where is this hopeling from?"

"His name is Isaac Conway. He lives in Farmington, Connecticut, in the United States."

Sim stretched out his hand, and the pad began to slow toward a stop. "We lucked out that he's from the U.S., given that's part of my territory. We house hairs by geographic location rather than alphabetically; it's just so much easier that way."

Ipsa traced circles on the metal wall beside her with her finger. Her wings pulsed with anticipation. She was so close. She threaded her finger in a long snaking motion along the wall. *I'm coming, Isaac.*

Their small open elevator came to a stop at a thin metal

walkway with two large glass doors at the other end. Ipsa sprinted toward the doors, placing her hand around a sleek metal bar.

Sim walked over to a pad on the wall and punched in a series of numbers. The doors immediately opened into a room aglow with soft light. "Let's see, let's see." Sim walked the length of one wall, glancing over the small boxes that ran from floor to ceiling. A wide smile broke across his face as he found the drawer he was looking for. "Ah! Here we go!"

But then, he frowned.

"That's impossible," Sim muttered, closing the drawer, rereading the front label and then reopening it.

"What's the matter?" Ipsa asked. Peering over his shoulder, she saw the contents of the drawer labeled "Isaac Conway": a felt-lined box with a round indent to hold a small tube about the size of a hot dog. There was just one problem: The box was empty.

Chapter Twenty-One

I swear to God, if he ever lays a hand on Nadine again, I'll kill him.
Why can't he just get hit by a bus and be out of our lives forever?
  —Janine

DHAVI OPENED THE DOOR BEFORE IPSA COULD EVEN LIFT her hand to knock.

Ipsa looked straight into his eyes. "Tell me who you were."

She'd come straight from the Statistics Department, where she'd stood beside Sim in front of an empty drawer meant to hold all hairs belonging to Isaac Conway of Connecticut. Instead, she'd found another dead end. Afraid the disappointment seizing her wings would give her away, she'd thanked Sim and bolted out of the department.

She sat down on the edge of a deep, soft chair. Dhavi looked tired and worn, as if he'd suddenly aged in a world without aging. He walked to the window, his hands bracing either side of its frame. His wings fell limp behind him. "Who was I…" he whispered.

He took a deep breath, and his wings inflated slightly. "What a question to answer." He paused again. "My name was Jim. I was a woodworker and…." Dhavi brought one of his palms close to his face, examining it as if for the first time. "I loved working with my hands, to create something that could withstand time."

"Did you make any of this?" Ipsa asked, extending her arm toward the room.

Dhavi chuckled, and the tension that had filled the room seemed to give way. "No, no, that's not how it works."

"Where did you live?"

"I grew up in England, on a small farm. When I was eighteen my father died. England had just entered a war. It was an uncertain time." Dhavi looked out his window past yellow roses, lost in some distant past.

"So, what did you do?"

"I sailed to America, got a job in a factory. I met a girl, I asked her to marry me and…" Dhavi's voice drifted off and Ipsa tried to fill the gap.

"You lived happily ever after? Isn't that how the saying goes?"

Dhavi looked down at his feet for a moment and shook his head slowly. "That is how the saying goes, Ipsa, but, as I think you saw in Annie's case, it isn't always true. We were happy, yes, for a short time. We had a son. But my *new* country was at war and I was sent to fight it. My wife was so angry! Leaving her alone with a toddler. I told her she'd be fine."

"And was she?"

"She was. And she needed to be, because I didn't ever come back to her."

Ipsa gulped. "The war killed you?"

"In a manner of speaking, yes. The war ended, but most of me died with it. I came home, but I was different. Wars change people. The things I saw. The things I had to do. I couldn't face my wife or my son. I wasn't well."

They sat in silence for what seemed like a hundred prayers, Ipsa with her hands folded on her lap. "What happened?" Ipsa's lips were trembling as she asked the question.

Dhavi turned around to face her. "I spent the rest of my life living on the street."

"But your family?"

"They tried to bring me home many times, but I was sick. The only thing that made me feel better was drinking. That and feeling like I was suffering. It's what I thought I deserved."

Ipsa glanced at his forearms, at the features she'd always taken as star marks: scars, red and raised. She winced, but her stomach growled for more information. "Where is your wife now? Is she Here?"

Dhavi's eyes filled with a faraway look. "She actually arrived Here several earthly years before I did; rather ironic, given my circumstances."

"You mean, she died first," Ipsa said. "And how long have you been Here?"

Dhavi chuckled again, moving from the window to a wooden seat by the fire. "I suppose it's been almost thirty years."

Ipsa leaned forward. "So, when you became an Implementer, did you look for her? Did you tell her who you were?"

"I came to my knowledge a bit differently than the traditional route. Actually, a bit more like you."

Ipsa paused, as if at a fork in the road. There were too many questions in every direction. "So, what happened?"

Dhavi smiled. "It was quite by accident. I'd only barely received my wings. I sat down one day at the same Repast table and stared straight into her eyes. She has the most marvelous green eyes." Dhavi said the last part almost to himself.

"And the memories…of There…they came back?"

"In pieces. Fits and starts, I suppose. I was so new, you see, that I didn't know any different. I just knew she was Marianne."

"And did *she* recognize you?"

Dhavi seemed to snap out of his daydream. "Not one lick, as they say. Of course, I look much different than when she would have last seen me; rather harsh living conditions will do that to a person. But even still, there was nothing."

"So, what did you do?"

The past seemed to vanish from his face, replaced with a half-smile. "I told Corintine, who ran my department."

"And he made you an Implementer?"

"That is a longer story for another day."

"But you could have found her again. Told her everything. Made her remember."

"Told her what? That someone she had no memory of had once been the most important person in another world that now held no meaning to her?" he asked.

"Do you see her now?" Ipsa said. "I mean, even though you didn't tell her, you could still be friends, start over?"

"Every now and then, I see her in the main square," Dhavi said. "Our eyes will catch and I'll think…" Dhavi's voice trailed off, wistful. "But the past is the past." Dhavi's words felt forced, rehearsed. "You can pick at a scab, or you can just let it heal over."

"I don't see why more angels can't know that. Why the Implementers think we need 'knowledge with prudence.' I think we deserve to know that." The firmness in Ipsa's voice surprised her.

Dhavi took a seat across from her on a chair woven in soft purple. He grazed its wooly arm. Ipsa reached into her pocket and pulled out the small tuft of Kluna she'd taken with her from the fields. The dried Kluna in her palm looked the same shade as the chair, the same shade as Implementer wings. Ipsa took a deep breath, ready to fire off another round of questions, but it was Dhavi's voice that broke the silence.

"Do you see this little pull in the fabric?" With his finger, Dhavi traced around one spot where a small loop of thread rose up from the chair. "Do you know why I resist the urge to pull it out?"

Ipsa shook her head.

"Because there is no end to this string. I could tease it out, but the snag would only grow bigger. Sometimes, by trying to solve one problem, you unravel another."

"Other problems?" she asked. "You mean other secrets?"

"Other considerations, unintended consequences," he said, standing up and walking back toward the window. "Considerations from long before you or I arrived. And there are angels Here who believe very strongly in preserving them."

"Eon."

"He could be a powerful adversary, Ipsa."

"Who was he? *There*, I mean."

"That's not for me to share. You'll have to ask him sometime." Dhavi said the last part somewhat wryly.

"He doesn't even care about hopelings," she said,

thinking of Isaac's crumpled prayer. "Or about making sure their prayers get answered."

"That's not true. Eon has more empathy for the human experience than many other angels. That's why he was chosen to be an Implementer."

Ipsa repressed the urge to laugh. "Eon is the least empathetic angel I can imagine."

Dhavi stood, his fingertips gently resting on the windowsill. "That may be what your eyes can see right now."

He glanced back at Ipsa. "I promise you: Isaac's prayer has been *read*, that's all that matters."

"I would feel better if I knew *how* they were answering his prayer." She shook her head in frustration. "And I guess there's something else."

"How did I know?" Dhavi said.

"I just want to know." Ipsa paused. "I know so much about her, but it doesn't feel like me—or at least, I guess it does some of the time, but other times, it's as if I'm watching this person who looks like me but who I don't understand." She looked down at her hands again. "Who I don't always *like*. Sometimes I can see myself in her, in something she says, or the way she fidgets and taps her foot when she's waiting for an answer. But other times..." Her voice trailed off. "She can just be so..."

"Human?" he finished her sentence. "We don't always like who we are. Or who we've been in the past." Dhavi turned back around toward her. "Think about the boy who...took your life. Imagine, one day, him arriving Here, being handed his file—imagine spending an eternity, not just the duration of a hopeling life—living with the worst thing you've ever done. With never being able to let go of that person you'd been. For many hopelings, this place is a second chance."

Ipsa reached her hand to the middle of her chest, tracing one of the rounded divots she'd always called a star mark. Six bullet wounds across her chest, and one on her arm. Mrs. Conway had prayed for that 'monster' to burn in hell for eternity.

"You mean, someday, he'll…be Here?" Ipsa asked.

"Everyone ends up Here," Dhavi said. "That's one of those 'other considerations' I was talking about."

Ipsa sighed. Dhavi sat on the edge of the chair and took her hand in his.

"Do you know Annie's story? Even if you don't understand it yet?"

"I think so," she said.

"Then put the file back. The understanding will come over time."

Ipsa nodded. Holding his worn hand, she imagined what it must have been like to sit across from his wife, to feel that rush of knowledge. A spool of thread rapidly unraveling.

"Should I tell Eon? That I know about the Arcanum?"

Dhavi looked at her with an expression Ipsa couldn't interpret. "Not yet," he said. "Not just yet."

Chapter Twenty-Two

I feel so lost right now. So lost, and all alone.
　—T.

"So," Muir said, leaning over a bowl of vismarati as she settled into the Repast table. "Isn't Sim great?" She leaned in closer and whispered, "Was he able to get Isaac's hairs?"

Ipsa's wings drooped. "The tube was missing. And don't eat those."

"Oh, right," Muir said, dropping the fruit in her fingers back into the bowl. "Where was it?"

"Sim had no idea."

"Do you think…"

At the same moment, Ipsa and Muir both looked down toward the stage below them, where they could see Eon in animated conversation with one of the Implementers, named Khan.

"What are you going to do?" Muir said.

"What can I do? I'm right back where I started." Ipsa rubbed her temples with her fingers, the way she'd seen Annie do when she'd had a fight with Mrs. Conway.

Muir placed her hand on Ipsa's shoulder and forced a smile. "I bet Sim will find it. Maybe there was just a mix-up."

"Thanks," Ipsa said. She thought about what Dhavi had said about not pulling the piece of thread, about how it was important to shield other angels from what she knew. Considerations—was that the word he'd used? She wanted desperately to share the truth with her friends. Sometimes it felt impossible to look at Muir and Elna.

Dhavi had asked her for patience, but they both knew that was not a strength for Ipsa. Or, she realized, for Annie. Dhavi had mentioned secrets. She tugged at the loop of thread in her mind. She tugged a bit more. He was right: The loop only got bigger. But Ipsa couldn't stop wondering: What more was there to pull out?

"I finished my last pair just in time!" Elna spread her mantel as she sank gracefully to the floor beside her friends. "What have I missed?"

"Ipsa didn't have any luck at the Hair Counting Department," Muir said, letting out a deep sigh.

"You're not still bothering about that silliness, are you?" Elna did not intend to scorn, but her words landed on Ipsa's ears like an irritating fly.

"It's not silliness," Ipsa said, her wings suddenly as stiff as cardboard.

"I just meant that if you really want to *help* hopelings, well, it seems as though you're doing that work already, just by reading their prayers and getting them to the right place! *Prayers must be heard to be answered!* Your department has its own Arcanum! If the Responders needed your help *answering* a prayer, I'm sure they'd ask the Implementers!" She smiled brightly, casting a confident glance down toward the group of Implementers assembled onstage.

"You'll have to excuse me if I don't exactly trust that the Implementers would do that," Ipsa mumbled to herself.

Elna gave Ipsa a funny look, but she shook her head and changed the subject. "I have to tell you about the last pair of wings I made! They were gold when I started, so of course I thought they'd be for a new Wreather, but they changed colors eight times while I was sewing. When I handed them over to Argo they were Contemplations blue, but we'll have to see, won't we!" Elna smiled.

She began to sing the welcome chorus as a new group of wingless angels climbed on stage:

Stardust to angels, your wings flock to thee,
Your soul shall it capture, then named shall you be!
From a place in the sky, like countless untold,
Angels to stardust, our circle unfolds.

"Please stop singing that!" Ipsa winced, holding her hands to her ears. "I can't take it anymore; I can't stand another moment of this ridiculous ceremony!" She was shouting, but her words barely registered, muffled by millions of wings flapping as the crowd welcomed the next set of angels to the stage.

Elna gave Ipsa a puzzled look. "What's the matter with you? We always sing that song! It's our history."

Ipsa looked down at the table, at the bowl of vismarati that Elna plucked one after another. She could not endure one more lie. Somewhere inside her wings, the thread snapped in two. "No, Elna, it's not our history, it's just a story—a story they've made us believe."

Muir cocked her head. "Ipsa, what are you talking about?"

"Those angels down there, the ones you made those blue wings for, Elna? They don't come from stardust." Ipsa's words rang with bitterness, anger. "Just look at them! Haven't you ever really *looked* at them before? They look like something, all right, but it's not stardust. They look like *hopelings.*" She looked up at Elna and then at Muir, hoping her words would register.

They did not.

"Of course they do, Ipsa!" Elna offered a wide smile as if hoping to calm her friend. "Because hopelings look like us! They were created in our image, after all!"

"No, no, no," Ipsa said. "You're not getting it. All of this stardust talk is just a fairytale—a made-up story. We don't come from some twinkling star in the sky; we come from There. *We* were those hopelings!"

Muir and Elna sat in stunned silence while, below, a pair of olive wings soared and looped above the crowd of angels onstage.

Finally, Elna laughed, cutting the silence. "Ipsa, this is another hopeling joke you've heard from one of your prayers, isn't it?! For a moment I thought you were serious! But it's just like the one about the bell!" She giggled again, a wave of relief washing her porcelain face.

Ipsa stared back at her, slowly shaking her head.

Muir looked back and forth between her two friends. "Ipsa, I don't understand. Are you saying that those angels on stage—were hopelings?"

"Muir, that's nonsense," Elna said, flustered. "This has to be another one of Ipsa's jokes, but I think it's gone on a bit too long, really."

"No, it's not," Ipsa said. "It's the truth—the truth they don't want us to know. I couldn't believe it either, at first, but it all made perfect sense. That's why I had such a

strange reaction when I read Isaac's prayer. He was—he is
—my brother."

"Ipsa." Elna's voice took on an uncharacteristic serious-
ness. "Please, keep your voice down. You're saying all sorts
of things right now that others could hear and misinterpret.
I think you don't know what you're saying. Your wings don't
look right to me. I bet you just need a good round of Meditation to relax."

"I do know what I'm saying, Elna," Ipsa said. "I know
exactly what I'm saying—all of this is a fraud."

Elna looked startled for a moment, like a deer caught in
the middle of the road with a large truck barreling toward
her. She seemed frozen in place, as if waiting to be hit
where she stood. But after a moment, her wings rustled,
determined to avoid the impact. She rose from her seat,
smoothing her mantle.

"No." Elna spoke with a finality that came from
spending hundreds of Repasts crafting wings for the very
ceremony Ipsa questioned. "I don't know why you're saying
these things, but they're not true. They can't be true. It's
making me *frustrated* with you, Ipsa. And I think I'm going
to find another table." Her golden wings were flustered,
trembling uncontrollably. "See you next Repast, Muir."

Ipsa watched her friend thread through the crowd, her
sun-kissed wings disappearing into the throng of angels.
Elna had been right about one thing: Ipsa's wings did not
look quite right. They sagged as if lined with cement. She
knew she should not have said anything—now she had
probably lost her two best friends.

She turned back toward Muir and met her brown eyes,
round as two walnuts.

Muir blinked once. "Do you know who I was?"

Ipsa's wings lightened. She shook her head. "I don't."

"So I died?" Muir spoke the words slowly. "And then came Here?

"I guess so. I'm not exactly sure how it works."

Muir looked around them. "Who knows? Just the Implementers?"

"Just the Implementers," Ipsa said. "And us."

Muir swallowed, turning her head slowly across the span of the amphitheater, taking in the millions of angels that surrounded them, all fluttering their wings in euphoric applause as the last pair of new wings below them found its mate.

"And us," she repeated.

Chapter Twenty-Three

Dios,

I need your help. We still haven't found a donor for Paulo. I know his heart won't make it much longer. Please help us. He's my heart. Why are you going to take him from me?
—Flavia

IPSA AND MUIR LEFT REPAST IN SILENCE. MUIR FLAPPED her wings methodically, as if in a trance. Ipsa stayed close by her side, holding her hand as they flew. Her wings ached with regret. She'd experienced a wave of relief as she unburdened her secret to Muir. But she also felt selfish, having put some of her weight onto Muir's small, delicate wings.

Seated back at her desk, Ipsa could barely focus on the prayer before her, Flavia's words unfolding in a frantic splay across the parchment. *Why are you going to take him from me?* Ipsa thought of how many of her own mother's prayers had been devoted to asking a similar question. The very same one that kept tugging at Ipsa's sleeve: Why? *Why...* The word whispered incessantly into the hollow of her ear.

Ipsa opened her mouth to mark the prayer as Highly Urgent, when she stopped herself. Something about the prayer triggered a memory—not an Annie memory, but a prayer-reading memory. The prayer she'd just read was familiar. She grabbed the hovering piece of paper and pulled it toward her, skimming it once again. Something about the phrase "He's my heart," struck her. Flavia and Paulo. She'd seen this prayer—or one very similar—before. Why was this hopeling asking the same prayer twice?

Questions swelled inside Ipsa, a reservoir ready to breach its dam. Getting up from her desk, Ipsa walked over to where Eon stood speaking with a group of Readers, her confidence draining from her wings with each step.

Ipsa gulped and forced her wings to straighten a bit. "Excuse me, Eon."

Her supervisor stopped speaking and turned around, arms folding across his chest as soon as he saw her. "Yes?"

"I'd like to talk to you about a recent prayer I submitted." Ipsa spoke slowly, just as she'd rehearsed. "From a woman named Flavia, about her husband who is in a hospital. I marked it Extremely Urgent. I wanted to make sure her husband was okay."

Eon's eyes narrowed suspiciously. "Do you need another introductory Prayer Reading session? Flavia's prayer is now in the hands of the Answering Department," Eon said dismissively, turning back toward the crowd gathered around him.

Ipsa was ready. "I—I realize that. I was just thinking that knowing the status of *Flavia's* prayer might determine the amount of future prayers coming from this woman's family and allow us to better prepare for them," Ipsa said, braiding her fingers nervously. "I thought if I could just—"

"My, my," Eon cut her off, his wings bristling as he turned back around. "A few productive prayer sessions and suddenly you're ready to go show the Responders how it's done."

"No, of course not, I just thought—"

"You just thought you knew better than every other angel Here," Eon said. "But then, what else is new?" Eon cleared his throat, and as he did his wings seemed to shake away some of his agitation. "I've got a great deal of *current* prayers to deal with, if you don't mind."

But Ipsa didn't move.

"I'd like to speak with someone in the Prayer Answering Department."

For a moment, it seemed as though The Hive itself ceased to churn. The normal, ambient chatter, the sound of chairs scraping the floor, the hum of prayers zipping through the air: all of it seemed to grind to a halt as Ipsa asked her question.

No Reader had ever asked to go to the Answering Department before.

Every angel within earshot seemed frozen, awaiting Eon's reply. Not a single wing fluttered. Ordinarily, eavesdropping, like gossiping, was unthinkable Here—but then again, so was asking about the Responders. If a request for information on a specific prayer's answer seemed bold, then asking to enter the Answering Department was downright audacious.

Even Eon seemed caught off guard. He puckered his lips in a fake smile and said to the group, "Let's continue this lesson in a few prayers." Then grabbing Ipsa's elbow, he pulled her toward him with surprising strength, his words forming a low hiss. "Follow me, *now.*"

Ipsa stumbled after Eon toward the far side of the Reading Room, a hidden door swinging open to reveal a spiral staircase. He climbed it with quick purpose, flicking his head back over his shoulder from time to time to make sure she was following him.

The stairs led to a large room with a massive window on one wall that looked down upon the Reading Room. Ipsa felt her wings shudder, recalling past moments when she'd believed herself safe from Eon's watchful gaze, wondering if all the while he'd been perched in his bird's eye lookout.

She glanced around, inventorying her surroundings. The room's floor felt as cold as prayers she'd read from blizzards. Like Dhavi's cottage, there were books every-where. But unlike the labyrinth of leaning book pillars that lined Dhavi's floor, the volumes in Eon's space—whose bindings looked to Ipsa nearly identical—were neatly lined along floor-to-ceiling bookshelves. In front of the overlook sat a large chair made of plush, red fabric. It was the only piece of furniture in the space, save a small table at its side. She ran her fingers across the chair's wooden frame. Carved in intricate loops, Ipsa read the Arcana: *Hopelings First. Knowledge with Prudence. Prayers must be Heard to be Answered.* The room had a low ceiling from which chandeliers dangled, casting the room in shadows. On the singular table lay a thick book held closed by something she'd seen on hopeling diaries but never Here: a lock.

Ipsa watched Eon glide toward the window. His violet wings pulsed to full wingspan, their edges almost blood red. When he spun around, his eyes seemed on fire, although

Ipsa assured herself it was simply the reflection from the flames above.

"You will not make a mockery of me or my department," he said. Ipsa watched as his wings seemed to clench back upward, the edges forming angry fists.

"I'm not trying to, Eon. I just want to know when Flavia's prayer will be answered." Ipsa choked out the words. "Why does that make you so angry? And why can't I ask the Responders?"

Eon's wings lost some of their tension as he walked slowly, purposefully, toward his chair. His long and slender fingers grazed the leather cover of the book perched beside it. He forced a grim smile. "So many questions!" Eon said, tapping the book's cover with his fingertips. "And such curiosity! Although, it's more of a *recent* curiosity. Yes, a sudden, almost insatiable curiosity about prayers." Eon paused, lifting his hand as if to investigate his fingertips. "New...and old."

Eon's eyes locked with Ipsa's and she felt her wings freeze in place.

"By 'old prayers' of course, I don't just mean your hopeling from the hospital. You've taken a rather special interest in one or two hopelings, wouldn't you say?" His voice sliced through the space between them, a hot blade through butter.

Ipsa considered feigning ignorance, but she knew her wings betrayed her: they lay shriveled like wilted rose petals against her back. She'd been so careful. Ipsa opened her mouth and stuttered, but no words came out.

"I'll mark this as the first time Ipsa had nothing to say," Eon said smugly. He sat down on the chair, which made him look like a king on his throne. "How prayers are answered—Flavia's or Isaac Conway's— is not for you to decide."

He'd said it. There was no longer anything left to hide.

"Why did you take his prayer? I *know* they can't be misdirected," Ipsa shot back.

"You know so little." Eon whispered the words without any harshness, his eyes following the glint of a prayer through the window. He looked tired. His skin betrayed none of the wrinkles that pulled at Dhavi's face, yet Eon seemed like an old man. Ipsa looked again around this empty room. She thought of Dhavi, alone and hidden away in his small cottage. Of Elna avoiding her at Repast. She wondered whether loneliness was the price of secrets.

"I know more than you think." Ipsa feigned confidence. "I know that I was Annie. I know we were *all* hopelings."

"Wonderful! Fantastic!" Eon clapped in mock enthusiasm. "Shall we have you fitted for your Implementer's wings?" He narrowed his eyes, his tone settling back to his usual frostiness. "Do you honestly think you're the first angel to stumble upon that truth?"

His question raised a dozen more in Ipsa's mind, but she bit her lip in silence.

"Have you sent it on to the Answering Department?" Ipsa held firm. "He needs m—he needs our help."

"You'd do well to remember with whom you're speaking," Eon said, resuming his icy sheen. "These ridiculous incursions have carried on far too long. Dhavi promised that this defiance was being handled. He kept me from resolving this problem myself. Clearly, I won't make that mistake again."

"Eon, don't you care what happens to any of them?"

He grasped the edges of the chair, leaned toward her, his teeth gritted. "I would appreciate it if you ceased making assumptions on matters about which you know almost nothing." The purple tips of his wings prickled up like porcupine quills behind him.

She glanced down at the rough, raised star mark that ran between Eon's fingers and thumb. A deep scar, as if from a knife's blade. Ipsa wondered again about who Eon had been There, what stories about his past looped endlessly through his mind now. As much as she disliked Annie at times, Ipsa could forgive much of her meanness, her insecurity. Annie had been a teenager, still figuring out what kind of human she was going to grow into. But Eon had died much older. He'd *been* who he was going to be There. And what if who he'd been wasn't pretty?

He smoothed out the folds of his robe. "Everything I do is to protect those hopelings from the likes of you. And you from—" Eon stopped short, pruning his lips closed.

"What do you mean: 'protect' them from me?" Ipsa remembered Dhavi's comment about empathy—the virtue that supposedly distinguished Eon as an Implementer. That he might be able to consider someone else's feelings—to want to protect anyone—seemed laughable to Ipsa.

"Understand that I am trying to protect you from *yourself*," Eon said quietly. "Isaac doesn't need your help."

"I don't understand," Ipsa began.

"You don't *need* to understand." Eon rose from his seat. "All prayers belonging to the Conways had better be back on their shelves by the end of this session. Or else we'll have to consider more *drastic* action. I will do whatever is necessary to stop this."

"Protect them from what?" Ipsa repeated.

"From an angel who thinks she knows what's best for —" Eon stopped, abruptly. "I have no need to explain myself further. But hear me when I say this: I've just asked you to stop your inquisition." He walked toward the door, before turning back once more.

"I'll only *ask* once."

With a flick of his robe, Eon descended the stairs, his fractured shadow trailing with each step. Ipsa's feet remained fixed to the floor. Her wings quivered, like a harp string roughly plucked.

Chapter Twenty-Four

Returning to her seat, Ipsa felt dizzy, her head spinning from her close encounter with Eon. Muir stood up at her desk, a look of concern on her face, but Ipsa shook her head and her friend reluctantly sat back down.

Sitting at her desk, Ipsa tried to register Mahir's prayer but struggled to focus. Her legs wobbled, her fingers seemed jittery, and her wings could not calm down. Ipsa had never felt anything like what she was feeling at this moment, but she had read enough prayers to know that this was fear, still reverberating through her wings. The idea that an angel could inspire fear was something Ipsa had never contemplated. *We'll have to consider more drastic action.* She had no idea what Eon was empowered to do as an Implementer—but she could guess he wouldn't limit himself merely to what was within his power.

Ipsa looked about cautiously. Her eyes drifted up to the top of the Reading Room, where prayers flipped and floated, making their way to the various chutes along the walls. She squinted against the light that flooded in from overhead. Silhouetted against the blue sky above, the prayers looked like pelicans, gliding about until diving for their destination.

She would return the files and leave it at that. After all, what made her think she could do anything for Isaac that the Prayer Answering Department couldn't do?

AT THE END SESSIONS, IPSA RETRIEVED ISAAC'S AND ANNIE'S files from her hideaway in the Contemplations Garden, then made her way toward the Archives. It was Recreation time and, peeking her head inside the large doors, Ipsa found no Archivists in sight. She walked inside, both Conway files clutched against her chest. She rested Annie's thick file on the glass floor. "Stay," she said firmly. As if in response, the file flipped over rather dramatically. Taking Isaac's file, she extended it upward with both hands. The slim book rested easily between her fingertips as she lifted it toward the ceiling. "Return: Isaac Conway," Ipsa whispered. The book soared upward and disappeared swiftly around the corner. Ipsa took a gulp of air, staring down at Annie's file fidgeting on the table. She placed one hand on its cover. Letting go seemed as unimaginable as parting with her own hand. She closed her eyes and remembered

Dhavi's words: She knew Annie's story, backward and forward. It was inside of her now, not just words in a book.

As if to say a final goodbye, her fingers opened the file and flipped through to a random page toward the back of the book.

Ipsa stared into the prayer and found herself in front of Annie's bedroom mirror, Annie's body turning from side to side in an indecisive manner. She wore an orange two-piece bathing suit that tied around her neck. Her hands fidgeted in different areas, pulling and tugging as she arched her back this way and craned her neck that way, trying to take in the view from every angle. Scraps of what looked like magazine cutouts were taped to the borders of the mirror, overlapping various photographs of Annie and her friends.

A small but persistent knock at the door startled Annie from her inspection of the bathing suit.

"GO AWAY!" she shouted.

There was a pause, and then a small voice replied through the door, "Annie, please?"

Isaac.

Ipsa could tell from the tenor of his voice that something was wrong. Annie seemed to notice too. She strode over to the door and, in an annoyed and dramatic gesture, unlocked the door and threw it open with a groan.

"What do you want?"

Isaac's eyes looked red and puffy and his left cheek below his eye was swollen with a hint of green under the skin. Annie grabbed Isaac by his shoulder and pulled him into the room, shutting the door behind her. "What happened to you?"

As Annie spoke she grabbed her pink terrycloth robe from the back hook of the door, wrapping herself in it before guiding Isaac over to the side of the bed to sit beside her. Taking his face in her hands, she softly pressed the pads of her fingertips to the spot around Isaac's cheek, the way she'd seen the school nurse examine her patients. He winced slightly at the touch.

"Annie, do you think I'm a theater freak?" Isaac's voice sounded small as a mouse.

"A freak? Of course I do." Annie smirked. "But you're my brother, so I'm supposed to think that. Did someone call you that?"

"It doesn't matter, just some kid from the pool."

"What's his name?"

"It will only make things worse. Besides, summer's almost over."

"Isaac, what's the point of having a cool older sister who knows cool older guys if you can't use it to your advantage once in a while?"

"Annie, you're, like, fifteen months older than me. You literally just turned fourteen two days ago."

"That's still older and cooler than you are."

Isaac sighed. "Justin Capaletti."

"I'll take care of it. Is he bigger than you?"

Isaac glanced down at his small, bony arms. "What do you think?"

"Well, you're about one thousand times smarter than him, so he's probably just jealous. What did Mom say when she picked you up? Did she flip out? Do not tell her this kid's name. That *would* make it worse. Let me handle it."

"She was on the phone with a client. I just mostly turned my head to the other side."

Annie got up and walked over to her bureau, rummaging around in a basket. "Here, let's try this." She brought over a small round disc. She took out a soft pad and started smearing something on Isaac's face.

"You're not allowed to wear makeup," Isaac said.

"Do you want my help or not?"

Isaac closed his mouth as Annie applied a thin powder to her brother's bruised cheek.

Annie leaned back, assessing her work. "Okay, that looks better." She lifted Isaac's chin slightly with her hand. "Now leave this Justin to me. And don't let him get into your head—he's just jealous because when you get on a stage, people stop and pay attention." Their eyes met, and both seemed to acknowledge the rarity of this moment.

But it was only a moment. Annie quickly needled him in his ribs. "Now get out of here and leave me alone. I have stuff to do."

Isaac hopped off the bed and walked to the door. Holding the doorknob, he turned back, digging into his back pocket. He dangled a pendant on a chain in front of her. "Happy belated birthday, by the way," he said. "Saw this at the mall and it made me think of you and me." He tossed the necklace toward her, but his aim was off, sending it flying toward the mirror. Ipsa felt the frame shift as Annie leaped up to catch it deftly. "Stick to theater," she said, teasingly. Ipsa felt the cool metal in her hand as Annie spun it around: A circle, half black, half white, divided in half by a snaking line.

"Yin and yang, that's us all right," Annie said, unclasping the latch and pulling it up around her neck. "Hey thanks, bro."

"Thanks, sis," Isaac slipped out, shutting the door behind him. Annie held the pendant between her fingers, tracing the raised curves. A circle and a squiggly line. Ipsa knew that pattern. It was the same gesture she'd made countless times when she was waiting for a prayer to materialize or Repast to start—she'd just never had the word for the shape she was drawing. Yin and yang. She and Isaac across the universe.

God, keep an eye on him. It's got to be hard being a 30-year-old trapped in the body of an eighth grader.

Ipsa forced herself to leave the prayer, opening her eyes. She shut the file firmly with both hands and took a deep inhale. "Return," she forced a cracked whisper. "Annie… Conway." The book rose slowly into the air, like a swaying helicopter that held too much weight. It rounded a large bookcase and flapped out of sight. Ipsa turned from the table to leave.

THUMP. Ipsa padded down several rows of shelves in the direction the prayer file had flown, through the labyrinth of human history that surrounded her. Turning the corner, Ipsa found Annie's file, which had fallen from the air. Scooping up the book, Ipsa once again called, "Return, Annie Conway," this time with a firmness that reverberated through the corridor. Up, up, up it went above her head, settling back into its nook on a high shelf with the rest of her family.

Ipsa crouched to the floor against a wall of files. Her wingtips drooped over her head, leaden. Her face felt warm and sticky. Her thoughts raced in every direction, amplified as though playing on a loudspeaker in the distance. Squeezing her eyes closed, Ipsa tried to clear her head, but the voices remained. Ipsa flashed her eyes wide.

The sounds were not inside her head.

Her wings frozen, Ipsa strained her ears, wondering if someone else was nearby. She couldn't make out whose voices she was hearing; it was muddled together, yet familiar. She sat up straighter, her head pressed firmly against the row of books behind her. The voices seemed to be coming from behind the bookcase that braced the back wall of the Archives. Ipsa turned her head to investigate. A sliver of light crossed Ipsa's face as she moved. The prayer files were stacked together as tightly as the walkway stones in the courtyard, yet in a few places where a shelf sagged slightly, a light illuminated the file from behind.

Slowly, gingerly, Ipsa reached her hand to touch one of the volumes. Her fingers slid up and down the binding, then, grasping it firmly, she slowly pulled the book from its place. Unaccustomed to being pulled from a shelf in this manner, the file wriggled and spasmed as she laid it on the floor. A flood of light spilled onto Ipsa's cheeks. Squinting, Ipsa tilted her ear against the opening; the blur of voices became louder.

Ipsa thrust her eye toward the opening but could barely make out anything against the backlight. She removed more files, revealing a cavernous room behind the wall. Something whizzed close by the wall, causing Ipsa to jerk her head back for a moment. Her eyes began to adjust. The room was enormous—from her small window Ipsa couldn't even see a ceiling. The flying objects whirled by at such speed she couldn't quite make out their shape, but still, the noise was so familiar. Ipsa hoisted her arm through the space and something flimsy and papery smacked her fore-arm. Several began pecking at Ipsa's hand, like seagulls diving for food. Opening her palm, she grabbed and missed. Finally, Ipsa steadied her hand in the air, her palm wide open and facing upward. She felt a wisp graze her hand and snapped her fingers shut, clenching her prize in her fist.

Ipsa stared down at the contents of her now open palm. It was a prayer. The rhythmic murmur finally clicked. The constant din of prayers that formed the background music of her life, this was the same noise she heard now.

Ipsa felt silly. Of course it was prayers. She looked up toward the ceiling at the trail of prayers that continually snaked their way toward their hopeling files to join them. She had found the source: The prayers were making their way out of a hole in the top of the room one by one, like a flock of earthly finches heading south for winter. She craned her neck to watch the procession. At the end of the row, the line broke apart in several directions as each prayer went off in search of its own file.

This must be the space where prayers arrived after being answered.

A murmur came softly from the prayer and, glancing down, Ipsa could see it was from an elderly woman in Japan, uttered only a few earthly hours ago, asking for help to purchase a fishing boat for her son.

"Strange," Ipsa muttered to herself. The prayer obviously wasn't Expired—the only type of prayer that would be immediately routed to the Archives—and it dealt with livelihood. She hadn't realized the Responders could answer a prayer so quickly.

Ipsa stood up, still holding the woman's prayer in her right hand. She reached for one thick file, then a second and a third, until she had cleared off a wide row of shelf space. Prayers were flowing in from chutes at the top of the huge chamber—chutes much like the ones in the Reading Room that routed prayers by their urgency and other categories. They were coming in at such a speed that the room seemed caught amid a hopeling snowstorm, paper flakes dancing about and meandering their way toward the floor, where they settled in a massive heap in the center of the room. Ipsa looked up again. Indeed the prayers were coming in from multiple channels, yet they were all ending up in one huge, shifting paper mountain. A single, clear tube above the pile seemed to then vacuum them up, guiding them, Ipsa suspected, up and into the Archives in an orderly fashion.

She stuck her hand in and fished for another prayer. This one was also from that same earthly day, this time from a little boy who wanted his mom to order pizza for dinner. Trivial. She grabbed another, then another—each one a different category of prayer, each seemingly recent, but not recent enough to be Expired. It made no sense.

Remembering she still held several prayers in her hand, Ipsa released them back into the blizzard. She collected the files at her feet, putting each back in its proper spot, caulking up the last remains of light that shone from the secret room. She had come to the Archives to put her investigation to rest, but her visit had only surfaced more questions.

Ipsa felt like a firefighter staring at a burning building, knowing they needed to go inside when instinct told them to run the other way. Eon's threat still rattled around in her mind, as did Dhavi's cautions, but Ipsa could feel the answer in her wings: she knew she needed to finish what she'd started.

It was time to go to the Prayer Answering Department to get some answers for herself.

The Answering Department stood in plain sight, as visible as any other department. It was not shrouded in any fog of secrecy; it simply didn't concern most angels. The building was round and smooth, without windows, facing out in a semi-circle from the edge of a steep cliff that hemmed one edge of their community.

Ipsa smiled nervously at two angels as she walked along the path near the building. It was still Recreation time, and so a few angels meandered by this space on their way to the main square or some social activity. There was no sign of anyone coming or going from the Answering Department, despite the fact that Responders didn't typically take time for Recreation.

Standing at the great main entrance, Ipsa paused, unsure how to proceed. What would a Responder say if she just walked right in? How would she explain her presence? What if they had the same reaction to her questions as Eon? Her wings shivered.

The door was massive. She grazed the wood panels with her fingertips, following the intricate carvings of prayers and hopelings that decorated them. In the center of the door, a massive pair of wings appeared so lifelike that she half-expected them to burst forth from the door and fly into the sky.

Breathing deeply, Ipsa put her hand on the doorknob, determined to enter and find her fate.

But the knob wouldn't turn.

Ipsa stepped back in confusion. Wiping her hand against her mantel, Ipsa seized the handle once more. She twisted with greater force, but it held firm, leaving her palm burning and sore. Pulling the door toward her, Ipsa could not even force a rattle. It was as if the door were sealed shut. Ipsa had never come across a door that would not open at the touch. She stumbled back a few steps, disoriented. Why would a door Here be locked?

Chapter Twenty-Five

Dios,

Today I'm a big brother. His name is Luca but I'm gonna call him Chino, cause he's got lots of curly hair. Mama says his heart isn't working right. Can you please hurry up and make it better?

—Diego

"I NEED TO KNOW ABOUT THE ANSWERING DEPARTMENT," Ipsa said, her voice as thin as paper. She'd pounded on Dhavi's great oak door, only to collapse on the nearest chair.

"What do you want to know?" Dhavi said.

Ipsa looked up at Dhavi in surprise. "I went to Eon last Repast to find out the status of a prayer—not Isaac's, another prayer—and he threatened me." She paused, recalling Eon's dark and lonely room. "I went to the Archives to return Isaac's and Annie's files. But there was this noise. There's a whole other room just filled with prayers, almost like they're coming right from the Reading Room and being dumped into one big pile. But that can't be. If they were all sent to the same place at the same time, then why would my job even exist? And when would they get answered?… So, I just needed to go there. I figured if I went to the Prayer Answering Department I could understand and make sense of all this."

Dhavi's voice remained steady. "And so, you went?"

"I couldn't get in. The door was locked. Well, more than locked, really. It was as if it wasn't even meant to be opened."

"You can't go into the Answering Department," he muttered, his back turned away from Ipsa.

"But WHY?" Ipsa said, raising her voice.

Dhavi led her by the hand across his threshold, taking to the sky in the opposite direction of the Rest Houses, where, with sunset as their guide, angels were settling in for evening meditation. Soon, night would fall and stars would appear. *Stardust to angels.* So the song went. The pair landed in front of the Answering Department's great door.

"If you said I can't go in, why bring me here?" she said.

The elder angel put his finger to his mouth to silence her. Taking his other arm, he raised his hand in front of the door, his eyes never leaving the carved wings at its center. Ipsa watched him carefully and then shifted her gaze toward the door itself. It began to wobble. The door became translucent, like a screen, before disappearing all together.

Ipsa stepped toward the opening; her face wrinkled in confusion. She tried to adjust her eyes but there was nothing to adjust them *to*. The great workspace of the Responders—the place where all prayers were answered—

was empty. Or, perhaps the better word was "absent." Ipsa stood at the precipice of a cavern, her feet half dangling over the edge of a mountainside that gave way toward a steep slope. There was no building behind this wall, only an ever-expanding sea of air, dropping down from the side of the cliff at her feet and disappearing into the misty, blue abyss of the Endless Lake.

Here's great Answering Department was nothing more than a wall with a door.

Dhavi seemed to read her mind. "You can't go to the Prayer Answering Department because there *is* no Prayer Answering Department."

There is no Prayer Answering Department. There is no Prayer Answering Department! The phrase repeated itself in Ipsa's mind on a loop, though each repetition brought only more confusion.

Ipsa cocked her head to the side, trying to make meaning of his statement. "No physical department? You mean because the Responders answer them in the Archives?"

Dhavi slowly shook his head from side to side.

"Where are all of the Responders?" Ipsa asked. They don't come to Repast…or join us for Recreation because of how many prayers they must answer." She peered over the edge of the cliff as if searching the slope for pumpkin-colored wings.

"When they leave Repast after their assignment, it's to get *new* wings. There aren't Responders." He gently pulled her back from the overhang, and as he dropped his arm the empty landscape disappeared behind the thick oak door.

Ipsa grazed her hand across the carvings, pushing the door with all of her weight. It stood as solid as it had been moments before. She turned around to face Dhavi, a look of confusion plastered across her face.

"What do you mean, Dhavi? If there's no department, where are the prayers sent? How do we answer them?"

Dhavi seemed lost in some facet of the great door. "We don't."

Chapter Twenty-Six

Cheon-ju,

Jin's been in a car accident. Please, please give us a miracle.
—JiYoung

Dhavi's words made little sense to Ipsa: No Answering Department. Prayers *not* being answered. Those were absurd statements. As absurd, Ipsa realized, as telling an angel she'd once *been* a hopeling.

So she laughed. The kind of manic laugh she'd heard in prayers from hopelings so delirious with fear or worry that there was simply nothing else to do. In fact, Ipsa could not seem to stop laughing, a hard belly-aching cackle that forced her to bend over. And then gasp for air. And then, finally, sob very wet, very real, very hopeling-like tears.

Dhavi picked her up, a crumpled heap, and pushed off into the sky. Ipsa's eyelids felt heavy, and the rhythmic beating of his wings made Ipsa close her eyes. She had never felt so helpless.

When she opened her eyes again, Dhavi knelt beside her, an anxious look on his face, his hand trying to clasp her own tightly balled fist.

She lay on the small couch in his cottage and didn't speak for some time. She'd learned more in a dozen Repasts than most angels ever would. And while Ipsa had been shocked to learn about her life as Annie, she'd mostly felt as though she were reading a book about someone else.

But prayer reading, that *was* Ipsa's life, the only reality she could ever remember. Her only real purpose Here. And even though she'd spent most of her Repasts hating her job, now it all seemed hollow: her studies, her textbooks, her sessions reading and sorting, reading and sorting. All for what?

After a silence that felt like a million prayers, Ipsa opened her mouth. "There is no Answering Department?"

"That's right."

Ipsa kept her gaze trained on the ceiling above her, feeling too weak to even lift her neck to face Dhavi. "There are no Responders answering the prayers I file every session?"

"No."

"Those prayers are just sent directly to the Archives?"

"Yes." Dhavi's hand clasped hers even more tightly with each short answer.

Millions and millions of prayers she and her fellow angels had read flashed across her mind. Ipsa felt betrayed —but worse still, she realized, *she* had betrayed those hopelings: the woman whose fiancé was in the car accident, the husband desperate for a transplant, the girl who'd lost her brother, Isaac, and millions of others like them. They had trusted her.

She felt the smarting pain of a million *why*s like a slap to the face, infinite as the pinpricks of stars above her. Each question offered a dozen more, such that the entire fabric of her existence seemed not a cloth pinpricked by questions but rather sewn together with them.

"Why would the Implementers lie about something like this? Why go to the trouble of having a department that doesn't even exist? Why concoct this story to begin with?" Ipsa pummeled Dhavi with her questions.

Dhavi held her hand firmly in his larger one, his eyes never faltering from Ipsa. "It's not that simple, Ipsa," he said. "This wasn't some story pulled from thin air. It *was* our past. It's just …not our present."

"So we used to answer prayers, but now we don't?" Ipsa said, hoisting herself up onto her elbows.

"That's right."

"Why did we stop? And why did you Implementers think the rest of us didn't really need to know?" Ipsa said the last part with a biting anger in her voice.

Dhavi let out a long sigh. His wings looked small and limp, not ready for Ipsa pounding at his door of secrets, demanding that he open up the shades, let the sun shine in and send the dust flying.

He walked to a door in the corner of the room and opened it, beckoning to Ipsa to follow. The door opened to a spiral staircase which, as Ipsa peered over the railing, seemed bottomless. As he led her down the stairs, Ipsa brushed her hand to the wall. She couldn't say how many times they'd looped down when the wall began to reveal lines, like the crude outlines of mountain ranges and riverbeds, peaks and valleys and oceans of a thick black line. Above and below the line were sketches and notes. Dates with names, pictures of tall buildings and airplanes, guns and computers. As she traveled down farther and farther, the line continued its jagged ups and downs, sketches of cars were replaced by ships, then horses, then hopelings walking. Finally, Dhavi paused a few steps below her. He reached his hand out to lay his palm flat on the wall. Ipsa studied the spot where Dhavi's hand rested: The smooth transitions of peaks and valleys that she'd seen looping their way across the page for so many turns of the stairs suddenly went haywire. The paper looked like a readout from one of the machines Ipsa had seen in hospital prayers, the computers that monitored the beats of a human heart.

"This is a timeline of There?" Ipsa asked.

"It is.

"What happened?" Ipsa said, pointing toward the sharp turns and skyrocketing peaks of the timeline before her.

"Everything has a ripple effect, Ipsa. Dropping a small pebble in a stream could affect the tide in a distant ocean. It took many human centuries for the Implementers to realize that." Dhavi brushed his hand in a wide circle around the swath of wall where the lines went haywire. "But what happened was like dropping a boulder into a cup of water."

Ipsa followed him still lower down the spiraling stairs of hopeling history until they'd reached the bottom, a picture of two hopelings drawn crudely at the base. Ipsa grazed her hand across the beginning of time. The wall's surface felt dry and stiff, as if it might crumble in her fingers.

"It was the angel, Fortula, who realized that they had the power to answer prayers. The world There was still so young, the requests so basic, so tied to the very survival of humanity: warmth, food, protection. Neither Fortula nor Yuka could say for sure how the answers happened, but if they read the prayer, they found they could control an outcome. And so they began to grant those prayers. Fire. A good harvest. A cave for protection. When the pace of answering those prayers became too great, they tasked other angels—some to sort and some to respond, even though those angels were blissfully unaware that they'd once been hopelings themselves."

"The Answering Department," Ipsa whispered, placing her fingertip on the wall. Dhavi motioned for them to return back up the stairs. Ipsa never took her eyes from the cresting peaks and valleys of hopeling history. They paused again at a moment when the timeline's course seemed to hemorrhage in either direction.

"Fortula had already answered her call to swim the Endless Lake when the Great Rift happened," Dhavi said, motioning to that moment on the wall. "She wasn't Here to understand the unintended consequence of one prayer answered. It was, on the surface, a simple prayer for survival. Half of the fledgling human race was gone in a matter of weeks."

"How is that possible, Dhavi?" Ipsa asked, alarm in her voice. "Why couldn't Responders just answer the prayers to stop whatever was happening?"

Dhavi sighed. "All those prayers flooding in only compounded the chaos. Imagine: one person's prayer to keep a loved hopeling—a healer—safe from the sickness meant that another person's prayer—to be treated by that healer—could not be answered. The hopeling world had grown exponentially larger than when Fortula had answered her first prayer, and an individual prayer impacted the larger system in unforeseen ways. The prayers grew more complicated. Sometimes, they didn't know what they were really asking for. Or one person's prayer was another person's worst fear. Sometimes answering one prayer could cause others to experience great harm or pain. It was something they'd never considered."

Ipsa remembered the pages and pages in Mrs. Conway's prayer file pleading for "that monster" who'd taken Annie away to burn in Hell. Her wings felt icy. She climbed a few more steps, watching the lines finally stabilize, hovering between high and low in an even horizon line of mostly small hills.

She leaned closer toward notes scribbled above and below the lines. "This is when they stopped answering the prayers?"

Dhavi nodded.

"I still don't understand about the Responders—why keep up the ruse? Why pretend we're doing something we're not?"

"Yuka feared this decision to stop answering prayers could wreak havoc on the hopeling world," Dhavi said. "It's also the backbone of our world, our purpose. What if she'd chosen wrong? Why bother the community needlessly if she realized they should go back to answering prayers?"

"What happened to the Responders?"

"They became Implementers."

"But if they eventually proved that answering prayers wasn't a good thing, why didn't you just explain that decision to the community? They would have understood." Ipsa spoke slowly, trying to make sense of everything Dhavi was saying.

"The Implementers weren't so sure about that," Dhavi said. "I suppose that's the problem with secrets. Once you get used to living with one, it becomes easier to add more."

Ipsa rose to her feet, her wings flared out in anger, pulsing a vibrant red. "So you just let us Readers waste our time opening prayers for no reason?!" Her voice echoed up the stairwell.

"Not for no reason. *Reading* prayers is our purpose."

"And why is that?" she asked incredulously. "Why does my department even exist?"

"Hope," he answered softly, almost as a sigh.

"Hope?" she retorted bitingly. "Hope for an answer that never comes? What is that worth? When has hope ever saved someone's life? Or put food on their table?"

"Fortula knew there must be a reason that they had been chosen to *hear* from hopelings. Instead of flailing around Here like a fish out of water, jerking and writhing, the prayers became almost tranquil. They still came in droves, but their wording changed. Somehow, these hopelings knew that someone out there was listening. They needed us to listen. And that was how Fortula came to know: *Prayers must be heard to be answered.*"

"But they're not being answered," Ipsa said bitterly.

"How do you know?"

"Because you just told me there *is* no Answering Department, that we don't answer their prayers." Ipsa threw up her arms in exasperation as she began climbing the deep staircase.

Dhavi followed behind her. "Who is to say their prayers don't get answered?"

"If we're not answering them, then who is?"

"*They* are."

"Do hopelings have special powers I didn't know about?" Ipsa scoffed.

"Of a sort. They can help each other, I promise. They just don't get it right every time."

"But we should let them *know* that we're not answering them!" Ipsa spoke with real alarm. "That they need to be responsible for each other! That relying on us means they're not relying on each other!" She turned on the stairs to look back at Dhavi, her brow furrowed.

Dhavi glanced down at his feet, chuckling. "So many of them call themselves religious, but if another hopeling told them a winged angel visited them with a message, what do you think they would do: Believe him, or think he was crazy?"

Ipsa grimaced; Dhavi had a point. She turned around and continued her ascent. "But letting them figure it all out on their own—it just feels irresponsible."

"Think about our situation in hopeling terms: If a parent wrote their child's papers and took his tests for him the whole way through his schooling, could the child really take credit for his good grades? In the same way, if we took care of every problem humans faced, like some puppeteer pulling the strings from behind a curtain…" Dhavi paused as Ipsa digested the analogy. "Humans deserve to take credit for their achievements—and their failures. "

"But how do we stop them from hurting each other? And how do we make sure that those who need help get it?"

"Sometimes humans make good choices," Dhavi replied thoughtfully, "sometimes they make bad ones. But, Ipsa, what I've come to realize is that a world without pain would be phony and contrived. Those living in such a world would never be capable of real joy or love or triumph, only holograms of those emotions. To me, it's the difference between a living tree and its reflection in a stream. One is real, the other vanishes in the breeze."

Ipsa emerged from the dim light of the stairwell into Dhavi's living room. "So experiencing pain is better than *not* experiencing pain? That's ridiculous."

"I guess what I'm saying is that, without at least the

possibility of pain's existence, there is no real celebration when they avoid it." Ipsa's face folded in confusion. Dhavi continued: "Is there any real accomplishment if a hopeling rushes into a burning building to save a child, when we knew all along there was no risk of harm?"

Ipsa hated when Dhavi spoke in such philosophical terms. Breaking from his gaze, she rose and began pacing the length of the room. "But isn't that a pretty big gamble? What about all the hopelings who are in real pain, with no one coming to their rescue?

"These are all important questions. You can see why the Implementers always felt it was...*easier* not to trouble most angels with such questions."

Ipsa's bottom lip began to tremble as she looked out the window at the endless ceiling of stars above. She thought of all the suffering she had read recently, all the need, all the helplessness.

She shook her head decisively. "These people needed *help*, not hope."

Chapter Twenty-Seven

DHAVI WALKED OVER TO JOIN HER BESIDE THE WINDOW, pulling out a worn piece of parchment from the pocket of his mantel. Unfolding it in his thick hands, he handed the paper to Ipsa. A prayer. He spoke gently. "Look inside."

Ipsa obeyed, giving herself over to the scene unfolding within the prayer: A chalky dust cloud hung above barren ground. There were thousands of people, as far as Ipsa's eyes could see, mostly women and children. It was not a village or city, just what looked like makeshift tents hemmed together by broken tree branches and thin pieces of garment. A stench caused Ipsa to wince.

"What am I seeing, Dhavi?" Ipsa looked away from the prayer, unable to breathe inside of it.

"A refugee camp. These people have fled their villages."

"What happened to their homes?" she asked.

"Another group of people decided they wanted the land, decided these people didn't belong, were unworthy. These are the survivors, though I'm not sure how lucky they'd consider themselves to have survived. Many are dying from disease or famine, others have been separated from their families, saw their husbands or fathers killed before their eyes."

Ipsa could scarcely bear to look. "Why are you showing me this?"

"What am I showing you?"

"Devastation, hunger, the worst that humanity has to offer. Why show me this when we can do nothing but watch them die?"

"Look closer," he instructed.

Ipsa forced herself to return to the squalor of the camp and a bulletin board, every inch of its surface covered with photographs. The photos showed the faces of children, small forms with big eyes, separated from their families in the melee, faces waiting to be recognized and reunited with someone. Ipsa looked down as this hopeling, Amal, picked up another photo, tacking it to the board. Dirt embedded in her fingernails, she wiped a stray hair from her cheek with her forearm. *Please let someone recognize this one.*

Ipsa slowly folded the prayer back in half. It jerked nervously in her hand.

"Even in the midst of human suffering, there are other hopelings working to end the violence or care for these victims. To do this work requires hope. That is how *she* has the strength to answer their prayers. Prayers must be heard to be answered." As he spoke, a tear rolled down Ipsa's cheek. It fell in one swift dollop, onto the paper still wiggling in her hands.

Lifting his hand and placing it on her head, Dhavi

followed Ipsa's eyes out to the roses blooming outside his window. Beyond them, the reds and oranges of a new daybreak smudged the horizon line. "Earth is a complicated place." He placed a hand on her shoulder. "It's nearly time for sessions. You'd better go."

Ipsa shut the door behind her, but one piece of their conversation stuck out like a stubborn tree root.

A world without pain would be phony and contrived. Those living in such a world would never be capable of real joy or love or triumph, only mere holograms of these emotions.

She couldn't help thinking that the world Dhavi described sounded a lot like Here.

Chapter Twenty-Eight

I take refuge with the Lord of the dawn, from the evil of what He has created. And from the evil of the dark night when it comes. And from the evil of those who practice secret arts. And from the evil of the envious when he envies.

—Asha

Ipsa headed toward the Reading Room on foot, slowly, like a boulder headed up a mountainside. She was not yet ready to give her mind over to reading more prayers. Her head was swimming, but she felt strangely empty inside, lost. As she threaded the stone path, she passed the bench under the sycamore trees where she once sat with Dhavi, free from this knowledge.

How could just a few angels be empowered to keep such staggering secrets? She thought about the contentment with being content she observed everywhere. She remembered the fear in Elna's eyes from last Repast. Ipsa suspected that it was not a fear her words were true, but rather, a fear those words would disrupt Elna's predictable world.

Ipsa thought about Annie's frightened final prayer, uttered from a dark closet. What harm could have possibly come from saving the life of a fourteen-year-old girl?

She headed toward her favorite bench, then realized another angel was already sitting there: Sim.

"Ipsa! I've been looking all over for you!" Sim's eyes twinkled. "Muir said I might find you here." Ipsa rushed toward the bench and, without thinking, gave Sim a hug, releasing as she did some of the weight tethered to her back. Sim's black wings turned the color of burned beets. He grinned, then stammered to collect his words. "I think I found your hopeling."

"Isaac Conway, right?" Sim said, reaching into his pocket to pull out a long silver tube.

"How? Where?" Ipsa practically shouted.

"I was in another compartment logging tubes. I'm working on a new algorithm for cataloguing hairs at the time of input so that I can properly calculate the function of —oh." Sim's wings blushed again. "Sorry to get all technical. Basically, the formula alerted me that this one was totally out of place. I can't even understand how it got there."

"Eon," Ipsa murmured.

"There are three or four hair samples in there, and it looks like they don't overlap, but they should give you a pretty good timeline," Sim said, opening the case to show Ipsa. "I guess you've never watched hairs before, but it's kind of like watching a hopeling movie—except the movies usually end with someone brushing their hair." He smiled.

Sim closed the lid and stretched out his hand. The small metal tube was no bigger than the length of his open palm.

Ipsa reached out to take it. Her hand trembled slightly, resting on top of the tube.

"This is in strict violation of every Surveyor procedure I can think of," Sim said, as he searched Ipsa's eyes for an explanation.

Ipsa lifted the cylinder from Sim's hand and slipped it into her pocket. She thought about how good it had felt to share her secret with Muir. Then she remembered the way Elna had looked at her: as if she were a stranger.

Ipsa took Sim's hand. "I can't even begin to thank you. I hope one day I can tell you everything. But for right now, can this be enough?"

Sim nodded. "Although any other Surveyor would think I'd really lost my wings. You and Muir are different from most of the angels in my department. They're kind of boring, to tell the truth." Sim smiled.

Ipsa wondered just how much sand was left in the top of the hourglass before Sim stopped noticing the content- ment that surrounded him and started embracing it.

Anticipation pawed at Ipsa as she turned the tube over and over in her pocket. She thought about all the prayers in which Annie had gotten things so wrong with her brother. Perhaps, in some small way, she could redeem Annie now, be the sister she never had the chance to be There.

Ipsa gripped the tube tighter in her palm, as if it might slip through her fingers. Dhavi's warnings about Eon rang in her ear. She needed to get to her session but was so distracted she almost bumped into Elna as she passed through the central square in front of the Wreathing House.

"Elna!"

"I've really got to go inside. We have a lot of wings to make this session," Elna said, her eyes glued to the ground.

"I'm sorry about the last Repast. I shouldn't have shared it with you like that. I know it's a lot to take in. Could we meet at next Recreation, find somewhere quiet and talk about it?"

"There isn't anything to talk about. And I don't think I'll be able to sit with you at Repast. One of our newer Wreathers needs some help behind the stage wrangling. I offered." Elna took a step backward, toward the doors of the Wreathing House. "See you around, Ipsa."

Ipsa stood in the courtyard for what felt like several hundred prayers, watching as her best friend practically jogged toward the large doors of the Wreathing House, disappearing inside. Ipsa's lips trembled. Perhaps Elna had been Here too long to change. Ipsa wondered whether this was how it felt for a human heart to break.

Chapter Twenty-Nine

IPSA ENDURED AN ENTIRE SESSION WITH ISAAC'S TUBE sitting in her pocket. At Repast, she spoke of it only in the briefest whispers to Muir. The pair sat mostly in silence, watching the proceedings below as if in a daze while all around them angels fluttered their wings and sang their happy chorus of welcome to the new angels.

When Recreation time finally arrived Ipsa practically leapt into the air and headed straight for the Contemplations Garden. That this small container might yield answers about Isaac's prayer excited and scared Ipsa all at once. She knew once she opened that tube, she could not go back.

"I'm going to find a way to help you, Isaac," Ipsa spoke

softly as she rolled the tube back and forth between her hands. "Not just *hear* you and give you a bunch of crummy hope."

Taking a deep breath and looking over her shoulder once more, Ipsa opened the small metal lid.

Inside the box were four red hairs of different lengths. Ipsa stared at them for what seemed liked hundreds of prayers, delicately examining them, holding them to the light. Isaac's first hair was delicate and fine, curling slightly at the edge, but the most recent hair was coarse, straight.

Ipsa picked up a curlier strand from Isaac's childhood. It was the longest of the four hairs, measuring about four inches in length when pulled taut. Ipsa pressed it back into the velvety cradle in which it was nestled. The inside of the tube's open lid revealed a screen, not unlike a miniature television. Below each strand of hair was a small, black button. Slowly, Ipsa pressed the button for that first hair.

The moment she did, a transmission flashed on the small screen: Mr. and Mrs. Conway, honking the horn in the driveway, Isaac wrapped up like a hopeling burrito in the backseat, his bush of downy hair covered by a small knit cap. Isaac's grandmother raced out the front door, calling behind to Annie who, at fifteen months, was just learning to walk.

Ipsa replaced the hair, realizing it would not give her the information she needed. She paused, passing over the second hair from Isaac's boyhood. Tracing the third hair, Ipsa's finger drifted down to press the third button. She skipped forward, as if fast-forwarding a hopeling movie. Isaac was around ten years old—she saw the debate championship she recognized from one of his prayers, which it turned out he'd won. And a community theater production of *The Lion King*. She lingered over the moments between

Annie and Isaac; found herself wincing as she watched Annie behave cruelly toward Isaac, cringing at each mean word, each shove or door slam. Ipsa witnessed other moments, millions of them, flashing across the screen like a movie reel: improv camps, debate tournaments, boyhood crushes. Just as Sim had promised, the third stream ended abruptly, with Isaac picking up his father's electric trimmer.

Taking her finger from the button, she realized ruefully that she might know the "who" of Isaac better than Annie ever did. Finally, she picked up the last hair, wondering if every memory of Isaac's past was preparation for what she was about to see.

Chapter Thirty

Lord, make me an instrument of Thy peace; where there is hatred, let me sow love; where there is injury, pardon; where there is doubt, faith; where there is despair, hope; where there is darkness, light; and where there is sadness, joy.
—Anthony

IPSA PRESSED THE FOURTH BUTTON. THE IMAGES CAME quicker and more vividly; the hair was still so new, so freshly shed. She was anxious to skip ahead to the end, to find out if the end was the prayer she'd been searching for all this time, but she forced herself to slow down, realizing any small moment could offer a clue to Isaac's current trouble. She skimmed through more play practices, an awkward first kiss with a boy from debate club. She saw Justin Capaletti calling Isaac a string of horrible names, saw the shove and the punch that sent Isaac to Annie's room with a swollen eye. She observed the night Annie died, when Isaac had uttered the prayer in which he'd sworn to never forgive whoever was out there listening: "*If you really do exist.*"

She paused, thinking about the idea of a prayer being heard. There was no sufficient answer Isaac could have possibly received after losing his sister. He simply needed to say those words to the universe. And he had.

Ipsa closed her eyes as she pressed the button down, fast-forwarding through the immediate aftermath. But she paused on a day when Isaac had pushed his way up to the front of a crowd assembled at the steps of Annie's high school. Saw the surprise on his own face when the words came gushing out, with a passion and eloquence that forced the angry mob to pause, to listen, and then, to weep. Sibling dynamics and boyhood crushes, those were tree roots to be tripped over for Isaac. But stagecraft and a watertight line of argument, those were like a perfectly molded shoe. Ipsa witnessed Isaac separate his pain from the action required, like he'd taken a sopping wet shirt and twisted every last drop from the cloth. This, he said, would be the last tragedy of its kind. We, he said, would make it so. This group would band together to make sure teenagers who struggled the way that this young shooter struggled had the supports they needed. And most of all, they needed to restrict access to a machine gun that had killed his sister and thirteen other people in the time it took a group of schoolchildren to recite the Pledge of Allegiance.

Ipsa saw the reporters jump over each other to get to Isaac, heard Mrs. Conway's cell phone buzzing on the countertop incessantly, with calls for Isaac to appear on local then national television. She saw the planning sessions by Annie's schoolmates, to which Isaac, still in eighth grade, became a regular invite. She also saw what the televisions and spotlights didn't capture: the purple half-moons forming under his eyes caked over by concealer, just like Annie had showed him, the tossing and turning in his bed until the first streams of light slit through his blinds. Saw the way his ribs seemed to protrude more, how much less he ate. How the calls came from people he hardly knew, when what he needed was his other half. His yang. Saw the way he swung the pendant around his neck like a pendulum, back and forth. Annie's pendant that he'd taken from the envelope in the hospital.

Ipsa paused at the first threatening note. It came in a business-sized envelope with no return address, the letter inside oddly spaced and riddled with typos. It told him to stick to learning pre-algebra and to stop creating lies about guns. Isaac stuffed it in the trashcan beneath a grocery store circular, hiding it from his parents. Ipsa observed him scanning messages on his computer. Somehow, strangers had found how to reach him, had sent him angry messages filled with capital letters, exclamation points, and profanities. Accusations that Isaac wasn't even really Annie's brother. That he was an actor, hired by someone who wanted to take away all the guns. Each time, she saw him take his computer cursor to a small picture at the top of his screen that looked like a household trashcan, and the angry letter would vanish from the screen. He said nothing to Mr. or Mrs. Conway. He started his freshman year at Booker T. Washington. Annie's high school. He joined the school's debate team and ran for student council. His Tuesday/Thursday group began to organize a national rally, tied to the anniversary of the shooting. Isaac would address the crowd. To the outside world, Isaac appeared invincible.

Ipsa slowed the reel at a moment when Isaac was leaving the library, an odd piece of paper taped to his handlebars. His name spelled wrong. Ipsa felt certain: This was the note that he'd twisted and turned in his hands when he'd prayed to Annie—when Ipsa had started this whole crazy adventure. She watched Isaac tug on the paper, his fingers trembling as he unfolded.

WE KNOW YOUR NOT WHO YOU "PRETEND" TO BE. I HAVE FRIENDS IN THE GOVERNMENT AND THEY TOLD ME ALL IS NOT WHAT IT SEEMS WITH THE BOOKER T. "MASSACRE." A HOAX FOR A POLITICAL AGENDA BECAUSE YOU WANT TO TAKE AWAY MY GUNS AND FREEDOM. CANCEL YOUR PROPAGANDA MARCH OR I PROMISE ILL MAKE SURE YOU SEE THE SECOND AMENDMENT UP CLOSE AND PERSONAL. AND I KNOW WERE YOUR "PARENTS" LIVE.

Ipsa paused the transmission for a moment. The letter writer had called her death a hoax. Ipsa had no idea what the second amendment referred to—it had never been mentioned in any prayer she'd read—but she assumed it was a phrase used by Americans. It sounded like a threat.

Isaac teetered on his bike, folding the note twice in his hands. Ipsa's wings tensed, and she leaned closer to the small screen, realizing she had seen this moment play out once before, this very moment, in the prayer that had caused Isaac and Ipsa's worlds to intersect.

He didn't get off the bike, simply straddled it and reached into his back pocket to retrieve his phone. Dozens of messages and alerts lit the screen. He swiped them away and chose something inside the screen to hover on. Ipsa tried to focus: In large letters at the top of the screen it said, "The No More Memorials March." The day listed underneath, October 1st, was the same day as Annie's last prayer.

He shoved his phone deep into his back pocket and read the note again. Then, he cleared his throat.

"Wow, I guess I've really hit rock bottom if I'm resorting to praying," Isaac muttered, a half-whisper to himself. "I haven't even uttered your name in a year, and we both know that I'm not exactly 'religious.' I got another note." He took a hard gulp. "It said we'd better call off the march or I'd see the Second Amendment 'up close and personal.' I can't tell Mom and Dad; they've been through enough. But if anything happened to me, I don't think Mom would survive. Annie, if you can hear me, I'm not sure what to do. I guess I'm scared. I need your help to know what I should do."

Isaac crumpled the wad of paper in his hands into a tight ball and threw it with all the force in his arm, but it sputtered and caught the breeze, landing only a few feet from his bike. He grabbed two fistfuls of his hair in frustration.

The screen suddenly went black. Ipsa opened her eyes. She unclenched her fist, her fingernails piercing the soft flesh of her palm. Desperately, Ipsa pressed the button again and again, but there was no point: The hair had reached the end of its transmission.

Chapter Thirty-One

Help, Please Lord! We've been in the attic crawlspace since the flooding started. I keep hearing helicopters flying around. When will they come for us?
   —Cindi

IPSA FOUND HERSELF IN A SITUATION SHE HADN'T considered. She'd been so singularly focused on the *what* of Isaac's prayer that she hadn't considered the *how* of helping him.

Ipsa felt as though she'd arrived at another dead end. The date she'd seen flash on the screen for the rally was October 1. She knew from the dates on prayers at last Repast that it was September 28th There. She had three earthly days to find an answer to this prayer.

"Where do you go from here?" Muir asked. The pair had huddled outside the entrance to the Reading Room as Ipsa recounted Isaac's hair transmission. She looked over both shoulders as other Readers bustled past them through the great doors for the start of the session. Once they entered, there could be no more conversation about Isaac.

"I wish I knew," Ipsa said. "I've racked my brain for any other division within Statistics or other department that could help me, and I'm coming up empty."

"What would you even do if you could get to him?" Muir asked, her head cocked in confusion. "I mean, now that you know what he *needs*, can't you just ask the Answering Department to rush his prayer?"

Ipsa had to remind herself that Muir still didn't know that other enormous secret of this place. Muir hadn't stood beside Dhavi as he'd revealed the Answering Department to be nothing more than a wall and a door. She didn't realize the ceremony of escorting the Responders toward their new work was nothing more than a charade. Muir knew they'd all been hopelings first, but Ipsa couldn't bear to heave a second blow to the crumbling foundation upon which Muir stood. At least, not until she knew how to answer Isaac's prayer. How could she share the truth about the Answering Department and then send her in to read prayer after prayer of need, just to ensure some measly bit of hope? Knowledge—she grimaced—with *prudence*.

"I just—need to be able to talk to him myself, Muir. I can't really explain why."

"Of course, of course," Muir said, her eyes trusting. "I've asked around during the past few recreation periods," Muir said slowly. "Nothing obvious, just gossiping about angel lore and all that." She leaned her face in close to Ipsa's ear, her wing forming a protective barrier behind them. "Someone mentioned dream visitation."

"Angels visiting hopeling dreams?"

"Yes, a pair of angels said they'd heard old stories about being able to visit hopelings in dreams and speak to them.

But they made it sound like it was an old practice, and something that only a few Implementers could do."

"Hopeling dreams," Ipsa repeated. She happened to know an Implementer, but would Dhavi be willing to help her?

"I can't imagine knowing who you were There," Muir said, turning her gaze to the ground. "Mostly, I'm relieved I don't know, that I don't have to know how my hopeling parents lost their child…" Muir's voice trailed off and her crimson wings let go a long shudder from their base to the tips. "But then other times, I realize how frustrating it is just to keep guessing. I read prayers from all over the world and can't help but read each one thinking: Am I from there? Did I know this person? It's as if I'm waiting for the session when I touch the prayer that unlocks everything for me, the way Isaac's did for you. I'm waiting, but I also realize that prayer will probably never come, and that makes me really sad." She paused, lifting her gaze back to meet Ipsa's own. "Does any of that make sense?"

"It makes perfect sense, Muir." Ipsa bit her lip, trying not to let her eyes scan Muir's body for some evidence of how she'd died, some hint of "star marks" like Ipsa's own bullet wounds, some clue that might tell the story or give Muir even an inkling of her past. But she also thought about her own violent end and her wings winced at the thought that Muir might ever learn of a similar, painful story. For a moment, Ipsa saw more clearly the ramifications of sharing each hopeling's past—and all of the sordid details that might go with it. She thought of the young man who'd killed her. Dhavi had said that everyone came Here, that everyone deserved a fresh start. Ipsa scanned the crowd of angels walking in, wondering: If they crossed paths someday, would some cosmic connection cause a glint of recognition?

Ipsa shook away the thoughts running through her wings. "Muir, are you sorry I told you?"

Muir's eyes widened and she reached out to grab Ipsa's arm. "You should never be sorry. You told me the truth when everyone I trusted was lying to me, to everyone," Muir said. "Now, everywhere I look, I see that lie, see the subtle ways they keep us believing that lie, honoring it: like at Repast, or the texts we recite in class, or the silly angel bard in the courtyard at Recreation that sings about our history. It's like I can't get away from the lie, but I would never choose to unknow it."

Ipsa placed her other hand over top of Muir's and held it tight. "Muir," she said, "the angel you talked to about dreams, did they mention—"

A voice interrupted just behind them. "Good session to you, angels." Eon had appeared out of nowhere, placing his hand on Muir's shoulder. "I'm sure you're both looking forward to a wonderful round of prayers."

"Yes, Eon," Muir said, a nervous smile on her face. Her wings trembled slightly, turning a shade brighter.

"Good, good," Eon said. "Now Muir, today, I'd love for you to spend some time with DeNira. I was speaking to her last session and it occurred to me she has a lot to teach you about some of the *classifications* you've been wondering about. I'm sure you can see Ipsa on another occasion, yes?"

"Um, sure. DeNira. I'll make sure I find her." Muir gave Ipsa a quick look as she eased out from under Eon's grip and slipped through the doors.

Ipsa looked at Eon, unsure whether she too, was being excused, her wings itching with discomfort. She remembered Dhavi's allusion to Eon's past and wondered what must have happened to him to make him so fiercely protective of their rules.

"Eon," Ipsa began, unsure of what she was even going to say.

His eyes narrowed into two slits.

"I just…I don't know who you were or what you went through There, but I'm sorry that—"

Eon grabbed her fiercely by the arm and pulled her close enough to feel the heat of his breath. He was small, but his grip was powerful.

"Hear me well, angel: Don't think for one earthly millisecond… You know *nothing* about me, and whatever you think you know about how our world works, whatever you think you understand from that white-haired, overly nostalgic angel hiding in the woods, you know *nothing*. Do you hear me?" Eon's eyes narrowed further, searching Ipsa's face.

"Eon, no, I—" Ipsa started to interrupt, but Eon's voice, though hushed, overpowered hers. He leaned his face in close, his nose just below Ipsa's own, never taking his eyes off of hers.

"I followed the orders I was given, and I won't stand here and be judged by the likes of you."

"I didn't…" Ipsa began, but her spool of words had run out of thread. Finally, she swallowed hard. "I know we both just want to help."

"Help?" Eon's voice mocked. "I *protect* our world. You simply meddle in things you can't possibly fathom. If it were up to me, I'd have had your wings removed. But there's still time." He let go of Ipsa's arm, smoothing his cloak with his hands. "I warned you to leave well enough alone."

Ipsa's arm throbbed from Eon's grip. She grasped at her

wings, as if seeking to confirm they were still there. They didn't just house her memories; they were her very soul. "Removed?" she managed to croak. "You can't do that." She lifted her chin to feign bravery.

"You have no *idea* what I can do," Eon said. Whatever fierce anger had taken hold of Eon disappeared back under the surface of his cool exterior. He called out to another Reader and, placing an arm on their shoulder, followed them into the Reading Room. Ipsa leaned against the building to steady herself. She took three deep breaths, willing her wings not to betray her fear in front of Eon.

❧

ONCE AT HER DESK, IPSA FORCED HER GAZE AWAY FROM Cindi's prayer. She couldn't read another word. The idea of a family trapped by rising water turned her stomach.

"Highly Urgent," she said, nearly choking on the words. She watched the prayer weave its way upward through the sky, knowing it would end up right in that swirling chaos of prayers in the Archives. Heard but not answered. And yet, what could she do? Not stop attending sessions. And so, she continued what felt like the charade of prayer sorting. Perhaps reading it and categorizing it as 'Highly Urgent" would give Cindi more hope, but she really had no idea.

Another prayer began to unfold before her:

God, this can't be happening. Tell me this is some horrible dream I'm going to wake up from and tell Luis all about. Why did he have to be so stupid and brave? Who runs into a building on the brink of collapse? Didn't he realize he might not come out? I'm so angry at him for leaving me. I hate myself for wishing that it had been another firefighter and not him. Why did you take him from me?
—Veronica

Ipsa raised her eyes from the prayer. The knot that had been forming in her stomach with each new prayer seemed to twist further on itself, as if her insides were a battleground for some savage war. So many questions and she still had no answer. This Luis was just the sort of hopeling Dhavi said would help answer other hopelings' prayers; yet his life had ended in tragedy and brought immeasurable pain to Veronica.

Ipsa looked up, scanning the Reading Room for any sign of Eon. Before the prayer had a chance to find the air, she slipped it into the inner pocket of her mantel, where she could feel it pulsating with life. She did the same with the next prayer, and the one after that, and the one after that, hoping no one near her would hear the faint murmurs and squirming coming beneath the folds. She had no idea what she'd do with them, but the thought of filing one more prayer to nowhere was more than she could bear. If these prayers were not to be answered, at least they would not be forgotten. If hearing them did anything to help, then she would read them again and again and again.

She read a prayer asking for good weather for a party and felt a sigh of relief. It occurred to her that while hard times might ebb and flow, the practice of praying was constant. To assume a hopeling knew when to turn off this reflex—to use it for a sick loved one but not for a green traffic light—went beyond the earthly compass; Ipsa could see that now. She read another, this one a prayer of thanksgiving over the birth of a healthy baby with a sense of unexpected fortune, like a hopeling finding change on the ground.

Ipsa commanded that prayer toward the Thanksgiving shoot, as a new prayer began appearing on the page before her from a hopeling named Kim. Ipsa found herself kneeling in an alleyway over the body of a teenage hopeling watching as blood tentacled out along the concrete. She felt Kim's body heaving.

Please make them stop shooting!

A police officer tried to pull Kim away, but her hands clenched hold of the front pocket of the young man's sweatshirt. "No," she shouted at the air. "This wasn't supposed to happen to him." She looked up at the officer above her, but tears obscured Ipsa's view. "Don't you understand? He was going to college at the end of the summer on a scholarship. We were just trying to walk home. They weren't even aiming for Chris." Kim's voice buckled under the weight of her reality, like an ant holding up a brick.

Don't let him be dead. Please God, don't take my big brother.

But Chris's eyes were glassy. The officer wrapped a blanket around Kim, slowly leading her away from the scene.

Looking up from the prayer, Ipsa glanced over her shoulder, half expecting Kim's brother to enter the Reading Room at that moment. Ipsa thought back to a conversation she'd once had with Muir—what felt like a thousand Repasts ago. Muir had wondered whether a certain randomness and constant change made life more interesting There. Ipsa felt certain that it must be terrifying. How differently each life could begin…and end; and how little control anyone had over it.

Somewhere inside Ipsa's stomach, a rollercoaster car looped the tracks. Kim's prayer was tied to Isaac's in a way neither hopeling could fathom. What she was asking for was exactly what Isaac and his friends were trying to do.

Ipsa lowered her head and closed her eyes as she clasped Kim's squirming prayer in her hands, her fingers pinching a sharp crease in the fold. She felt as helpless as she had the moment she'd first heard Isaac's voice, so many sessions ago. In the meantime, Ipsa could do nothing but read more prayers. Prayers she couldn't answer.

&

"WHAT YOU'RE EXPERIENCING IS EMPATHY," DHAVI TOLD her later at recreation time, when Ipsa had shown up at his doorstep. She'd brought her stash of unfiled prayers to Dhavi's door as a child might bring a broken toy to their parent, hoping they'd know how to fix it.

"I liked it better when I wasn't experiencing *anything*," she replied. "I don't want to know all this pain, and I don't want to know that all I can give them is some lousy hope." Her shoulders ached, and Ipsa wondered if she needed to have a Wreather look at her wings; not Elna, of course, since her friend seemed to be avoiding her.

"But I don't understand: Wouldn't it be better if everybody felt empathy? Wouldn't it be better if everybody experienced real emotion instead of watered-down peace and Repast pleasantry?" Ipsa said.

Dhavi's hands fell back to his sides, and he sat down in the wooden chair behind him, the folds of his robe spilling over its arms. Ipsa knelt beside him. His eyes seemed heavy with exhaustion. "You have to understand, the other Implementers see that knowledge as unleashing a tidal wave in a lake with no current."

"An endless lake," Ipsa quipped.

The fog that had settled over Dhavi cleared, and he took both of Ipsa's hands firmly in his, shaking his head. "This can't be your battle to fight, Ipsa. Eon has already called the Implementers together about you."

"About *me?*"

"Yes, and if Eon convinces them that things Here must remain the same, I won't be able to stop them."

"Stop them from what?"

"You know about the Arcana. They won't let you just walk around with that knowledge."

"You mean removing my wings?" Ipsa's voice cracked.

"Where did you hear that?" Dhavi looked at her with surprise.

"I tried to apologize to Eon, but it didn't go so well," Ipsa confessed. She swallowed hard; her wings trembled. "He mentioned something about his past," Ipsa said. "He was so angry. Like he needed to defend himself. Dhavi, I know you see that this is wrong. That there shouldn't be secrets."

Dhavi chuckled softly, his wings sending a ripple down the back of his mantel. "Ipsa, you remind me of..." His words drifted off softly. "If you could, would you go to Isaac at this very moment?"

"Of course!" she exclaimed. "Will you tell me how?"

"Would you protect him? Would you tell him what to do? Prevent something bad from happening to him if you had that power?"

"Oh Dhavi, yes! Can I do that? Is there a way? Muir said something about dreams." She clutched his knee again, this time in excitement. She opened her mouth to tell him about the scene she had observed with Isaac and the threatening letter, but she bit her tongue.

"Whether you *can* help is not the point. The question is, whether you *should*." Dhavi took a finger and thumb and delicately placed a lock of Ipsa's hair behind her ear.

"You once told me that angels had knowledge—that it was what separated us from hopelings. It feels like all we really have are secrets. *Secrets* with prudence," she said bitterly, playing on the Second Arcanum. Her eyes searched for an answer in the deep pools of his eyes.

Dhavi's face brightened. "There is something I wanted you to read!" he said. He walked across the room to a sea of papers and books in the corner. He lifted a heavy paperweight from atop a writhing piece of parchment.

Ibrahim was reunited with his sister and mother today. Thank you, God! –Amal

The hopeling from the refugee camp.

"Are you saying that I helped make this happen?" Ipsa asked.

"Prayers must be heard to be answered," Dhavi said gently. "Ipsa, I know it's hard for you to see why your work is necessary—but I promise you, what you're doing matters. It is far from meaningless. Hopelings like Amal need you. They need to know someone out there is listening. Don't give up on them."

Chapter Thirty-Two

They bombed the marketplace today. When will this madness end? When will there be peace?
    —*Kadhim*

"Ipsa, there's something you need to see," Muir said. Ipsa turned her head away from Kadhim's prayer, surprised to see Muir at her reading desk. Nervously, Ipsa's eyes flashed up toward the wall above her, in search of Eon.

Muir leaned in close to Ipsa's ear, speaking in a hushed whisper: "It's okay, he's on the other side of the Room. I think I just overheard Isaac praying again."

"What? Where?" Ipsa shook her head in confusion. "How do you—"

"I sit next to a Reader named Tegan, and he talks to his prayers like he's on a phone call with each hopeling—it's a little weird," Muir said.

"Anyway, I just heard him say something like: 'Hello, Isaac from Farmington, Connecticut, what can I do for you?' and I thought, 'How many Isaac's from Farmington, Connecticut can there possibly be?'"

"Probably a lot? And anyway, why would he be—"

"Ipsa, stop asking questions and go see if it's him. NOW. Tegan's desk—three rows in from the far wall. I'll distract Eon with…something."

Ipsa stared up at Muir, barely recognizing this assertive angel conspiring to break every rule.

"Ipsa, GO!"

Muir's words woke Ipsa from her daze. A moment later, she was peering over Tegan's shoulder as words appeared on the parchment before him.

…the rally is tomorrow. My dad found a nail in his tire this morning. He said it's probably from the Stinson's kitchen renovation, but what if it's not? How can I get on a plane and fly to DC and stand up in front of thousands of people if these crackpots know where I live? But I'm the one sharing our agenda, and if I don't… I'm scared, Annie. I don't know what to do.

—Isaac

"Do you need something?" Tegan cocked his head over his left shoulder, one eyebrow raised.

"What? No, I just—hey, could I see that…"

The prayer sprang from the desk and began taking flight.

"That one?" Tegan said, his eyes following it upward. "I'm sorry. I had just filed it as you came over." He turned back to Ipsa, squinting. "Can I help you?"

Ipsa bit her bottom lip. "Never mind." Looking around, she saw Muir motioning for Ipsa back by her desk.

"I couldn't find Eon anywhere, which I guess is good news?" Muir said.

"He just disappeared?" Ipsa bit her lip, glancing up toward Eon's hidden overlook.

"I don't know. I swear he was over there a few prayers ago," Muir said. "Was it Isaac?"

Ipsa nodded. "It's tomorrow. Or not, I guess. Tegan filed the prayer before I could see many more details."

"So what will you do?"

"I have to convince Dhavi to let me help Isaac. Not just because he's my brother. I think it could affect lots of hopelings. And I'm worried he might get hurt—or worse."

"I really think you need to talk to a Responder in the Answering Department about this!" Muir pleaded.

"I—it's more complicated than that. I wish I could tell you, but I can't. I hope someday I can, but right now, will you just trust me?"

Muir nodded. "Just tell me what you need me to do."

"If you see Eon, distract him. He can't notice I've left the session early."

Ipsa backed toward the front doors of the Reading Room, opened one of the doors a crack and wedged through, all the while keeping her eyes on the room, scanning it for any sign of Eon. Ipsa was so preoccupied that she nearly bumped into an angel pacing nervously just outside the doors.

Ipsa gave a startled cry, then a confused greeting as she realized it was Elna: "What are you doing here?"

"I came to find you." Elna looked around as if she was nervous to stay in one spot too long, her normally elegant wings crouched limp and low on her back. Her naked scalp glistened with sweat.

"What's the matter?"

"That hopeling you told me about a few Repasts ago. Isaac. What exactly is it that you're trying to do?" Elna's eyes were wide. Angels didn't know fear, but Elna's face reminded Ipsa of her own scared reaction in Eon's chamber. Ipsa reached out to grab her arm in concern.

"Your wings are shaking. What's going on?"

Elna stuttered. "I…I was finishing up a set of wings in the Wreathing House and I heard your boss come in."

"Eon? What did he want?"

"He was speaking in a very low voice with Thodius, so I couldn't hear everything. But I made out a few words." Elna drew a deep breath, her hands clasped over her stomach. "He said your name, I'm sure of that. And he was asking about the process for—not a fitting—but for *new wings*. Ipsa, I've never even heard of that. What is he trying to do?"

Ipsa looked past Elna's shoulder toward nothing in particular as she murmured: "He wants to take it all away."

"Take what away?" Elna tugged on Ipsa's arm. "Ipsa, whatever you've been doing—this silly nonsense about us being hopelings—you need to promise me you'll stop. You have to make Eon see that you've realized your mistakes. Please!" Elna implored.

"You don't understand."

"I know!" Elna stamped her foot. "But I also know that he has the power to hurt you, and it seems like you're asking questions you shouldn't be asking," Elna said, taking Ipsa's hands in her own. "And besides, you just haven't been acting like yourself lately. It's like you're a different angel or something."

Ipsa bit her lip. In fact, she felt more like herself than she'd ever felt. But she also felt Elna slipping away, like sand from the hourglass. She feared the dazzling angel she'd met three hundred sixty-some Repasts ago, the one that had egged her on over the Endless Lake, was slowly disappearing.

"Maybe I am, a little bit," Ipsa said.

"Well, I think I liked things better before."

Elna hadn't intended to be hurtful, but Ipsa winced.

"This isn't some hopeling prayer to laugh about, Ipsa. I heard it in Eon's voice. If he can do this, he will. Unless you make things right."

Ipsa paused. "You're right, Elna."

"Will you promise me you'll do something about this?"

"Yes, I promise."

Ipsa saw a wave of relief wash over Elna and a switch seemed to flip inside of the Wreather, restoring her carefree manner. "Oh, that makes me feel so much better. I'm going to get back to the Wreathing House!"

Before she could leave, Ipsa grabbed Elna and pulled her close, holding her in a tight embrace. "I've missed you."

"Everything will be back to normal now!" Elna spoke in the same singsong voice she used for the Repast welcoming chorus, her golden wings practically dancing.

"Normal," Ipsa replied, her voice cracking slightly. Giving Elna a final squeeze, she turned and quickly walked away, not wanting Elna to see her crimson wings drooping. She couldn't blame Elna—the only thing that had changed in their perfect world was Ipsa.

IPSA HEADED STRAIGHT FOR DHAVI'S COTTAGE BUT PAUSED behind a thick hedge, overhearing a pair of voices fighting for airspace. She recognized the other voice instantly.

"This rogue behavior WILL end," Eon said. "I'll see to that. You're so blinded by love that you can't see you're abetting her reckless insubordination. Did you know she's actually stolen hairs from the Surveying Division?" Eon said, incredulously.

"I do," Dhavi said, his voice even.

Dhavi's answer seemed to catch Eon off guard. Ipsa's own wings burned with shame.

"Well, that's actually better. Even better." Eon said. "You're making my case to the other Implementers very easy."

"Has it really not occurred to you that we might be wrong?"

"Is this about your little lecture to the Implementers?" Eon scoffed.

"It's dangerous for us to think that our ways of operating can never evolve. Did the Great Rift not teach us that? Ipsa has helped remind me of that. If you weren't so focused on maintaining your own secrets, I think you would admit that this knowledge has changed her—for the better. There's a passion within her that wasn't there before that has impacted her reading. I think it's worth consider—"

"You're delirious," Eon said. "You came Here a crazy old drunk and you're just the same as an angel."

Dhavi's voice remained steady. "So long as we're dredging up past lives, you came here a fairly proficient executioner. Are you still obsessed with exacting vengeance?"

Neither angel spoke. Ipsa feared the silence would reveal her chattering wings.

Dhavi cleared his throat, his words softening. "Eon, I understand why you hold the Third Arcanum so sacred— you would know better than anyone the unintended consequences of answering prayers. But why—"

"What do you mean: '*You* would know better than anyone?'"

"The Great Rift," Dhavi paused. "You were the Responder."

Ipsa grabbed at her wings to keep them from shaking.

Eon, usually quick with a retort, said nothing.

"You know better than anyone what can go wrong when we meddle in the lives of hopelings—even if we're trying to help them," Dhavi said.

Eon spoke so softly that Ipsa strained to hear, the side of her face brushing up against the wall as she pressed her ear toward the conversation.

It was Dhavi's voice she heard next. "Your what?" He sounded genuinely surprised by whatever Eon had said.

"Her life was in danger."

Several moments of silence hung in the air. When Dhavi finally spoke, it was in a low voice. "Did you know who she was?"

"Once I read the prayer, yes. I had only just arrived Here—maybe it had been a half dozen Repasts—and I'd been assigned to the Answering Department. I was so new. And then I received her prayer." Eon's voice sounded hollow. "So I saved her."

Ipsa's wings pressed tight between her back and the wall. Somehow, as much as she'd wondered about his life There, she'd never pictured that other human beings had loved him, and he them.

"Your daughter…Eon, I…" Dhavi stumbled over his words.

"Don't pretend to care," Eon said, snapping out of whatever time capsule he'd stepped into, resuming his usual tone of indifference. "I've had a few billion prayers to get over it. And the world did not end. It was another lifetime, another person. But it was a mistake I won't allow repeated." He said these last words with an iciness that made Ipsa's wings rigid.

Ipsa heard nothing for some time. Finally, Dhavi spoke, so softly she had to strain to hear. "Eon, I'm sorry I brought up your past There."

"The words you scatter in my direction are of little concern to me. But we have the Arcana for a reason. They're bigger than you or me. And they're *certainly* bigger than her," Eon said. "You've been complicit in this debacle. You're a prime example of why angels shouldn't know about their pasts—you just couldn't stay away. And trust the others will find out."

"The others?" Dhavi sneered, as if baiting Eon.

"I'm requesting another emergency meeting of the counsel. This can't carry on one prayer longer. I plan to detain your little protégé lest she cause more trouble. One more misstep on her part, and I think I'll have no trouble getting those new wings approved."

"Stay away from her," Dhavi growled. Ipsa felt the wall rattle.

"This is her own fault. And I don't mind saying, yours too." Eon paused, and then spoke once more. "I've spent the past several Repasts wondering how that prayer landed on the table of a former earthly relative. But now, I wonder if you might have been able to help me solve that riddle all along. I guess that's just another mystery to share with our colleagues."

Whatever Dhavi said in response, Ipsa didn't hear it. She had the good sense to crouch her wings low, hiding herself beside a blueberry bush. A moment later, she heard the door swing wider, the crackle of pebbles underfoot. Eon disappeared.

Chapter Thirty-Three

Lord,

Dad's cancer is in remission! The doctors say his new drugs combined with his determination and exercise really helped, but you and I know the real reason.

Thank you.

–Laura

Ipsa sat crouched in a tight little ball for what felt like an entire Repast. She knew Eon was gone, and yet her body would not seem to unclench itself. Slowly, she raised her head. Dhavi leaned against the doorframe, staring off into space. His wings and shoulders hunched forward, as if being pulled down toward the ground.

Ipsa finally rose to her feet. Her legs wobbling like rickety stilts; her wings leaden. She had clearly startled Dhavi from his daydreams, but he rushed to her and folded his arms tightly around her.

"Eon..." Ipsa said, unable to finish her sentence.

"Did he see you?"

She shook her head.

"That gives us a little time—but not much."

"Dhavi, I'm sorry I didn't tell you about the hairs," Ipsa said. She pressed her nose against Dhavi's cloak, which smelled of pine and spices. She inhaled deeply.

"It's all right." Dhavi leaned back slightly from their embrace so he could look into her eyes. "How much did you hear?"

"Enough," she said, squinting as she stared back up into his eyes. Her wings shuddered, remembering Dhavi's revelation about Eon's murderous past. "How does a hopeling like him end up Here?"

Dhavi gave her a funny look. "Is the hopeling world filled only with people whose lives have never taken a wrong turn?"

"Of course not."

"Then why would another world be any different?"

Ipsa remembered something Eon had said in the heat of their argument. "Do you really love me, Dhavi?"

"I do," he said, drawing her back in toward his chest, his chin resting on the top of her head. They stood in silence for many prayers.

Ipsa turned her head upward to meet Dhavi's eyes with her own. "What did he mean when he said that you couldn't stay away from me?"

"You know, Ipsa, as old as I was when I died, my disease kept me from some of the greatest moments of my life on earth, like getting to watch my son grow to be a young man and marry and have children of his own."

"Did he?"

"He did. A boy and a girl. I only had the briefest taste of

fatherhood, but *grand*fatherhood, I think, would have been something indeed." Dhavi's eyes stared off in the distance wistfully, and a sad smile formed between his wrinkles.

"But they'll become angels," Ipsa interrupted. She bit her lip, remembering the look of pain in his eyes when he'd recalled the story of staring into his wife Marianne's vacant, unrecognizing eyes. The past was the past.

"Yes, you see that's the challenge—and the burden—of knowing what you and I know, Ipsa. There is much we can't say, even if we want to say it. But that didn't mean I couldn't watch over them." He squeezed her tiny hands in his, filling her palms with warmth. "And so that is what I did the first opportunity I had—though it was much sooner than I would have liked."

Ipsa's brow crinkled.

"So you see, Ipsa, I can't be mad at your curiosity." A smile broke across Dhavi's face. "You get it from your grandfather."

Ipsa blinked hard, hoping that when she opened her eyes again, she could better understand Dhavi's words.

"Grandfather? Was I, I mean, Annie—was she? She was your granddaughter?" Ipsa said.

"Not *was*. You are my granddaughter. Always will be." Dhavi searched her eyes for a reaction. "Does that make sense?"

Ipsa nodded. It felt like a key sliding into a lock. She reached her arms around Dhavi and squeezed tight. Ever since she'd learned of Isaac, she'd felt this aching to feel the way a hopeling sister was supposed to feel about their sibling: to love him. But love was something earned over time; through friendship, trust, and caring. This was the love that she genuinely felt for Dhavi.

She realized this was also the love that Isaac must have felt for Annie.

Ipsa kept her cheek pressed tightly against Dhavi's chest as she spoke. "I came because I need to see Isaac."

Dhavi gently unpeeled himself from Ipsa's embrace. "We've talked about this. Isaac is my grandson; you know I want the best for him. But we can't go There and solve his problems." Dhavi lifted her chin so that her eyes met his. "He's not some puppet for us to play with. Say what you will about Eon, but he has that part right."

"But he's asked for help—he's asked for *my* help." Ipsa bit her lip. She reached for his hand and as she did, the sleeve of his mantel slipped up his forearm. She turned his palm over in her hand as she examined Dhavi's wrist. The skin there told a story: scars of raised, pink flesh on his forearms and dark circles across his skin. She lifted her other hand to Dhavi's cheek where, just above his beard, a long purplish-brown line cut deep into his skin and ran down the length to his chin.

"You were homeless?"

Dhavi let out a long exhale and placed his hand over top of hers on his face. "For many years, yes."

"You must have prayed. I mean, it must have hurt so much to be away from your family. Didn't you pray?" Ipsa said.

"Just about every minute of every day for thirty years," Dhavi said, a sad smile breaking the pained look on his face.

"Surely someone Here could have answered you— releasing you from that pain—reuniting you with your family. That wouldn't have made you a puppet on a string," she said, recalling something Dhavi had once said. "Why didn't you ever stop praying? I mean, after a while, why didn't you just give up?"

Dhavi let out a low laugh. "So many questions." He turned her hand over in his. "Who said that my prayers weren't answered?"

Ipsa folded her arms. "But how could they have been? You died on the street. You died without meeting my mom or me and Isaac."

"Ipsa, at first my prayers were for myself. And they were answered. Your grandmother found me, again and again. She brought me home. She bathed me. She told me she loved me," Dhavi said, his eyes glassy. "But I saw what my sickness was doing to her, to your father. So after a while, my prayers changed. They were prayers that my wife would find someone who could love her the way she deserved. That my son would grow to be a better father than I was." He paused. "Those prayers were heard."

Ipsa grabbed hold of Dhavi's arm. "I need to see him. It's not even about the prayer anymore. I was a horrible sister most of the time and…I just need him to know that I'm sorry."

Dhavi took a step backward and studied her for a moment before speaking. "Eon could be back any moment; if he can convince even one or two other Implementers, I won't be able to stop them."

"I know the risk. Please, Dhavi. For me." Her eyes looked up at Dhavi, wide and desperate. Her bottom lip trembled slightly. "I just need to see him, face to face."

Dhavi took Ipsa's chin in his hand and tilted her face up toward the sky, staring deeply into her eyes. Letting go, he turned away and walked to the window, bracing his right arm against the wall. His wings hunched forward like question marks. He let out a long, slow exhale and then, with his left hand, he reached into his mantel and pulled out a shiny disc. With a pinch, the lid flipped open to reveal two small arrows and a circle of numbers: a hopeling pocket watch. Dhavi glanced at it for a moment before flicking it shut again. Outside the window, a field of roses stood perfectly still, for they lived in a world without wind.

"It's nighttime There," Dhavi mumbled to himself. "The risk is so great. But if she could really do it—then they'd have to see." He turned back to Ipsa.

"Lie down and close your eyes," he said. "Hurry."

Chapter Thirty-Four

If there is to be peace in the world, there must be peace in the nations. If there is to be peace in the nations, there must be peace in the cities. If there is to be peace in the cities, there must be peace between neighbors. If there is to be peace between neighbors, there must be peace in the home. If there is to be peace in the home, there must be peace in the heart."

—Laozi

When Ipsa opened her eyes, she was no longer seated in Dhavi's cottage. Where a moment ago she'd seen the open doorway unfolding acres of wildflowers beyond the threshold, behind her now was simply darkness. The only way was forward.

She tried to get her bearings. This place didn't look like prayers she'd read, but it wasn't Here, either. She stood in a snow-covered field, yet at her feet lay a coconut the size of a hopeling basketball. Ipsa looked up to find a palm tree burdened with the ripening fruit. She reached up to touch the palm leaf tipping down toward her head, a sliver of icy green snapping off in her fingers.

"Watch out!" a voice called from behind her. Ipsa jumped, just narrowly avoiding a young boy and girl in bathing suits sledding down the hill past her. Ipsa blew a few flakes from her hands and they hung in the air, like specks of dust, before making their way back to the ground. Kneeling in the snow, the palm trees on either side began to pass her by. But Ipsa realized it wasn't the trees that were moving—she was being carried forward by some invisible conveyer belt.

"Where am I?" Ipsa called out.

What Muir had heard must be true: She was in the world of hopeling dreams.

Ahead there was no longer snow. Ipsa blinked and she was no longer outside, but in a building with large marble columns and shiny tile floors. Glancing down at her feet, her mantel was gone, replaced with jeans and a T-shirt that read "Farmington Falcons."

A bell rang and the hall filled with a swarm of hopelings scattering in every direction. An elephant walked by lazily, with a beautiful female hopeling on its back, covered in a bejeweled yellow costume.

The elephant's tail swished out of sight, and the crowds cleared to reveal a young man standing in the middle of the hall. He was tall for his age, and wiry. He wore a gray sweatshirt with the letters "BTWHS" and rumpled khaki pants. His orange hair looked equally rumpled. Ipsa knew him—but not just from his prayers or hair transmissions. When Ipsa looked at Isaac, she saw pieces of herself.

"Annie?" he said.

Ipsa stepped toward the young man.

"Annie? Is it really you?"

"Yes, it's me."

The left side of Isaac's mouth curved upward. Ipsa knew that smile, because it was also her smile. "Why have I never dreamed about you until now?" Isaac's eyes searched her face. He slid his parted fingertips through his hair—the way Ipsa did when she was trying to make up her mind where to send a prayer.

Ipsa took another step toward her brother. She had learned so much about him, but always like an outsider peering through a glass door. Now she was stepping inside. She reached her hand up to softly graze the outline of his cheekbone, her palm brushing a patch of red fuzz covering his cheeks.

"Watch your step," he said.

Ipsa glanced past her brother. The end of the hallway pulled toward them, sharp edged, like the end of a photograph. Beyond the marbled floor she saw a beach.

"I think we're changing scenes," Isaac said. "I toss and turn a lot as I get settled." He grinned. "Sorry about that."

"Where are we going?" Ipsa said.

Isaac held his hand to his brow to screen his eyes. "It looks like Cape Cod—near where Grandma Dorsett used to live. Do you remember?"

A soft breeze carried the smell of saltwater, lifting a strand of hair from Ipsa's cheek. Pulling at barnacle-covered crab traps as they waded into the tide. Their mother at home boiling a pot of corn—they'd pretend they were woodchucks grinding their way across a cob, fingers drenched in butter. Yes, she remembered.

"Why here?" Ipsa said.

"I was looking through some old photos the other night. Mom was talking about going there, the three of us. Thought it might be 'cathartic.' Oh—jump."

The water in front of them seemed to be spilling over the edge of an abyss, like a waterfall at the horizon line. Just ahead was a field of grass and a tree house Ipsa recognized: the Conways' backyard.

"You prayed."

"I did."

"Why? After so much time?"

"I don't know, exactly. I guess I was scared." Isaac scratched his head. "But mostly I just really missed you."

A slow parade of sea turtles crossed their path.

"National Geographic is the only thing that helps me sleep these days. Mom gets pissed at me for falling asleep on the couch." His gaze followed one turtle as it padded by. "I've decided I'm not going to go to the rally. It's tomorrow. I'm not going to give the speech." Isaac swallowed hard, his eyes glued to the turtle's hard shell.

Ipsa opened her mouth to speak and then closed it, unsure of what to say.

"It turns out I'm a fan of self-preservation—I'd like to blame it on your death, but to be honest, I guess I've always been a little bit self-absorbed."

Ipsa recalled so many scenes from Annie's file. "You think?" she said. They both started to laugh.

The Conways' backyard turned to train tracks, steel beams running endlessly into the distance. Ipsa stepped onto a wooden railroad tie. Through the slats she saw blue sky with nothing below them.

Isaac reached back to take her hand. Standing side by side, their shoulders reached the same height. They were both, she realized, fourteen—Ipsa had stopped growing a year ago, while Isaac had shot up nearly six inches. In that moment, she knew that she desperately wanted him to keep growing, keep aging, keep living. She wanted to hide him away in a bunker, keep him safe from scary people sending him letters and following him to the library. She closed her eyes for a moment, hoping she could wish him away somewhere safe.

"So maybe I quit, they leave me alone. There's a family of a shooting victim—a first grader—they've had to move five times to get away from these people. Just because they wanted to change the legal gun-owning age by three years."

Losing his balance slightly, Isaac dropped his right hand down to steady himself on the metal rail, his left hand still firmly holding Ipsa's. "I've played out every possible scenario. There's no winning."

"Maybe that makes your decision easier," Ipsa said.

"Thanks a lot." Isaac offered a wry smile.

"It wasn't a joke," Ipsa said. "If there's no winning either way, then maybe just go with your gut?"

"As a debater, I make decisions by analyzing all the evidence, preparing an argument for both sides, and then determining which is more valid." He winked. "But it seems easier if you could just tell me what I should do."

Isaac's eyes seemed to be pleading with hers. "Please, Annie."

Ipsa held on tight to her brother's hand. As a dreaming Isaac stared deeply into her eyes, she felt strangely powerful. She could tell Isaac what to do, in this moment, and somehow she knew he would do it.

Ipsa swallowed.

She stared back at him.

Finally, she spoke.

"I can't."

"Please, Annie." Her brother squeezed her hand tightly. "I can't figure this out alone."

"I don't think you have to." Ipsa nodded her head

toward a spot further along the tracks where they abruptly stopped, running into a dense field of corn. Their parents stood at the edge of the field. Mr. Conway waved at Isaac. Ipsa could see their mother, extending an open hand toward him.

A storm cloud, heavy and black, formed overhead. Ipsa thought she heard someone calling her name in the distance.

"You're going to leave soon, aren't you?" Isaac shouted over rumbles of thunder.

"I'm sorry. I don't have much time."

The two of them paused. The Conways and the cornfield were closer now.

Ipsa reached her hand up to touch her brother's mess of red hair. "I'm sorry for how I treated you. I'm sorry I wasn't a better sister."

Isaac cocked his head, a look of confusion transforming his face. "What are you talking about?"

"I was so mean to you; I didn't show you how much I loved you. I wasted all our time together."

"Are you kidding me? You were an amazing big sister," Isaac said. "Remember that awful kid…oh, what was his name?"

"Justin?" Ipsa offered.

"Justin Capaletti!" Isaac smiled, as if she'd turned the light switch on in a distant closet. "Man, I *hated* that kid! And you got him to *apologize*! I always meant to ask how you managed to make him do it!" Isaac's hand slipped under his shirt collar, pulling out a silver beaded necklace, three pendants dangling from the bottom. He held them out in his open palm: two metal plates and the yin and yang pendant that he'd given Annie for her fourteenth birthday, the summer before she'd died.

"You're my yin, remember?" he said. "I keep it with Grandpa Conway's dog tags. Makes me feel like you're still with me."

Above them, the rumbling grew louder. A bowling ball crashed down between their feet, splintering a wooden railroad tie.

"Whoa," Isaac said, jumping back.

"Let's get you back to Mom and Dad," Ipsa said. They broke into a run as more bowling balls began to drop as if from cannons in the sky. Their parents disappeared between two stalks just as the pair arrived at the field's edge. Ipsa turned around. What was left of the train tracks were vanishing into the sky, track by track, like dominoes tumbling down into the abyss. Above was nothing but air. A splintering crackle of thunder made her teeter slightly.

Isaac covered his ears to muffle the noise. "Annie!" He shouted her name as loud as he could, but it registered as barely a whisper. "Please, what should I do?"

Ipsa said nothing. Instead, she pulled him close as a hopeling life preserver. All around them, a hurricane of bowling balls crashed down. She tilted her face toward his ear. "I believe in you. You're going to figure out the right decision. I know you will." Breaking free from their hug, she began to push Isaac toward an opening in the field.

"Wait!" Isaac shouted back, his body halfway into the field. "I haven't even asked: Where are you? *What* are you?"

Ipsa felt a smile breaking out across her lips. "My name is Ipsa now. I read prayers."

"Ipsa." Isaac's lips formed the word, but the sound couldn't reach her ears above the crackling overhead. Then he said something else Ipsa couldn't make out.

"What?" She cupped her mouth with her hands.

Isaac, too, cupped his hands and raised his voice. "I love you."

Ipsa had never said those words before, but she knew now that she felt the same. "I love you, too." Ipsa rushed forward and gave her brother a final hug before pushing him into the cornstalks.

Chapter Thirty-Five

There is a new constitution in our country today! I will now be able to go to school. All girls will be. My father says that I can be anything I want to be, just like my brother. I have big dreams, Allah.
—Noomane

IPSA BOLTED UPRIGHT. SOMETHING WAS WRONG. HER WINGS felt as if tiny icicles had suddenly formed on each thread of Kluna. Eon stood above her. His steel gray eyes seemed colder than the iciest regions of Earth. Ipsa searched the unfamiliar space for Dhavi, but he was nowhere.

"What have you done with him?"

"Perhaps you should be more concerned with what I'm going to do to *you*." Eon said. "Or to your friend in the Statistics Department. The Hair Surveyor—Sim, is it? Allowing sensitive materials to leave the department?" Eon made a tutting sound.

Ipsa's mouth opened wide. Her wings clenched into two small ruby red fistfuls.

"We've had this conversation so many times." Eon said. "How I loathe having to revisit a headache."

Ipsa noticed two large angels standing beside a door. Her wings felt weak and wobbly, two blades of grass. Cocking his head back toward the open door, Eon nodded.

The angels took Ipsa by the arms and brought her down a flight of stairs and through a doorway. Ipsa heard the door slam behind her, a key turning in a lock.

She looked up and was startled to see Annie all around her. But this Annie had wings. She was seeing her own reflection. Cautiously, she walked toward the image on the wall directly in front of her and pressed her hand flat against the surface. She'd never examined her reflection this closely; Here possessed no mirrors. She'd seen only hints of herself—on the smooth marble floor of the Reading Room or the tranquil sheen of the Endless Lake. Never had she explored such a flat, perfect image of herself. Ipsa forced herself to remember this wasn't Annie standing before her. Suddenly conscious of every small gesture, she turned away, only to be met by another pair of Annie's eyes watching, waiting. She turned again and again and again, but the eyes were everywhere. The room felt circular, with a dozen flat walls displaying every angle of her body, casting reflections of reflections. Each surface projecting hundreds of smaller replicas of Annie/Ipsa, reaching back into the distance until they seemed no larger than a keyhole. Each one seemed to be watching, waiting for her to move.

Ipsa backed away from the nearest wall, toward the center of the room, and squeezed her eyes shut. A trickle of liquid grazed the side of her face as it rolled down her cheek. She reached up to wipe it away. Her cheeks and forehead seemed to be sprouting tears, and her arms burned. Confused by the sensation, Ipsa rolled up her sleeves and began to pump the air with the skirt of her mantel. She leaned against a mirror for support, but her slick frame slid down the smooth surface. Her hair, matted and damp, clung to her neck. The heat was unbearable—as if she'd opened the door to an oven and crawled inside. And unlike reading a prayer, the sensation was not fleeting and painless —it enveloped her.

She heard a crackle overhead and looked up but could see nothing. The room had no visible ceiling, reaching up into a dark abyss.

"Hello?" Ipsa yelled up into the air above her, her voice echoing and bouncing off the mirrors. She heard another splintering noise and suddenly a torrent of water fell from above her head, drenching her until her mantel clung to her limbs and her sopping hair sent small streams of water snaking down the small of her back. Ipsa tried to look above her to find the source of the rainfall, but she could see nothing but the constant stream of water pellets hitting her face.

"Where am I?" she shouted.

For a moment, the downpour stopped. "Oh, don't you like it?" Eon's voice reverberated through the echo chamber. "I know how fond you've grown of Annie, so I figured you'd enjoy spending some time with her reflection. I wanted to bring some of her world's charm right to you. I just wasn't sure which season you preferred," he said, feigning real curiosity. "Oh dear, I didn't think about proper attire. It appears you could have used an umbrella."

His voice disappeared, replaced with a gust of rain. Ipsa wasn't sure how long the downpour lasted—she only noticed when it shifted from the heavy pelt of raindrops to something softer and icier, falling slower, like bits of white Kluna floating to the ground, forming small piles at her feet. She'd read enough prayers to know that this was snow. Every fiber of her wings, hair, and skin felt saturated with frigid water. Ipsa curled her knees up closer to her chin, wrapping her arms around her legs in search of warmth—a sensation she'd never sought before. Her wings shivered violently. The room grew dark as a moonless night. She shook her head periodically, shaking off the buildup of flakes on the tip of her nose and the back of her neck. Her wings, which otherwise might have served as the perfect canopy to shield her, clung to her body in a shriveled, frigid heap.

An icy blast of air began to swirl around her, whipping her cheeks until they felt raw. Ipsa huddled in the corner of two mirrors, hoping to shield her back from the merciless wind.

She began to distinguish another sound behind the wind. A million whispers filled the room, bouncing off walls and amplifying into a crescendo. She knew at once that these were prayers, but they chorused together in one painful note, as if this room housed all the hopeling pain in the entire earthly world—as if she were sitting inside The Hive itself. Ipsa heard desperate pleas: hopelings begging for mercy to end their suffering. Her eyes darted back and forth as she edged further against the wall—all the while, the wind created a swirling blizzard around her.

"Please," she yelled, drowning the room in her own voice, "help me."

A key turned in the door's lock and the howling wind disappeared. So, too, did the voices. Light poured into the dark room, forcing Ipsa to squint and shield her eyes.

"How are you finding your accommodations?" Eon said. A path emerged through the snow as he walked, as if cleared by some invisible shovel.

"What is this place?" Ipsa said. "Where is Dhavi? Just let me explain what happened," she croaked.

"YOU'LL DO NOTHING OF THE SORT!" Eon roared. A swirl of hot air reached the hallway candles, leaving shadows to dance across the snow. Eon's wings flared open, a violent shade of purple. "You'd have us open up the curtains! Let the light of truth shine in! What would that knowledge really give our community? You think that your friend Muir would feel comfort in knowing she'd drowned in her family's pool? Or that Elna should understand that, as cancer ravaged her body, the hospital bills bankrupted her parents? You think that would somehow give their work more meaning? You're a foolish angel."

Eon smoothed his robes. "I've had enough 'explaining' from your protector, and quite frankly, I'm bored of it," he said, his face composing itself once more. "I'll not have our entire world unhinged by the likes of *you*. You'll meddle no more."

Ipsa's wings crushed against her back. She clenched her fists to steady herself. "Why do you hate me so much?" Ipsa said.

Eon started to laugh. "How much you think of yourself! Do you think hopelings hate *flies*? I assure you; they don't exhaust that much emotional energy." Eon came closer now and leaned in toward Ipsa's face, his voice like ice. "They just find a fly swatter and crush them."

He turned from Ipsa, walking back toward the open door. He stood in silence for a moment.

"You've fed your own curiosity and risked two worlds in the process." He paused. "But that ends now."

Eon rapped on the open door with his bony knuckles. In the far corner, a mirror slid open and a flood of light revealed the silhouette of a willowy angel, her scalp perfectly smooth. She stepped forward and the door groaned shut, leaving the room in the soft shadows of candlelight that spilled in from the hallway.

"I can't trust that the other Implementers will fully grasp the gravity of this situation," Eon said, still addressing Ipsa. "I need to take matters into my own hands, unfortunately."

The figure remained at the edge of the room.

"Don't just *stand* there, Wreather," Eon commanded.

Elna took a step forward into the candlelight. Her normally regal shoulders sagged, and her wings seemed to tremble.

"Are...are you certain?" Elna said.

"Why are you wasting my time? Do I need to cut yours off as well?!" he snapped.

Elna moved to stand behind Ipsa. "Ipsa, I thought you said you'd fix everything." The words were laced with confusion.

"I've asked you here to perform a *task*, Wreather, not to socialize," Eon said. "Do as you've been instructed."

Elna slowly lifted her arm, revealing something long and shiny in her right hand. Ipsa's eyes widened in terror.

"Eon," Ipsa said. "Please, you don't have to do this. There must be another way!"

"How many times did I tell you to leave well enough alone, Ipsa?" Eon said. "That *was* the other way, but you wouldn't listen. This is the only way I know to protect them."

Elna laid her left hand on Ipsa's shoulder.

"I'm sorry, Ipsa. I don't want to have to do this." Elna's voice cracked. Clearing her throat, she squeezed Ipsa's shoulder. "But now you'll get a new pair of wings and forget all of that nonsense about us and hopelings. And then we can be like we were before."

Ipsa winced in anticipation, her mind dizzy. Elna's grip tightened slightly on Ipsa's shoulder and she leaned in close, the glint of a blade visible in the dancing light.

But it was another voice—not a knife—strong and steely, that cut through the air.

"Eon, what is going on here?"

Chapter Thirty-Six

Grant us peace.
—Hanif

AN ARM PUSHED PAST EON, AND IPSA SAW THE SPEAKER'S face, slender and charcoal-colored, two perfect cheekbones sloping toward a noble chin. A face so beautiful that, for a moment, Ipsa had to glance away.

"What are you…How did you…" Eon stumbled on his words.

"I'll ask the questions," the angel said sharply. She turned to Elna: "Please leave us at once." Elna slipped out, looking over her shoulder in confusion as the door shut behind her.

"What in the name of Here were you just about to do?" the angel said. "We have procedures, protocols. I told you we would meet to discuss this. I asked you to keep an eye on her, not remove wings without authority."

"I couldn't be sure that the group would agree," Eon

said, a desperate ring to his voice. "We can't risk another breach."

"Eon." She softened her tone, placing her hand on his forearm. "I realize this has been hard for you, how much of the past this situation has surfaced. But Ipsa deserves to stand before the Implementers, just as you did so very long ago."

Eon looked down at the other angel's hand, resting on his sleeve. When he spoke, his voice sounded weak and hollow, like a tree drained of its sap. "I'm sorry I've disappointed you. I just hope that the rest of the group has the courage to agree with me."

The other angel turned toward Ipsa. A single crease wrinkled her forehead. She extended her hand down to help Ipsa stand. With her touch, Ipsa's clothes and hair dried instantly and she felt a warmth tingle through her body. Ipsa knew this face from every history book she'd ever read, from every class and Repast chant. She knew it from the threads of Kluna that pulsed through her wings. The gift of magic they'd provided.

Yuka's gift.

"Come with me," Yuka said.

THE PAIR WALKED IN SILENCE FOR A THOUSAND PRAYERS. Ipsa following one stride behind as Yuka walked with purpose through a narrow tunnel that led them away from the room where Ipsa had been held. Ipsa studied Yuka's wings—a more vibrant purple than any Implementer's she'd ever seen. They flared wide and majestic, stretching out beyond the length of her extended arms. Yuka. The first angel. Ipsa had never seen her at Repast, never even considered she could still be Here, after all this time. That she had not long ago joined the cast of Departing at each Repast.

"You're still Here," Ipsa managed to blurt out. The edges of her wings blushed beet red. "I meant, um, I would have thought, by now…"

"That I would have gone by way of the Endless Lake?" Yuka turned to speak to Ipsa over her shoulder. Her eyes sparkled in a way that might have made Ipsa believe their world's origin stories of stardust. "I guess my wings think I've still a bit more work to do. I keep wondering myself, but here we are."

Yuka opened the door and Ipsa stepped into a large, open room, empty except for a cluster of chairs on which a group of angels were seated, each with purple wings, save one pair of marbled brown: The Implementers.

At the front of the group sat an empty chair.

"Would you take a seat, please?" Yuka said to Ipsa, waving her hand toward the chair.

Ipsa glanced across the room. Her eyes stopped on Dhavi, his lips pursed together in a small, stoic smile. Ipsa forced a smile in return. Eon leaned against a column off to the side, his expression one of disgust. He walked over to take a seat amongst the counsel. Almost automatically, she drew her right hand behind her back, grazing the bottom of her wing protectively.

Yuka, who had taken a seat amidst the other Implementers, rose again to speak. "It goes without saying that Ipsa's actions were brash and ill-counseled."

Ipsa's wings clenched at the sound of her name.

Yuka seemed to glide across the length of chairs. Her mantel made the slightest swoosh as she turned around. "But something Dhavi shared with us caught my attention.

He said that Ipsa's knowledge has made her a better Reader."

"A more dangerous and reckless reader," Eon muttered.

"I'd thank you to hold your comments for now, Eon." Yuka's voice was firm, though not harsh. She turned back toward Ipsa. "The relationship between Here and There must be protected at any cost. Without our oversight, the hopeling world might long ago have collapsed. Your knowledge has the potential to risk that relationship, that delicate balance. Knowledge *without* prudence.

"As I think you've gathered, while we've taken certain safeguards to shield most angels from that burden of our shared history, occasionally, another angel comes to the knowledge of the First Arcanum on their own."

Ipsa stared at the floor, afraid she might accidentally glance over at Eon as Yuka spoke.

"In a few of those cases, that knowledge became like an itch: Scratching only intensified the itch, until the skin was raw. The knowledge seeded an insatiable curiosity that became, in our view, unhealthy and dangerous. In each case, it had nothing to do with *who* they'd been There. But knowing their human connection became almost a purpose in and of itself. They could do practically nothing else besides seek out information about that world. We feared they might share their knowledge with others outside of this group, and that this insatiable curiosity would spread across Here, almost like an infection. It reaffirmed that this knowledge must be guarded."

Yuka paused, the single crease in her forehead more prominent. Her eyes seemed many earthly centuries away as she stared into the distance.

"When something like that happens, it can feel very unsettling. And so, I hope you can understand why the idea of sharing the knowledge of our hopeling past with the broader community might seem preposterous to many of us. There was a strong fear that such tampering had the power to unhinge the very fabric of Here. The Second Arcana—that idea of rationed knowledge—is one that we protect fervently."

Eon cleared his throat.

Yuka turned her head toward him, as if to silence him with a look. Ipsa's mind raced with this flood of information.

Yuka sighed a heavy exhale. "I don't pretend the Arcana are perfect, Ipsa. But they have worked for a long time."

"You've built our world on lies," Ipsa said.

"Levels of knowledge," Yuka answered.

"Just two levels," Ipsa said. "The Arcana mean one thing for you—the truth—and one thing for everyone else."

"Ipsa, think about Repast for a moment," Yuka said. "The words Thodius shares, those words are our creation story—at least the story that every angel in that arena knows. It is what they trust in, what they believe in. You speak of sharing our hopeling past—or the truth about the Answering Department—but what purpose would that serve except to unhinge everything they believe in? Why do that when our community is content and the risk is so great? Imagine if, given this new information, Readers just stopped listening to prayers."

"But what they believe is a lie."

Yuka shook her head. "We did not bring you to this forum to debate, simply to get more information as we weigh our decision. Ipsa, we've had other knowledge breaches in our history, and we've handled most in a similar way: We removed those angels' memories—all of their memories of Here. They received new wings and a new identity. Did you have any idea that was a possible outcome of your search?"

Ipsa glanced at Dhavi. "Yes, I did."

Yuka's perfectly shaped eyebrows arched toward the sky above. "Yet you continued on anyway. Why?"

Ipsa looked around at the room of faces, all waiting for her response. Her fingers gripped the edge of the seat. "I guess at first it was because of how I'd been on earth, how I'd treated Isaac. I felt like I owed it to him."

"Owed it to him to meddle in his life?" an Implementer named Khan asked from across the room.

"No, that's not what I did." Ipsa turned back toward the crowd of Implementers. "I mean, I thought about it. But he didn't want me to make the decision for him. I realized that as soon as I saw him. He just wanted to know I was out there. I don't even know what he decided. I don't know if I ever will."

"That may well be true," Yuka said.

"But that's not why I did it," Ipsa said, her voice growing stronger. "I know why I did it now."

An Implementer named Jana asked. "And why is that?"

Ipsa turned and looked straight at Dhavi as she continued. "Dhavi once said something to me about how a world without pain would be phony—that the people who lived there would never feel real joy or love, just some hologram version of it. He was making the argument for why we shouldn't answer prayers. But to be honest, it didn't sound like earth; it sounded like our world. It sounded like Here. I want to feel those same emotions. I deserve to control my own destiny," she said, "not have a bunch of angels in purple making decisions about how I should feel."

She heard a rustle as a few angels shifted in their seats.

"I did it because we *deserve* to know that we came from There, not from some heap of stardust. I did it because Muir and Elna and Darius and Sim and every other angel Here deserves to know, too."

Yuka turned toward her fellow Implementers. "Well, then. Does anyone have any other questions for Ipsa?"

Eon stood up, his chest puffed out as he walked the length of the floor and slowly circled Ipsa's chair. "Yes, as a matter of fact, I have several." He paused just behind her chair, his nearness to Ipsa's wings making them wilt slightly. "I think we've rather glossed over the *how* she came to much of this information."

"It sounds like you know the answer already, Eon." Dhavi's voice rose suddenly from the crowd.

Eon glared back at Dhavi. "I suppose I do. I was just wondering when we might get around to *that* part of the conversation. It seems to me that such a breach from within our own circle should be met with some kind of...examination."

Dhavi stood up to address the group. "I realize I took a risk and acted alone and without your counsel. I did it because I trusted Ipsa to make the right decision, even given the extraordinary knowledge she now possesses. And she did, I might add. I hoped that her example might show us that there needn't be danger in sharing this knowledge with other angels Here."

Ipsa watched the faces of the other Implementers seated around him. A few murmured quietly to each other. Ipsa glanced at Yuka, but her face was a book with no cover.

Eon folded his arms indignantly. "What are we going to do about this breach?"

"Eon, I'm not sure you're in the best position to lecture

on rogue behavior." Yuka looked around the room. "Are there any more questions for Ipsa?"

"I have one," said Pytho, who oversaw the Harvesters. "If we make the decision to re-assign you, where should we send you?"

Ipsa felt her wings pulsing. How much longer would she have her memories of Isaac? Of the truth about Here? She paused to consider the question. "The Prayer Reading Department, please."

"I will speak to each Implementer individually and they will help to inform my ultimate decision. In the meantime, you'll need to be separated from the community," Yuka said.

She lowered her head and then, as if she'd rung a silent bell, the doors opened and two angels appeared to escort Ipsa out of the room. To wait.

Chapter Thirty-Seven

There's been so much violence after the police killed that boy—answering hate with hate, anger with more anger. I can only pray that you've seen fit to turn our city upside down, so that eventually, it might be right side up. In your name I pray.

—William

COMPARED TO EON'S ROOM OF MIRRORS AND WHIPPING winds, Yuka's method of confinement seemed a gift. Ipsa's angel chaperones touched down on a familiar curved path at the edge of a field of wildflowers. They were outside Dhavi's cottage, the haven to which she'd run to so many times to make meaning of so many secrets, of the knotted and tangled loop of thread at which she'd tugged and pulled. It seemed a fitting place to wait out what might be the last Repast she'd know in her own wings. Ipsa felt a wave of relief when she saw it, when she realized she would be with Dhavi. Even if the news was bad, even if she would no longer be Ipsa or know about Annie Conway, at least she would have a chance to say goodbye.

Her guards had the hazel wings of Archivists and pleasant, if vapid, smiles. Ipsa marveled at their genial apathy; that they could be tasked with something so obviously unrelated to the Archives, so out of the norm as keeping an angel under house arrest, and yet offer a smile and pleasantries as if they were all gathering for Repast. They nodded at their prisoner, closed the door, and took their positions just outside the cottage entrance.

As soon as they were alone, Ipsa rushed to hug Dhavi. A wave of warmth washed over her, like the sun escaping a cloud. She leaned her head against his chest. The smell of fire seemed sewn into the fibers of his mantel. Ipsa inhaled and closed her eyes, content to stay there for a thousand Repasts.

Dhavi broke the silence. "I'm proud of you."

"What do you mean?" Ipsa lifted her head to meet Dhavi's eyes.

"About the way you handled Isaac's prayer."

Ipsa gathered the folds of fabric around Dhavi's sleeve, clutching them in her fingers. "Has—has there been any word from him? I mean…has he prayed again?"

Dhavi shook his head slowly. "I don't think so."

Ipsa let go of Dhavi's sleeves, rushing over to his worktable, shuffling piles of papers and hopeling calendars. "What day is it There? How much time has passed? I need to figure out what day it is…"

Dhavi walked over to the table and, taking her small hands in his own thick, worn palms, stilled her search. "October the first."

Ipsa's wings drooped, her gaze falling to the floor. "October first…That was the date of the rally."

"And why do you look so crestfallen?" Dhavi said, tilting his head. He cupped her chin in his hand, lifting her head as he spoke.

"What if he made the wrong decision?" Ipsa asked.

"And what was the 'right' decision, Ipsa?"

She bit her bottom lip and thought for a moment. "I… don't know."

Dhavi offered a raspy chuckle that reached from his belly to the tips of his dappled brown wings. "Well, then, that takes some of the pressure off, doesn't it?" He pursed his lips, and his expression grew serious. "Ipsa, isn't that the point? There's no easy answer to most questions. Isaac needs to figure out the right answer for *Isaac*. And we must trust him."

"Can I ask you something?"

Dhavi smiled. "Anything."

"Did you have something to do with me finding Isaac's prayer that Reading Session?"

Dhavi's eyes sparkled. "I'm sure I don't know what you mean."

"Well, then," Ipsa said, looking around the cottage. "What do we do now?"

"We wait."

❧

THE TWO ANGELS WAITED FOR THREE REPASTS. IPSA watched the sun rise over the fields beyond Dhavi's window each morning, watched each predictably perfect transition from a pinpricked night sky to red, then orange and then, finally, blue. And she watched it set from his front door each night, the colors draining toward the horizon line like wet hopeling sidewalk chalk running downhill. She thought about the billions of prayers being uttered while she watched the sun make its way across the blanket of blue sky. She thought about the hopeling who'd scrawled that threatening letter to Isaac and wondered what *his* prayers sounded like. And then she thought about Muir, sitting at a Repast table without her. If Ipsa was given new wings, if she remembered nothing about what Hopelings First really meant, would Muir remind her? And if she did, would Ipsa believe her? Or would she flutter her wings in fear, as Elna had done?

At daybreak on that third Repast, the guards opened the door, smiled, and asked Dhavi to please come with them. Ipsa hugged him as if it were the last hug she'd ever give, then watched from the open doorway as they vaulted upward into the sky, receding from her view. She stood there, no watchman guarding the threshold, and imagined running away, taking with her the knowledge she still had— of Dhavi, of the Arcana. She thought of the recreation period she and Elna had spent flying over the Endless Lake so many Repasts ago. She wondered what lay beyond the horizon, if her wings could get her there. Instead, she closed the door.

The sun's light was nearing the end of its daily arc when she heard a gentle rap at the door. Ipsa opened it and was surprised to see Dhavi, this time unattended.

He offered a smile that seemed inscrutable. "It's time," he said, extending his hand for hers.

As they approached the large doors to the Implementer's meeting room, Ipsa stopped. She realized that nothing more than a piece of wood stood between her and her fate. She thought of Isaac tossing Annie the yin-yang pendant; of the look on Sim's face when he'd handed her Isaac's tube; of Muir's voice, firm and honest, when she told Ipsa she was glad to know the truth. Ipsa thought about how much she had seen, how much she'd learned in less than a dozen Repasts. She considered, for a moment, if it had been worth the potential price, if she'd do it all over again.

She realized she would.

In that swirling moment of realizations, Dhavi placed his hand on the knob.

"Dhavi, wait," Ipsa said, placing her own hand over his.

"Yes?"

"If—if things don't go my way in there, will you do something for me?"

"Ipsa, don't—"

Ipsa shook her head firmly, cutting him off. "Please."

Dhavi sighed. "Anything."

"Will you look after Muir? You know, see how she's getting on with her prayers, make sure she's not spending an eternity deciding between Urgent and Highly Urgent." She wondered whether she should tell Dhavi that Muir knew the truth about their hopeling past. He could help her navigate that knowledge—avoid whatever fate lay in store for Ipsa. But something in her wings told her to swallow that secret.

"Of course."

"I haven't even asked about Sim. He shouldn't get in trouble for the hairs—he really had no idea what he was getting into; he was just being nice. And please," Ipsa said, wincing at the memory of Elna holding a sharp blade in her hands, "if there's any way you can avoid it, don't let Elna be the one who takes my wings."

"I won't let that happen, Ipsa, but we really need to go inside."

"Just one more thing, Dhavi," Ipsa said.

"Yes?"

"Thank you for everything. Thank you for breaking the rules since it meant us getting to know each other. Thank you for risking the pain of getting to know me, after how much it hurt you to meet Grandma Marianne. Thank you for helping me sort everything out, and not getting too mad at me when I didn't do what you asked—which I did a lot. And most of all, thank you for letting me see Isaac." Ipsa leaned in on the tips of her toes to give him a peck on the cheek. "I love you," she said.

Dhavi's brown wings turned the color of a ripening apple. "You're welcome, my child," he said. "I love you, too." And he pushed open the door.

Ipsa looked around. The group mingled near their chairs as before. She noticed Eon in their midst this time, his hand grasping Yuka's elbow as he whispered something in her ear. His head tipped back with a laugh. Ipsa's wings felt leaden. She looked to the middle of the room for her chair but saw none. Another angel came up to Yuka and tapped her on the shoulder, motioning toward the doors. She turned toward Ipsa.

"Everyone, please take your seats so we can begin," Yuka said. "Ipsa, would you be so good as to stand over here? This won't take long." She pointed to a spot at the front of the room. Ipsa forced her feet, which felt like two rocks, toward the space.

"I've had the opportunity to speak with each of you individually," Yuka spoke directly to the Implementers. "And I feel confident that we are at a place of consensus. Again, it is not easy to look inward—especially when so much of our world is built upon looking outward, at another world and way of life—but I commend each of you on your openness to this process."

She extended an arm toward Ipsa. "This angel engaged in flagrant violations of our rules."

Ipsa noticed Eon nodding his head almost violently in agreement. She knotted her hands together on her lap, twisting and turning them.

"She also recklessly endangered an angel in the Statistics Department by asking him to conspire in her search—although I should say that Jana interviewed him extensively and he had no knowledge of Ipsa's purpose in obtaining the hairs.

"And yet," Yuka continued, "we must also acknowledge that she has taught us something valuable. She taught us what reading can look like when we truly focus on understanding hopelings and deepening our perspective through greater knowledge of them. Much of the subsequent examination we've undergone has been, I think it's fair to say, a little uncomfortable." She paused, slowly turning her head to make eye contact with every Implementer. "I think this is a time for us to be bold."

Ipsa held her breath.

"And sometimes that means change," Yuka said.

Change. Ipsa's mind raced with possibility and excitement. Here could change. She wanted that world so much, wanted Muir and Elna and Sim and all of the other angels in their community to live in that world.

"And that is why," Yuka said, beaming, "I am recommending that we focus our efforts to train angels around empathy in a way we've never done before, so that not just Readers, but all angels, can treat their understanding of hopelings as more than just an academic pursuit." Yuka spoke in an animated tone. "I'm imagining a space where angels would have to experience some of the hardships of the hopeling world, like a heat wave or land dispute. Angels could engage in that experiential learning. We will also be revamping our coursework. More case studies around actual hopelings—putting names and faces to some of the scenarios we talk about in class." She smiled wider. "I think this will be an exciting moment for our entire community."

There was silence in the room for a moment, followed by the sound of eleven pairs of wings flapping in approval. All except Dhavi and Ipsa's.

"But they still wouldn't know?" Ipsa blurted out. "Every other angel Here. They still wouldn't know about their old lives? Or about the way we interact with prayers?"

The Implementer Khan spoke up. "They would have all of the benefits of that knowledge without any of the burdens," he said with a satisfied smile.

"But that's no different than how things are now!" Ipsa's voice clamored through the chamber.

A few Implementers murmured to each other, wings fluttering nervously.

For a moment, Ipsa had been swept up in a tide of possibility: Yuka's talk of greater knowledge of hopelings, of change, and a need to be bold. She'd been so certain that the Arcana could be revealed in their true form—that a curtain could be pulled back. Somewhere in her mind, she'd heard a door creaking open, saw light spilling into a dark room. It was the light of knowledge and transparency —of understanding who they were, and who they'd been, of the role they really played There. Instead, that door slammed shut with a steely bang. Somewhere, in the abyss, a bolt slid into place.

"But you said…change. You said…we needed to be

bold." Ipsa grasped for words, as a blind hopeling might fumble in a room of unfamiliar objects.

"And we do," Yuka said kindly. "I'm sure this is a lot for you to understand, but this will be a big change for us. It will mean an entirely different way of training new angels. And it will require intensive *re*training for those angels already in our community."

"But the secrets…" Ipsa's voice trailed off. Her eyes felt watery.

"Not secrets, Ipsa. Knowledge, with prudence," Yuka said, repeating the well-worn Second Arcanum. "But of course, you're concerned. We've said nothing of your situation. Please forgive me. Here we are talking about things like broad institutional changes, and you're probably very preoccupied with your own wings!"

"No, that's not—" Ipsa began.

"As I said at the outset, regardless of the manner, you brought many important learnings to light," Yuka said. "And we still have much to learn from you, Ipsa. That is why I'm recommending you help us as we construct this new empathy training." Yuka smiled brightly. "In order to do that, it will be important that you retain some of the knowledge you've gained from this process."

Ipsa looked up at Yuka, her brow furrowed. "Some of the knowledge?"

"Your connection with your hopeling family bordered on dangerous. You will not be able to keep your memories of Isaac or anyone else in your family."

Yuka's words landed like massive boulder into deep water: After the initial impact, there was only quiet as it slowly dropped into the mud below. *You will not be able to keep your memories of Isaac.*

"Of course, after we remove those memories, we'll sit

down and share portions of the Arcana's highest levels of knowledge with you—that's really the important part," Yuka said. "Ipsa, I want you to think of this as an opportunity. A chance for you to release the burden of caring so much about one single hopeling."

Ipsa stared at Yuka, unable to find any words. She'd considered so many outcomes, but not this one. She squeezed her eyes shut and thought about embracing Isaac in his dream. The warmth she'd felt pressing her cheek against his shoulder. The moments they'd spent together on Earth as hopelings, the life she'd watched him live out after she'd died—gone, or at least replaced by some black and white transcript of events.

Then she had another thought: "You said 'any members of your family.'" Ipsa's eyes jerked in Dhavi's direction.

"We've had a lot of discussion about this, Ipsa," Jana said. "We believe it will be better if we *reset* the relationship. We still don't know why exactly you had a reaction to Isaac's prayer. One hypothesis is that meeting someone you had a connection to There—even though you two never met while on earth—caused something special to happen. A glitch."

"I won't do anything reckless again, I promise. Please, Dhavi is the most important angel in my life. I can't exist Here without him."

This caused Jana to chuckle. "Oh, well, I'm certain that's not true. I think you'll be just fine. Isn't that right, Dhavi?" She offered her fellow Implementer a knowing wink. "But Ipsa, think of this as allowing you to have more capacity to feel that friendship and fellowship with an *entire* community, not just one angel."

"The important thing to remember is that you'll still

hold this greater knowledge," added an Implementer named Roz. "About the Arcana."

"Ridiculous." It was Eon who spoke, the little color on his face draining down his chin. He walked across the room, his arms reaching out to the group, pleading. "Think about what she's done. About the precedent we'd be setting by allowing her any access to the Arcana." His upper lip twitched in anger.

"Thank you for your concern, Eon," Yuka said. "But it has been decided. And I would remind you about certain precedents you helped set long ago." She turned her back, signaling the discussion was over. Eon looked over at Ipsa, his eyes narrowed and cold. Gathering up his cloak in his arm, he stalked across the floor, opening the door wide before slamming it shut behind him with a bang that rattled chairs.

Ipsa looked desperately at Dhavi, but his head was lowered toward the floor, his reaction hidden by the canopy of his wings.

Yuka came over to Ipsa. "I can see that you're troubled, angel. I know this is not the outcome you had hoped for. I have a feeling you'd have given your own memories if it meant changing our rules, am I right?" Their eyes locked, and Ipsa felt as though Yuka was privy to every thought racing through her mind. She couldn't even bear to nod.

Yuka continued in a low voice, her words meant just for Ipsa. "You must understand that—as hopelings say—it takes time to turn around a large ship. These bigger questions we will continue to explore, likely for centuries to come, but you must be content with small steps. I've seen what can go wrong when knowledge is freely given. I'm not prepared to let the light in all at once and risk the entire fabric of our world."

Yuka, who stood a head shorter than Ipsa, lifted her arm and took the Prayer Reader's chin gently in her ebony hand as she spoke. A sensation of calm swept over Ipsa like a breeze on a stifling day.

Turning back toward the crowd, Yuka raised her voice. "Thank you all." The other Implementers stood and, pushing open the doors, began to leave.

"So, I can just go?" Ipsa squinted toward the courtyard.

Yuka walked over and placed both of her hands on Ipsa's crimson wings. Yuka closed her eyes, her lips moving silently. "You are free to go, Ipsa," she said. "When you walk outside of this room, you'll be the same, but lacking those memories." She lifted a hand to Ipsa's cheek. "Take as much time as you need before coming out. I'll wait just outside."

"What about my friends? Elna knows that I almost lost my wings…" Ipsa said.

"You can go back to all of your friends and enjoy Repast just as you always did, without remembering all of this recent bother. Elna's memories regarding your— detainment—and its surrounding circumstances have been modified. It will be like no time has passed since she saw you last, and you will remember none of the strain those encounters caused."

The Implementers filed out of the room, but Ipsa barely noticed. She stayed standing, dazed, as they walked by, some of them offering an encouraging nod. Yuka stepped just outside the threshold, waiting patiently for Ipsa to cross. Soon only Dhavi remained.

"I'm sorry," Dhavi said. "You know this isn't what I wanted."

"I thought it could be different," Ipsa murmured.

"It still can be," he said.

"But how? You heard Yuka. Everything I did feels like it was all for nothing," Ipsa said, sinking down to the floor. She placed her palm against the smooth marble.

"I'm sorry you feel that way," he said. "I certainly don't. In fact, I'm feeling quite—what's the word? Hopeful. Something I haven't felt in a long time."

"Why?" Ipsa asked, searching the wrinkles and scruff on his face.

Dhavi reached for Ipsa's hands, pulling her back up from the ground, then led her over to a table against the wall, on which sat a single leather book. It was not some dusty remnant from his cottage shelves. The cover looked clean, the corners crisp.

"Before you go out there. I wanted to share something with you—some reading that I thought you'd be interested in—a few prayers I compiled this Repast. They're dated October 1st."

Ipsa grabbed her grandfather and clung to him like a hopeling life raft. "Dhavi, I love you."

"And I love you." Dhavi's voice broke as he spoke.

The pair stood in silence for many hundred prayers. Dhavi stroked her chestnut hair with his palm as Ipsa leaned on his chest, breathing him in.

Finally, he spoke. "It's probably time for me to leave you," Dhavi said, still holding her hand.

"Once I go through that door, Dhavi…" Ipsa's voice trailed off. The burden of losing him felt like stones tied to her ankles, weighing each step.

"I know. But we found each other once. Perhaps we might just find each other again," Dhavi said, a twinkle in his eyes.

He kissed the top of her head, then stepped into the

doorway, nodding again toward the book. "Give it a read. Goodbye, my child."

Dhavi disappeared past where Yuka stood, still and unobtrusive as the columns that braced the room. Ipsa leaned against the wall and exhaled a long, deep breath. She thought about seeing Elna at the next Repast, with no memory of reading that crumpled piece of parchment beneath her desk. She thought about returning to her life without the journey to this knowledge, without Dhavi's love or the memories of embracing Isaac.

Ipsa looked beyond the open door to the courtyard as angels of all sizes and shapes passed by. She watched one cross the square who looked a bit like Muir, her black hair fastened into several small buns.

Muir! A smile spread across Ipsa's face. That truth would carry on in her wings even after the memories of this journey left Ipsa's. Maybe there was a world in which sweet, little Muir held the key to unlocking their secrets.

Ipsa watched another angel walk by with deep olive skin and a crop of short pink hair. Who had he been There? And how would he react if he learned that story? Would he be grateful for that knowledge, as Muir had?

"I hope we'll see someday," Ipsa whispered.

She would step across the threshold of that room in a moment, losing so much that she cared about. She couldn't seem to move. She wanted to stay in this room forever.

Ipsa turned back toward the book. She gingerly traced its cover. The leather smelled fresh. A thick ream of paper squirmed beneath the covers. Prayers.

Slowly, she opened to the first page, which held a single line with four words scrawled in a familiar scribble that made Ipsa smile.

Thanks for listening, Sis.

She thumbed through the remaining prayers, page after page. Hopelings didn't always get it right. But sometimes… sometimes, they did. Together, the swath of people within these pages, young and old, from so many corners of their world, were coming together to be the answer. Each person taking a risk, choosing to dive headfirst into uncharted waters. Isaac had chosen bravery over safety. Risk over comfort. Others over himself. And he was far from alone.

There was a lot to learn from humans.

Ipsa closed the book.

"Yuka," she called from inside the room. "What if there is another way?"

❦

"You're certain about this?" Yuka said some prayers later, staring out at the rippling tides, the first throws of sunrise skipping across the shifting surface. "You're quite certain you can't live without that knowledge?"

"I am," Ipsa said.

"You know that even I can't tell you what's beyond—or if there even *is* a beyond," Yuka said, motioning toward where the sun and its reflection met in a radial symmetry of color and light. "There will be risk."

Ipsa smiled toward the beckoning water. "Someone once told me that without risk, life isn't really worth living."

"Then good luck, Ipsa," Yuka said, placing her hands on the other angel's wings.

At Yuka's touch, Ipsa's wings detached from her back and began to coast upward, through the air. They flew toward the rising sun, across a sea of dazzling colors. Soon, the soaring red of the Reader's wings blended into the morning sky.

Ipsa waded into the water. She felt a lightness about her, as if she, too, might drift upward toward the sky. But untethered, she remained with her feet in the wet sand. The water felt cool as she stepped further in. She did not look back to where Yuka stood at the shore. Ipsa looked only toward the horizon line, which was bright. She took a breath and started swimming.

Acknowledgments

"You will forget someone. You will forget someone important."
 —Gerald the Elephant, *The Thank You Book*

I started this book in 2004, while I should have been focusing on my graduate coursework in journalism; for that, I must first thank Northwestern University for the opportunity to audit my first fiction class. While it rendered my journalism degree dead on arrival, that class opened up an amazing world of stories.

Carol Casey's early enthusiasm for this story offered reassurance at a pivotal time. Nike Carstarphen and Alex Gardner astounded me with their commitment to this project. As an unpublished author, asking anyone to read my manuscript felt monumental. So those who proactively offered, like Nancy Crawford and Meredith Bloom, among others, gave me a great gift. My sister Beth: I will forever remember standing in Home Depot when you called me in tears after finishing the manuscript.

In 2013, I signed up for a writing workshop at Johns Hopkins University. There, I met two people who changed the course of my professional writing life: Elissa Weissman, the group's instructor, and YA author Karen Hattrup. To have mentors and peers whose work I vastly admired believe in this project provided necessary fuel. Karen has read pretty much every word I've written in the last decade, and certainly every iteration of this book: every query letter, every cautiously optimistic email from an agent or editor, and, much more, has offered me unwavering support in my lowest moments. Elissa edited every version of this story, introduced me to my first agent, and insisted, more than once, that I keep going, despite serious doubts. She helped get this over the finish line, with both her incredible editorial eye and unflappable belief in this idea, and I'm forever grateful. In a similar vein, I count myself unbelievably lucky to have met and learned from writer Margaret Osburn, a mentor whose confidence in me has, at times, outshined my own.

Several literary agents helped me in big ways, by believing in this project on some level and offering smart feedback. Thank you to Steve Malk, Hannah Mann, Julia Kardon and Rick Richter. Thanks to author Laurel Snyder for gifting me with the title, which was there all along.

I'd pretty much given up on ever seeing this story appear on a shelf when, in April 2023, I lost a cherished mentor, Omari Todd. Out of that grief came a renewed determination to publish this book. Omari always knew the right answer and always helped others tease out that answer for themselves. Thanks for helping me get there, friend. And Emma Snyder, thank you for truly listening and helping me articulate what mattered most.

Thank you to my father and siblings, John, Kate and Bryan. It's a rare gift to have siblings celebrate a win for one as a win for the rest, and I've felt grateful to share the road of highs and lows with you, always knowing that you'll be my biggest cheerleaders.

To Jamie, my much better half. It is not easy to live in a house filled with female extroverts. Thank you for showing us all the wisdom of silence and for being a steady compass of kindness, integrity, compassion, and reason. Your soulmate is probably in that bar, indeed.

And to my mom, who would be the least surprised of anyone to see this day come. Thanks for being my greatest champion and my first and best teacher: You showed me that hands are for helping others (and for weeding). I hope you're running the show up there.

About the Author

Maggie Master grew up outside of Philadelphia and chose her writing career at age eleven. Since then, her work has appeared in *The New York Times*, *The Washington Post*, *The Baltimore Sun*, and other publications. *The Hopeling* is her first novel. Maggie lives in Baltimore, Maryland, with her husband, three daughters, and a cat and dog who do not get along.